Acclaim for
Worth Fighting With

"Vincent Quinn's *Worth Fighting With* is an acerbically funny comic novel about academic life at a university in the English provinces. The plot focuses on hapless Danny, a forty-something lecturer whose career is as stagnant as his emotional life (focused on appealing young soccer players). A tale of passions requited and passions denied, the book is peopled with sharply observed characters and situations and is enormously entertaining. This is a debut to be applauded."

—Peter Burton,
Author of *Talking To: Writers Writing on Gay Themes*
and *Amongst the Aliens: Some Aspects of a Gay Life*

"The anxieties and resentments of the faculty committee scarcely hint at the bizarre domestic circumstances and emotional life of Dr. Danny Whelan and Dr. Barbara Barnes. They hardly expect love or sex, but the genial author, in his wisdom, finally allots them some of each. The enemies, on campus and in the bedroom, are mean-spirited, dishonest, but finally ineffective. I compare Vincent Quinn to Iris Murdoch for wit and insight: not a word wasted, and a rattling good story, with bravado, set-piece episodes."

—Alan Sinfield, DLitt,
Professor of English, University of Sussex;
Author, *The Wilde Century: Effeminacy,
Oscar Wilde and the Queer Moment,
Out on Stage: Lesbian and Gay Theatre
in the Twentieth Century,*
and *On Sexuality and Power*

NOTES FOR PROFESSIONAL LIBRARIANS
AND LIBRARY USERS

This is an original book title published by Southern Tier Editions™, Harrington Park Press®, the trade division of The Haworth Press, Inc. Unless otherwise noted in specific chapters with attribution, materials in this book have not been previously published elsewhere in any format or language.

CONSERVATION AND PRESERVATION NOTES

All books published by The Haworth Press, Inc., and its imprints are printed on certified pH neutral, acid-free book grade paper. This paper meets the minimum requirements of American National Standard for Information Sciences-Permanence of Paper for Printed Material, ANSI Z39.48-1984.

DIGITAL OBJECT IDENTIFIER (DOI) LINKING

The Haworth Press is participating in reference linking for elements of our original books. (For more information on reference linking initiatives, please consult the CrossRef Web site at www.crossref.org.) When citing an element of this book such as a chapter, include the element's Digital Object Identifier (DOI) as the last item of the reference. A Digital Object Identifier is a persistent, authoritative, and unique identifier that a publisher assigns to each element of a book. Because of its persistence, DOIs will enable The Haworth Press and other publishers to link to the element referenced, and the link will not break over time. This will be a great resource in scholarly research.

Worth Fighting With

HARRINGTON PARK PRESS®
Southern Tier Editions™
Gay Men's Fiction

Worth Fighting With

Vincent Quinn

Southern Tier Editions™
Harrington Park Press®
The Trade Division of The Haworth Press, Inc.
New York • London

For more information on this book or to order, visit
http://www.haworthpress.com/store/product.asp?sku=5902

or call 1-800-HAWORTH (800-429-6784) in the United States and Canada
or (607) 722-5857 outside the United States and Canada

or contact orders@HaworthPress.com

Published by

Southern Tier Editions™, Harrington Park Press®, the trade division of The Haworth Press, Inc., 10 Alice Street, Binghamton, NY 13904-1580.

PUBLISHER'S NOTE
The development, preparation, and publication of this work has been undertaken with great care. However, the Publisher, employees, editors, and agents of The Haworth Press are not responsible for any errors contained herein or for consequences that may ensue from use of materials or information contained in this work. The Haworth Press is committed to the dissemination of ideas and information according to the highest standards of intellectual freedom and the free exchange of ideas. Statements made and opinions expressed in this publication do not necessarily reflect the views of the Publisher, Directors, management, or staff of The Haworth Press, Inc., or an endorsement by them.

This is a work of fiction. Names, characters, places, and incidents either are the products of the author's imagination or are used fictitiously, and any resemblance to actual persons, living or dead, business establishments, events, or locales is entirely coincidental.

Cover design by Kerry E. Mack.

Library of Congress Cataloging-in-Publication Data

Quinn, Vincent (Vincent R.)
    Worth fighting with / Vincent Quinn.
        p. cm.
    ISBN-13: 978-1-56023-672-6 (pbk. : alk. paper)
    1. Gay college teachers—Fiction. 2. Gay men—Fiction. 3. Midlands (England)—Fiction. I. Title.

PR6117.U37W67 2007
823'.92—dc22
                                                            2007009191

Don't let us forget, old fellow, that the minor emotions are the guiding lights of our lives.

Vincent Van Gogh

Of course, a man must have meat.

Barbara Pym

Acknowledgments

Yael Raz was the first person to read a draft of this novel and I may not have persevered without her encouragement and advice. I would also like to thank Helen Barr, Vicky Lebeau, and Alan Sinfield for reading the manuscript before publication; their support was invaluable. Thanks, too, to Jay Quinn for commissioning the novel and to John Shire for the author photograph.

Fortunately my workplace bears no resemblance to the one depicted in this novel. On the contrary, my colleagues in the Department of English and the School of Humanities have provided a sane and stimulating environment in which to write and think. My students have also been inspiring. I would especially like to thank everyone connected to the Centre for the Study of Sexual Dissidence and the MA in Sexual Dissidence and Cultural Change.

This is in part a book about teaching. I am therefore particularly pleased to have a chance to thank Peter Mullan and Enda McAteer. Not only did they encourage my work, they provided me with models of what good teaching can be. Indeed without their kindness and interest I might not be in a position to write these words. And among the many friends who have sustained me over the years, I want to make special mention of Louise Hudd and Noam Raz.

My greatest debts are to my family, above all my parents, Sean and Lena Quinn, and my partner Alan Sinfield. This book is for the three of them.

doi:10.1300/5902_a

PART ONE

1

"Your Ronaldo has gross pustules."

It was difficult, in the crowded room, to know who had spoken, let alone what the words meant. Twisting backwards, Danny found Marcus Cranborne in the seat behind.

"Excuse me?" he flinched.

Marcus gestured at a man several rows ahead. "Your Ronaldo has gross pustules."

"Ronaldo? His name is Ronan."

"So what? Just look at the back of his neck."

Danny followed his colleague's finger.

Although he hated to admit it, Marcus had a point. With so much green and purple, Ronan's skin wouldn't have seemed out of place in the heathers section of his local garden center. Unable either to look or to look away, Danny peeked backwards and forwards until a bustle at the door announced the arrival of their guest speaker. By a miracle of physics that was all the more alarming given his enormous size, Marcus had already shot to the front, where he was laughing exaggeratedly with a well-dressed blonde. *Exactly his type,* thought Danny as he pondered the significance of the phrase "Your Ronaldo." In what sense, if any, could Ronan MacIntyre be considered "his"? Truth be told (as he took another peep), he thought Ronan highly trying.

"Pustules," he repeated. "*Gross* pustules."

It was a curious word. It made him think of pus—the type that oozes out of sores. Then he saw the kind that gets the cream. (Oddly enough, both images suited Ronan.) Danny screwed up his eyes, trying to make out the individual spots on the youngster's neck. They weren't so much open wounds needing plasters and antiseptics as self-contained humps—pithy, and dry, and strangely pleased with them-

doi:10.1300/5902_01

selves. (In short: just the sort of zits he'd have expected Ronan to have.)

They were truly disgusting.

Yet oddly compelling.

In fact, the more he watched them, the more he felt like slipping onto his hands and knees, creeping along the floor, and reaching up to squeeze one. Or to pinch it till it popped.

He giggled at this picture, then found that he was blushing.

"Really," he told himself. "You ought to be ashamed!" Yet the warmth of his flush, and the imagined sound of Ronan's yelp, were enough to block his guilt. "Pus, pustule, puss," he hummed, only pulling himself together when the glamorous newcomer started positioning herself behind the lectern.

Bill Roberts, the head of the English Department, followed her with a scrap of paper like an altar boy carrying a votive offering. His introductions were usually as terse as he could make them; he didn't believe in wasting words on other people. But this time he was positively eloquent. He even smiled once or twice.

"On these occasions it's customary to say what a pleasure it is to introduce such-and-such a person from such-and-such a place—although usually the visitor turns out to be some dreary old bore from one of our rival institutions. Tonight, though, it really *is* a pleasure to introduce Dr. Barbara Barnes, who is not only an accomplished scholar but is also the newest addition to our department—so new that most of you will not have seen her before. Dr. Barnes recently completed her doctorate at the University of Oxford—not *yet* one of our rival universities, I'm sorry to say. She has considerable teaching experience both at Oxford and, less glamorously, at the University of North East London where she had a part-time post in, ahm, Women's Studies and Gender Theory. I could, at this point, give you a list of Dr. Barnes' numerous publications, but tonight's paper will speak for itself. Its title, if I'm right" (and here he seemed to hesitate) "is 'Eager Eve or Endangered Species? Eco-Feminism and the New World Order.'"

While Professor Roberts handled the introductions, everyone else inspected the speaker. Far from being fazed, Dr. Barnes sleeked down her hair and stared right back. She thanked Professor Roberts for his "generous introduction," said what an honor it was to have joined "such a promising young department," and began her paper with an air of total self-possession.

As he watched, Danny Whelan wondered if he had been right to come. It was the first talk of the academic year—attendance was expected. But the English Seminar Room was depressing at the best of times. A cramped and ill-designed cube of glass, stifling in summer and freezing in winter, it represented everything that was makeshift about his profession. Add hard chairs and abysmal acoustics and you got a taste of life at the lower end of the university spectrum. Not for the first time he asked himself how he had come to be in such a place. No answer being forthcoming, he turned to the more pleasant task of seeing who was present, and with whom, and what they were doing to each other.

Two or three heads drew most of his attention.

With his dough-colored face and shifty-looking eyes, Marcus Cranborne resembled an overweight owl who hadn't quite abandoned the hunt. Although opinion was divided over whether he was cuddly or malign, everyone agreed he was a lech. Bill Roberts was of the same unreconstructed generation, but where Marcus was vast and ever-spreading, Bill had a tight face with pinched blue lips. While Marcus fancied himself as a dandy, Bill took an ostentatiously utilitarian approach to clothes. Let more famous academics prance around the world like peacocks; he was content to stay at home in his polyester sweatshirt and two-tone brogues.

When chairing the seminar Bill tended to rustle loudly in his Gladstone bag or tap impatiently on the desk. He sometimes used these antics to signal his disapproval of the paper. More often they were just a way of drawing notice from the speaker and towards himself—he was that kind of man. However, this week he listened closely. Though he'd usually have considered Dr. Barnes' paper prime snorting territory, he kept perfectly still except to scribble on his piece of paper. Marcus Cranborne—who often fell asleep—was similarly rapt. His gaze never left her face.

Bored with their adulation, Danny's eyes moved on.

Postgraduate students punctuated the room: balancing file blocks on their knees, they wrote with terrifying speed. How old they made him feel! They were so earnest, so serious—even the handsome ones, the pretty ones. Rather than laughing, as Danny did, at the oddballs that surrounded them, they screwed up their faces as if in training to join the faculty eccentrics. Could it really be that none of them had a sense of humor, not even the one by the door with the startlingly attractive scowl? (Though why physical attractiveness should promise a sense of fun, Danny had no idea.) Instead they pursued their studies with a laudable, if menacing, concentration.

Rachel Glover and Deirdre Waugh presented a more comforting sight. Had there ever been a time when these two hadn't boomed their way through faculty meetings, gushing with rapture at Shelley, Keats, and "dearest Jane"? (They had shared a house since 1968 but what that "meant," no one knew.) Ed and Susan Upshaw were also there, a marshmallowish couple whose publicly held hands reduced right-thinking people to nausea. (Interestingly, they sat next to a faculty pair who were famous for their rows.) Then there was the departmental administrator, an extraordinarily capable young woman—not yet thirty—who was possibly the sanest person in the room, and certainly the cleverest.

Without realizing it Danny returned to Ronan MacIntyre's jewel-encrusted neck and to the dark blond hair that lay above it, thick and wavy like a pageboy's. Ever since Ronan had joined the department Danny had felt disturbed by the younger man's ambition. With that sort of hair he should have been lying face-up in a stream like a Pre-Raphaelite heroine, not charging to every conference in the country and applying for promotion over his elders and betters (by which Danny meant himself). And you could tell he was a narcissist by the way he endlessly glanced round, flashing his face to the room's four corners. Young people ought to be more modest. But there he was, writing yet another withering question on the inside cover of his Penguin *Sons and Lovers*. *We'll be hearing* that *soon enough,* thought Danny, for Ronan was always the first to ask a question during the discussion period.

Meanwhile, Dr. Barnes was approaching her conclusion.

This consisted of a drawing up of shoulders and a rapping out of points. She emphasized each comment with a shake of the head and a point of her finger. No one would guess she was a junior lecturer in an ex-polytechnic. With her lacquered nail polish and pirated Chanel suit, she should have been running video-conferencing sessions for a multi-national, not talking passionately in front of a blackboard on which someone had drawn an oversized penis beside the university motto, *Long Is the Struggle and Long the Satisfaction*.

Danny Whelan closed his eyes.

He dreaded the rest of the evening. A drink in the bar did not appeal. A cheap and cheerful Italian meal "with the usual crowd" was even less enticing. Why bother when he didn't fit anymore? He was neither an old-timer nor a promising youngster. Ronan MacIntyre, who was ten years his junior, already had a book out. Barbara Barnes was finishing her first. But at forty-plus, Danny still carried the corpse of his doctoral thesis. He was supposed to be "turning it into a book" but it was really an albatross that refused to be cast off—a fight to the death he feared he wouldn't win.

Dr. Barnes put down her paper and Bill Roberts asked for questions.

Sure enough, Ronan's fat little hand shot up. He prefaced his question by stressing how much he'd enjoyed her paper, especially since it had reminded him of an essay—which she must *surely* know since it was highly germane to her argument—written by a hitherto untranslated Romanian who had died in mysterious circumstances during the last days of the Ceaucescu regime and whose work was only now getting the recognition it deserved. There was something insulting in his elaborate courtesy; he obviously felt he had to soften his question with endless, insincerely considerate sub-clauses. And he had such a silly voice: deep and baritone when it should have been as light as his complexion. The incongruity made Danny want to laugh.

To his satisfaction, Barbara not only knew the theorist in question, she was also able to correct Ronan's pronunciation. (Apparently he'd got his diphthongs wrong.) Enthused by her putdown, Danny went to the bar, where he got stuck beside Bill Roberts. Unable to avoid conversation, they viewed each other with antipathy.

Bill clicked his heels with an ironic bow. "*Dr.* Whelan," he said, in an arch parody of academic protocol.

Danny smiled as best he could. "*Professor* Roberts," he replied, raising an eyebrow in return. The ritual made him want to vomit. No one else insisted on titles. It wasn't 1912, for God's sake. But despite his south London origins, Bill could have been a minor Ulster Unionist—a smooth-shaven Puritan transplanted into an English Literature department. (His specialty was Anglican verse.)

For his part, Bill felt an impatient contempt for Danny Whelan. He liked feistiness, particularly in women. But there was no fun to be had out of a gangling man too timid to rise to your taunts. ("Teasing," Bill called it, although that wasn't the word other people used.) There was something about tall receding men with dark mustaches that made Bill queasy; he didn't ask why. Whatever it was, "Dr. Whelan" reminded him of an overactive marrow that had bolted up unseen until it was hollow and meaty and much too long for comfort. The way things were going Danny would be six inches taller and completely bald by the time his famous book came out, assuming it actually existed. And Bill, for one, had his doubts.

Needing to work off an aggression that was all the stronger for being irrational, he waited until the rest of the department arrived before grilling Danny on the book's progress. His teeth glinted yellow. "You must be almost finished. I remember you telling me the year before last that you were on the penultimate chapter."

Feeling like a nine-year-old who hadn't done his homework, Danny muttered the usual unconvincing phrases. He had made "rapid progress" and was on "the final 'final draft.'" Although it was true that he hadn't yet been offered a contract he had nonetheless had "*genuinely* firm interest from *several* firms of *big* and *important* academic publishers" and he had "*every* reason to be hopeful."

But no one was convinced.

Some projects have an aura of disaster about them and Danny's book was one such enterprise. He tried to change the subject but Bill kept turning the screw, like the sadist he was, until Danny had flushed to his armpits. Refusing to be fobbed off and making no concessions to the rest of the company, Bill pressed him about every single chapter. He even raised an eyebrow at Barbara Barnes, daring her to join the humiliation. (She looked away.) Faced with Bill's coffin-like grin (one couldn't call it a smile), Danny knew that it wasn't only paranoia that made him dislike his boss.

Half an hour later, having mysteriously lost his appetite for dinner, Danny cleaned a space on the steamed-up window of the number fourteen bus. He contemplated decaying city streets and tried not to think about the new term. Instead he inspected the other passengers and cooled his forehead with the back of his hand. The smell of wet wool was almost overpowering.

As usual, he came home to an empty house. He hardly minded though. It was enough that it was Friday and that he'd escaped the horrors of communal pasta. What did it matter that he'd forgotten to set the central heating and the house was like a tomb? At least he had the weekend to himself. Dropping his briefcase by the door, he wondered what he could have for supper.

Poached eggs on toast?

French bread and cheese?

Or pot noodles? (Just for a change.)

Having carefully laid the table, he ate a simple meal with pleasure. (Scrambled eggs and crisp bread with a single glass of wine.) Then he crawled into bed for an early night. Tomorrow—he promised—he would have a lie-in.

The last thing he saw as he drifted off to sleep was the formidable Dr. Barnes, all manicured nails and finely layered hair. Danny wondered how her evening had gone and what sort of colleague she was going to be. Then he heard Marcus Cranborne's sinister whisper "Your Ronaldo has gross pustules"—and he laughed out loud at the memory.

2

It was 9:27 p.m. and Barbara Barnes was locked in the ladies' room. ("Hands fine. Hair worrying.") As she set about the necessary repairs she remembered how she'd felt when she walked into the seminar room. Heart beating—self-conscious—everybody looking at her. The terror was still fresh: but also the exhilaration. Part of her enjoys these self-displays although another bit is terrified of failure.

So had this one worked?

She reviewed the signs as she returned to her table. There had been spontaneous applause, several useful questions, adoring looks from a female postgraduate, plus back-slapping in the bar. But there had also been cons—such as fat-faced Ronan's question. (He caught her eye as she crossed the restaurant floor; she waved a radiant acknowledgment.) It was less troubling that Rachel Glover had disapproved. Not only were Rachel and Deirdre close to retirement, their claim to be feminists mainly rested on the fact that they dressed like suffragettes. (Barbara reminded herself *never* to buy a cape.) But though Bill Roberts was attentive he hadn't said a word about her paper.

As she despaired—the day had been a disaster from beginning to end—she grasped the back of her chair and dropped gracefully into her seat. Then she smiled her fullest smile, rapped her fingers in Marcus Cranborne's direction, and started flirting as broadly as she dared. As she worked her favorite tricks (hair blazing, voice loud) she wondered what she'd done to deserve yet another goatish academic. She thought she'd left that breed behind in Oxford.

Not that Marcus presented any difficulties. Barbara had long since realized she attracted aging public schoolboys who wanted to be looked after. With their love of bossiness they were happy to accept her brassy public image provided they could get their leg over every other Saturday. Unfortunately for them, however, Barbara had other demands. For her, a man ought to be strong. She didn't go for losers,

doi:10.1300/5902_02

only her equals. Or better still, for men she thought of as superiors. But every now and then, when her ego felt weak, it was useful to spar with the Marcus Cranbornes of the world. Their guileless attention was a powerful restorative—like gin drunk straight from the bottle but considerably less dangerous.

Barbara realized that her new colleagues were trying to work her out. She liked it when people couldn't take their eyes off her. But she also wondered if the line beside her mouth was noticeable and whether her tweezers had missed any graying hairs. Being blonde, she had to search hard for them and was constantly anxious that whole colonies might be hiding unseen on the back of her head. For the fifteenth time that day she wished she could sink through the floor and rise up ten years younger. The yearning was more about self-preservation than vanity. Unlike the others, she hadn't always been an academic. In fact, until recently she'd had a proper job. "Tell us a few classroom secrets," said Bill—and she could have struck him for revealing her past. "So you used to be a schoolmistress!" exclaimed Marcus, picturing her in a starched pinafore with a pointer and a globe. "Tell us more!"

"There's nothing to say," she insisted. "It was a horrible job. If I'd had different career advice I'd never have done it." But that wasn't good enough. They demanded amusing anecdotes about drug-related playground violence. Anything to make them feel secure in their rather less "horrible" jobs.

Despite its social value, Barbara only saw wasted opportunities when she pictured her previous life. While she had been setting up reading clubs for the under-eights her rivals had stolen a decade's worth of marches. In those innocent days she had read feminist theory for fun and because she believed in it. She never guessed that every time she finished an interesting book she was supposed to write 6,000 to 8,000 words describing how its author had ignored a small but vital point, without which their argument was entirely worthless. As a result her early offerings had been embarrassingly upbeat. "What's this?" her PhD supervisor had asked of her first chapter. "Your job application for *Cosmo?*"

By the time she'd learned the necessary world-weary skepticism she discovered that the rest of her generation had moved on. These days postmodernism was where it was at—a bright and peppy place where anything could happen when you clicked your ruby-red slippers. Having abandoned Marx and de Beauvoir for cyberpunk, body piercings, and the Internet, those cunning bastards had opened up a new front while Barbara was still galloping to battle on a horse that might expire at any moment. Cursing her rivals as they disappeared over the horizon, she wondered if she would ever catch up with better-shod youngsters like Ronan MacIntyre.

It wasn't that she was old; she knew she wasn't. But every morning she worried they were there—more wrinkles, more white hairs. And they had to be eradicated. Although she feared becoming a sinister replica of her mother (a woman whose vanity would have given Cleopatra pause for thought), she needed whatever weapons she could find in her new career. English departments were full of people who would shake their wise male heads and say "She's under-published for her age"—and that would be that. To have a chance she had to pass as a bright young thing whose career was ahead of her. It was simple really. All she had to do was publish like crazy and stay eternally young. That way she'd stop cocky graduate students from leapfrogging over her in their callous search for Readerships, Senior Lectureships, and killer agents who could get them onto *Newsnight*.

Though she had mastered the party line of her new institution she wasn't sure that ex-polytechnics and cheap and cheerful Italian restaurants were for her. Some of her colleagues might believe their spin about "the excitement of life in a large provincial town" and the "intellectual adventurousness of the new universities," but Barbara—who had been born to a different set of social aspirations—wanted more status. That was why she'd gone to Oxford for her doctorate and why she dressed the way she did. With her armory of fancy letters and fancy clothes how could anyone stop her?

While academia was unlikely to earn her much money, the right appointment might recall something of the glamour that she'd known, way too briefly, as a child. She had decided against the United States. ("*Far* too vulgar.") Instead she fantasized about summer cocktails in a walled garden in Grantchester or North Oxford. Only then would she call herself successful. So when Ronan MacIntyre expressed surprise that a forty-year-old could still be "just a junior lecturer" she smiled benignly and took another drink. Why get riled? She wouldn't be staying there for long. Soon she'd be an academic superstar out of David Lodge or Malcolm Bradbury—a history woman for the new millennium. And in the meantime she smiled at Marcus Cranborne, enunciated firmly, and left her meal untouched.

Marcus looked inquiringly at her plate.

"It's fine," she explained, "really it is. Except it's not actually a *risotto*. They haven't used arborio, let alone *carnoli,* and I doubt if that yellow stuff is saffron."

Ronan smiled at her pointedly accurate pronunciation. "So wise of you not to attempt the accent," he murmured.

"What was that?"

"I was saying how wise I was to avoid the osso buco."

Barbara touched the line beside her mouth. She felt protective of it; it was a sign of things to come. Gulping down the plonk, she pulled a comic face as if to say "I am used to better things. I'm only drinking this to humor you." It was a way of expressing independence. "I do not seek your reassurance," she seemed to indicate. "On the contrary, *you* must seek *mine*."

Marcus, who was more gourmand than gourmet, joined the fun.

"A spiky young red," he suggested. "Redolent of—?"

"Wood chip?"

"Petrol fumes?"

"Bile!"

As she contemplated his swede-like face, Barbara reflected that although Marcus was a senior lecturer—and therefore worthy of attention—he wasn't a patch on her darling little Stevie. How lucky she was to have a partner who held her hand through every crisis. (And she had three of these a day.) He was so sexy, so supportive. If only she could be sure that he needed her as much as she needed him!

Overcome by the unexpected panic that can affect even the chirpiest of us, she forced herself to take deep breaths. Ronan looked at her inquisitively. She saw the glance—knew its meaning—and switched immediately to her most powerful mode:

"*Don't* you think that. . . ?"

"I really *do* believe that . . ."

"No, I *can't* agree with you *there* . . ."

"As far as *I'm* concerned . . ."

It was exhausting, but it had to be done. There could be no betrayal of her weakness. On she talked, often wittily and always firmly, until even Bill Roberts laughed once or twice.

He baffled her.

He greeted her best remarks with total silence but was inordinately amused by puns. (Perhaps they reminded him of the metaphysical poets?) Whatever it was, she didn't like him watching her. Being watched was different from being admired. Being watched was sinister. It was too much like being judged.

Instinctively, she hid her mouth with her hand.

As Barbara would soon find out, most people found Bill Roberts "difficult." He lived frugally and alone. In an academic such behavior usually signaled an obsessive dedication to scholarship, yet no one could claim that Professor Roberts lived for his research. His reputation rested on a book nobody read except to refute. It had been published twenty years ago, when professorships were easier to come by. In the current market he'd have been lucky to get a part-time lectureship let alone a Chair.

But if Bill didn't write during the evening what *did* he do? You couldn't imagine him curled before a cheerfully tacky quiz show. Nor was he the sort of bachelor who practiced haute cuisine. Danny Whelan often fantasized that his boss was the ringleader of an international gang trafficking in women, children, and stolen copies of Shakespeare's First Folio. However, the truth was more banal. Having realized he'd never be a big-name academic, Bill had turned himself into a career administrator.

These days poetry was merely a site for the exercise of power. He loved terrorizing the first-years with his superior humanity. (Not one of them could rival his sensitive appreciation of Donne's late verse.) Confronted by their vulgar interest in television, Game Boys, and fantasy writing, Bill felt infinitely refined. Indeed their ignorance was so pleasing that he could hardly bring himself to spoil it. Given this, and given the extreme unpopularity of his classes, he thought it advisable to avoid too heavy a seminar load. Weren't there other ways of serving his department? Restricting his teaching to a few specialist groups, he concentrated on nods and winks, secret deals, leaked memos, and committee meetings where he pulled the wool over his colleagues' eyes. If he looked more excited than they did on Monday mornings it wasn't religious poetry that sustained him so much as his anticipation of another week of intimidating orders, threatening glares, and loaded silences. (For he never raised his voice if he could help it. He preferred having people strain.)

His favorite arena was the interview panel.

As well as providing rich opportunities for bullying, appointment committees were invaluable for empire-building. His chosen candidates were fed supportive questions while rival applicants were blasted into orbit. However, his selections could be surprising. He didn't approve of Barbara's research but he had pushed for her appointment. These days everything was an "ism." Post-structuralism, new historicism, multiculturalism. Feminism was no better; if anything, it was worse. (There was nothing more upsetting, he thought, than a woman in a surplice.) But though he wanted "the ladies" to know their place, he was sufficiently ruthless to grasp that his career depended on his colleagues producing Important Research that would gain government funding and attract students to their courses. If he had to let the PC trendies in, so be it.

Thus it was that the feminist Barbara Barnes and the queer theorist Ronan MacIntyre found themselves in a university otherwise dominated by remnants of the sixties. Once they were in, it was never long before Bill passed his candidates confidential information about the people who'd opposed their appointment and how he had fought against enormous opposition to have them "on board" (as he archly called it). He had his favorites put on committees, where they would vote according to his "encouragement" and "advice." By contrast, colleagues such as Danny Whelan who had arrived before he became Head of Department were rigidly sidelined.

Bill's influence stretched beyond English. Besides dominating the Arts School he sat on the Promotions and Tenure Committee, another important forum for handing out rewards and punishing disloyalty. However, his thoughts were on higher things. He dreamed of the Arts and Sciences Liaison Group, the Finance Committee, and the University-Wide Working Party on Syllabus Reform. Then there were the vast resources of the Ongoing-Audit Committee, a Dickensian outfit that delighted in harassing and confusing the rest of the university by nit-picking their every word and deed. Higher still lay the Vice-Chancellor's Steering Party (a kitchen cabinet for people who couldn't cook) and the Forward Motion Group (a rival cabal that only existed to undermine the Vice-Chancellor's Steering Party). Bill grew restless imagining the influence he'd have if he sat on such committees. Oh, the teases he could set in motion for no other reason than that he enjoyed annoying people, especially the weak and the vulnerable.

Although he was confident he could do a better job than the current Vice-Chancellor (who had an absurdly old-fashioned belief in consensus government), Bill wasn't powerful enough to challenge for the succession. First he needed a base camp. Within the next two years he planned to be the Pro-Vice Chancellor with Particular Responsibility for the Humanities. It would be pleasing to have something attainable in mind: not so much a focus for his machinations as a star to wish upon.

Yes, that was a good way to phrase it: "A star to wish upon."

Put like that, it almost sounded poetic.

As yet Barbara knew nothing of Bill's determined way with colleagues but her eyes widened respectfully when he stopped an overexuberant Dr. Cranborne from entering her taxi. Without saying a word, Bill carried his point and Barbara rode home without Marcus's Latin quotations.

As she traveled, she scarcely noticed the stars that lit the sky. (For the rain had finally stopped.) All she knew was her triumph. The anxiety—the feverish rewriting—the application of layer upon layer of protective makeup—the retching—the walking into a chattering room and hearing it still, horrifically, as she approached the lectern. Everything had paid off, and for once she liked the face reflected in her window. The nose was not too big, the mouth was soft and small.

Out she bounded, key in hand, ready for music, dancing, laughter.

She giggled as she moved through the hall to the kitchen. "I'm home and dry," she thought as she poured a glass of red, opened a can of olives, and took out the Brie. "Home and dry with a man who loves me. I'm so happy I could cry."

Whereupon she laid her head on the table and wept until she thought she would die.

3

By the time he'd read the first question Danny's body was covered in a mess of stinking sweat. It was bad enough that the instructions were in German but his rushed translation didn't help: "Your municipal swimming pool is eighty feet by thirty feet. The deep end is ten feet and the shallow end is four feet. Two-thirds of the way across the pool shelves downwards at an angle of twenty-five degrees. If the pool keeper's hose is filling it at a rate of one cubic foot per thirty seconds, how long will it be before the pool is full?"

No sooner had he realized he was dreaming than his relief was washed away by new anxieties. When was his first class? What was he teaching? Had he finished marking the essays? Did he have a problem group? What time was it? Where was the alarm clock? Why hadn't it gone off?

It took several more seconds before he remembered it was Saturday. Almost delirious with pleasure, he wrapped the duvet close and went back to sleep. It was six a.m. The same sequences of panic and pleasure followed at six-thirty, seven, seven-thirty, and eight.

At eight-thirty he got up.

Rather than cluttering them with academic research, Danny spent his Saturdays with books he knew backwards. Sitting in his dressing gown with a pot of strong black tea, he read *Jane Eyre* for the hundred and nineteenth time. At forty-two he was still able to groan at Jane's reverses and rejoice at her good fortune. The final chapter was his favorite. He adored its air of quiet triumph.

Breakfast finished, he avoided the eye of his computer as he picked another book to accompany him to the toilet. After dangling over an unread copy of *Crime and Punishment,* his hand descended on *Mansfield Park*. Fanny Price was bound to do the trick. He planned his day between chapters, although "planned" was probably the wrong word. His Saturdays had only two fixed points: shopping in the morning and catching up with the day's soccer results on *Match of the Day* in the evening. Between these there might be a visit to an art gallery, a pub lunch, or a bit of desultory cruising in the kitchenware section of Habitat. Anything might happen. Anything or nothing.

Danny watched everything as he walked into town.

Across the street a woman reasoned sweetly with her children. He peered at her suspiciously but although the kids were called Ariadne, Sappho, and Hector, he didn't recognize her from the university. Relieved, he went on observing. Details amused him, like the black-and-white cat curled beside a Guinness billboard or the smell of Lapsang souchong that had begun to pervade certain roads.

The district had altered radically in the last ten years. Rather than working-class pubs, wine bars proliferated, along with VELUX windows and enameled tiles saying "Beware of the Cat"—many of them in Portuguese. Having been drawn to the red-brick terraces because they reminded him of childhood, Danny resented gentrifying newcomers and tried to keep his house as "authentic" as he could. While it sometimes occurred to him that his carefully kitsch décor represented a different sort of betrayal this wasn't something he dwelled on.

As on the previous three weeks, his first stop was a bric-a-brac market cum second-hand bookshop. Danny wasn't interested in first editions; a remaindered sports biography gave him more pleasure than an unreadable verse epic with marbled endpapers. However, if a book was to his taste, it produced an almost sexual delight. Its weight in his lap, his fingers on its pages! Here was a visceral joy he wouldn't dream of sharing with his colleagues. But books weren't his sole reason for visiting the shop. Fascinating though its "pieces" were, none was more intriguing than the plummy young man who worked there on Saturday mornings. "Freddie" he was called and he was one of Danny's rare blonds. ("I *prefer* brunets," he had often thought, "but when I *do* fall for a blond it's head over heels.")

The mechanics of the crush fascinated Danny. Some weeks he saw an object he wanted, only to leave without buying it. Other times, when he was determined to save his money, he got something ugly and expensive because Freddie had given him a boyish smile. A psychology was at work. To speak or not to speak? To be stern or self-indulgent? To leave the shop feeling happy—in a shame-faced way—after a harmless flirtation? Or to be sad but self-respecting after refusing to meet Freddie's eyes? There was no right way. Whatever happened he'd regret it later. And he never knew from week to week how things would turn out.

This time Freddie was busy with another customer. Danny had to grab his attention back. But what could he buy? He had too much junk as it was. At last he moved to the counter with a twice-rejected bit of china. Although they never managed more than a cheerful exchange about the weather there was no doubting Freddie's eagerness to please; he often held Danny's gaze. However, Danny would have been mortally embarrassed if Freddie ever did make moves on him. When he fancied someone the soles of his feet began to sweat and a thick-scaled snake twisted itself around his tongue until the most inoffensive of sentences came out as outrageous spoonerisms.

Anxiety made waiting a torture. The man ahead was haggling. (Danny *never* haggled.) Soon it would be time to pick his change out of Freddie's soft pink hand—a hand he wanted to put in his mouth and bite. *(Hard.)* Looking away, he glimpsed himself in the security monitor. "Who would go for *that?*" he groaned, horrified by his receding hairline and stooping figure. Panicked by a mixture of longing and dread, he wheeled around and left the shop. Six paces later—realizing what he'd done—he rushed back, smiled winningly at Freddie, replaced the plate, and returned to the street, blushing with shame.

Having blotted the morning with this moment of lust-driven forgetfulness, he saw nothing for it but to crash round Waitrose buying luxury goods for lunch. He felt dubious about their "fairy ring mushrooms" but was ready to rejoice—with every other gay man in town—at the start of the all-too-brief red banana season. The result was an exotic if unbalanced meal.

Danny often meant to spend Saturday afternoons at an exhibition or a matinee but these expeditions rarely happened. And today he had an excuse. The wind had whipped itself up and sheets of rain were cutting against his windows. A bang upstairs provoked fears of a camp version of the fall of the House of Usher in which the atrocious weather caused him to be buried alive by flying ducks and hostess trolleys. However, a glance in his study showed that it was simply a box file crashing off his desk. Rather than reshelving it, he left it on the floor with the rest of his book. How many drafts were there now? At least seven. (Not counting the notes waiting to be written up.) Ten years of work were sprawled around the room—a shapeless monster that threatened to take over the rest of the house.

He found he was sweating.

Then other worries crowded by. Things like his height (which had always troubled him) and his age (which was just beginning to). In general he was wise enough to ask little of life. The greatest pleasures he could think of were an absence of worry, a slackening of stress. But despite his efforts he sometimes longed—with a despairing force—for things he had lost, or given up, or had never had in the first place.

Lately a sense of failure had begun to permeate everything he did. He wasn't any good. He was too lazy, too timorous. Too old. He should have held out for love, money, fame—the things he'd dreamed of at sixteen.

But mostly he yearned for men whose looks he hadn't returned, whose numbers he hadn't rung. Men he'd run from because his fear had made him cram his mind with other things. Freddie was a no-body—a posh fantasy. But behind his blond hair and cut-glass vowels lay a man who'd given Danny more than a decade of pain—a man who rose in his memory, the image and the voice as clear as winter sun.

"Christian," he murmured, pausing as he spoke for a moment of lust, anger, pain, nostalgia, humor, self-disgust, elation, boredom, doubt, resentment, horror, longing, and fatigue. (*Deep* fatigue.)

He smiled at a memory.

"Christian Ellis," he repeated. "Christian fucking Ellis." And then, with a laugh: "The sexy bastard!"

It still baffled Danny that he and Christian had never gotten to-gether. Right from the start, they'd been so close their friends assumed they were a pair—and in Danny's head they were. The time he'd spent on daydreams! For eight years he'd pictured a Heal's double bed (king-size of course) in a north London flat where the only jarring notes came from the Stephen Sondheim scores playing in the background. But he never got round to sharing these plans with Christian. Instead he deferred his confession, and with it his desire. (And meantime Christian said nothing.)

It was a way of life. Danny grew used to it.

Then—without warning—Christian went away. "Disappeared," in fact. No one knew where to. They just knew he didn't want to be contacted. For he'd told them so in no uncertain terms. But Danny refused to let go. He wouldn't see anyone new. For five more years he'd filled his life with crushes while watching Christian's work becoming increasingly famous. One recurring nightmare had his friend whispering the latest news. "*Silence and Remorse* is in its twelfth edition," he'd boast. "Not bad for an academic monograph. Don't you think?" At which Danny wouldn't know whether to make a pass or to tell him not to be so fucking pushy.

He sighed.

With one thing and another the day wasn't going as he'd have liked. He wondered how he could stop his bitterness from ruining the entire weekend. It was half past three—far too early to start on supper.

But what, then? Not even *Wuthering Heights* would lift *this* mood. There was nothing he could do. Nothing.

Then, abruptly, he lightened.

There were ways and ways of spending a rainy Saturday and he knew one of the best. Dawdling up the stairs with delicious hesitation he pulled his bedroom curtains, took out some tissues, undressed, and got into bed for a long and comfortable wank while listening to the live soccer commentaries on Radio 5.

Ah, he thought, with a triumphant smile. *The romance of the no-score draw!*

4

"Playing with yourself again?"

The question stopped him dead.

Peering through a veil of dreams, Danny answered back—"cheeking," it would have been called when he was younger.

"Of course I am," he muttered. "Who else would I be playing with?" But gawp though he might, he couldn't see who had spoken.

On he slept, surrounded by used tissues, as the radio played in the background. (The matches were over and the phone-ins had begun.)

Football had always mattered to Danny—his earliest memories were of going to games with his dad. And perhaps those days came back to him as he turned on the bed. Maybe *they* were why he flinched, and smiled, and drooled, and tried to cry out in the mad, muffled way that dreams produce. It probably wasn't his mother he was seeing; she had died when he was three. Could it be his dad? (A man baffled by parenthood.) Or was it some other man, or men?

"Shut up!" he tried to say. "Shut up!"

But the words refused to come out.

Danny was seven when he saw his first match.

By then, nothing much remained of his mother except her photograph and a sense of not knowing what it was he was missing. Later, he sometimes wondered if football—in some weird way—had filled her empty place. Except it wasn't the game that made the difference, it was the experience of being there with his dad.

Normally, Larry Whelan couldn't speak without blushing, but for forty-five minutes at a time he had a new way of living. Danny was both scared and excited by these transformations. It was natural for him to imitate his father's gestures—the stamping and the yelling and the furious remarks. And it was equally natural for Larry to as-

doi:10.1300/5902_04

sume his son had gotten the hang of things. But Danny, who wasn't one for hanging out with other boys, hadn't a clue what was going on below him.

However, after several visits he noticed that the action ebbed and flowed.

The game had shape. It was like the dances they did at school. ("Free expression," Miss Lister called them.) Except rougher.

Men ran.

And then stopped.

They moved in a pack. Then one of them would strike out alone. They slid along the mud or rose into the air. Often they were knotted together. Other times they moved in pairs. They were controlled by a heavy brown ball. The object was to avoid the ball as it hurled itself towards them. Most times it made for their feet. Less often their heads. They usually managed to brush past it, but sometimes they were forced to touch it. (Fortunately this didn't happen very often.) Occasionally songs broke out, cheery refrains that faded as they started. Once in a while, the ball hid at the far end of the field. Some people liked this but others didn't. And when everybody had worn themselves out, they hung their heads and trudged home. (That part rarely changed.)

After a few weeks, when he was getting the drift of things, Danny tried a smile.

His father grasped it like a stroke patient fixing on a word. The boy often had the beating of him. Especially since they'd been on their own. But maybe they were on to something here? Wishing that *she* could have been there to take care of things, he pointed out the atrocious interplay between the midfielders and the striker. But his voice came out too loud and high. He hated what he said, and how he sounded. (Why couldn't he just *speak* to the kid?)

Although Danny couldn't quite follow what his dad was saying he was flattered at the man-to-man approach. He tried a comment of his own—something about the players' balletic grace—at which his Dad gave him a funny look and said the other side were just as bad, worse probably, though they were having the better of the luck.

Danny asked why the players were slipping. His voice was cautious—a youngster poking at a bruise.

His father's mouth suggested an uncharacteristically strong response. "Because they're a load of—" He stopped to rearrange his face. "It's the pitch," he explained. "It's wet from last night's rain."

Danny nodded. He sort of understood. But he wondered why the game went on when the players couldn't stand up straight. Apart from anything else, it made the dance monotonous.

He and his father traded comments as they walked home past high red walls and concrete funnels. (Years later, Danny would weep in public when he came across a L.S. Lowry in a London gallery. And he'd thought he hated Lowry's paintings!) Game by game, a momentum built. Much ground was covered, all of it mysterious. Sweepers and flat back fours. Set piece play. The offside rule. The words were symbols in a poem—the fact that Danny didn't understand increased their power. Then Larry would rouse himself, realizing what the boy's grandmother would say when they were late for tea.

What would she have made?

"Sausages," suggested Danny.

"Egg and chips," said his dad.

"She won't be pleased. We've been away for hours."

Larry winked conspiratorially. "Women!" he laughed. "They haven't a clue what's important!" But he saw his wife as he spoke—and was sorry.

For more reasons than they could explain, Danny and his father counted the days between home matches. Danny was proud to skip beside his big, tall dad, and Larry walked all the straighter for having escaped, for a couple of hours, from his mother's house, and the shame of being widowed.

Week by week, they prayed shyness wouldn't get the better of them. With quiet, nervous voices, they stretched a thread between their minds and hoped it wouldn't snap. To share a house, and half their blood, yet know so little about each other's lives. What flimsy words they had, and what stilted speeches they made, as they tried to understand the thoughts and feelings by which they lived.

Half a season passed, and still one saw modern dance where the other felt each lunge and kick as if he'd made them himself. Danny liked it when his dad lifted him onto his shoulders. It wasn't just the view, it was the way his father tensed and relaxed. The match played itself out on Larry's body so that Danny, with a leg hoisted over each shoulder and two hands on his Dad's bald head, felt the action on the pitch through the heat and sweat and anger of his father.

There was antagonism on the field, and on the terraces, and on the streets outside—and all of it was channelled, for Danny's benefit, through his dad's upper body. Like his father, Danny had found a release for needs he didn't know he had. And although they saw different things, they felt the same emotions. Whether jeering or celebrating, they broke from silence into a clear, aggressive joy: and in doing so, they became as one.

Their problems came when the playing stopped and Danny climbed from his father's shoulders. Where once Larry would have gazed shyly at the floor he now sought his son's gaze with the same ferocity with which he'd followed the game. He didn't use to speak in such an excited way. The raised voice made Danny nervous, especially as he never understood what his dad was going on about.

Even when he noticed Danny's expression, Larry was afraid to ask what was wrong; you never knew what the boy might say. But most times he barely saw his son, he was so absorbed by this weird new role he'd found in the land of the talkative. Even so, he always watched for Danny's response at the end of each story. Unable to make much sense of, say, the ten best saves of the 1940s, Danny couldn't bear to meet his eyes. He'd no idea how to act when his dad got that look that begged him to be impressed. He scarcely recognized himself: It was as if he'd changed into a stranger who had to be talked to in this frightening way. And though he knew he was getting his reactions wrong when he saw his father's disappointment, he didn't know what else to do.

And *still* Larry talked.

". . . so up comes Charlie Cook, and he was a cocky one, that Charlie, and he takes a swipe from twenty yards out. Jimmy Willis is off his line but he tears right back and—"

Danny put his hands to his ears.

He didn't want his special shapes taken away, not even by his dad. (Or rather, *especially* not by his dad.) So he stamped his foot and refused to hear. Larry was too deep in 1949 to see his son's unrest. He only noticed when Danny—who was enjoying the experiment more than he'd expected—turned his whimpers into full-scale shrieking. People started staring, and if there was one thing Larry hated it was being made a spectacle of.

"What *is* it?" he demanded, suddenly annoyed.

Danny squeezed his fists into his eyes and cried even harder. Which was worse, Larry wondered, his son's tantrum or his own attempts at conversation? This speechifying was no good. The boy didn't like it, and it made people gawp. He was foolish, and hot, and Danny was as odd as two left feet. A man could despair with a son like that to show him up.

Perhaps everything would disappear if he shut his eyes. Maybe he'd wake up with his life wide open—no wife, no son, no mother. And no false turnings in the road ahead. He felt like weeping at the pain of being who he was. But on bawled the child—the stupid fucking kid. He'd better see to it, he supposed, but Christ knows how. Its mother would have known but Larry didn't.

He moved his hand uncertainly. A pat might do the trick, or a nudge. He shifted nearer, his body awkward and his arm as stiff as if he'd been about to stroke some flighty animal—a Siamese cat, or a miniature dog. Unnerved at this development, Danny flinched, and his backward step triggered everything that his father had been trying to repress. Larry didn't care for overbred pets with curls and pedicures. In fact, they turned his stomach.

Such things were more to a woman's taste than a man's. Not that Larry had had much to do with women recently. (Well, how could he have?) He closed his eyes, the better to embrace the past, and to dream about a future. But when he opened them again he was stuck in the same gray scene. Then his dead wife seemed to rise before him:

half in memory and half for real—a vessel for his need. He leaned towards her. He wanted her as if it was his wedding night—his first time, and hers as well. He was young, he had desires. But she slid away from him to put her arms around the boy.

The failure felt total, and there was nothing he could say to lance it before jealousy, and loss, and fear, and desire, and shame, and frustration made him raise his hand as high as it would go then bring it down, with his fullest force, on the back of Danny's head.

(Was it this that made Danny call out so loudly that he woke himself? Stabbing at his bedclothes, he slowly stretched, then rose and took a shower.)

By the time he was twelve Danny knew what goals were and why they mattered. And he could see them better now that he'd shot up into a beanpole. Though he and his dad still went to home matches, silence closed over them after those first few months of speech. Silence was safer. It discouraged false hopes, and it matched their personalities. It wasn't that they disliked each other. (For never again did Larry hit his son.) They were just too awkward to talk about the things they loved. Mutual respect became a way of holding off closeness.

Danny still wasn't interested in tactics. As far as he was concerned, team performance was just an excuse to watch individual players. Even when they were off the ball their forceful presence commanded his attention. He was moved by their delicacy and strength, and by their sudden shifts of pace. One moment a guy would be getting his breath back, his hands on his hips and his thighs gently steaming. Then he'd whirr towards the action, steering through hostile players while his teammates streamed ahead. Another second later he'd be alone on the edge of the field, his arms poking awkwardly from his shirt, the play having moved somewhere else.

Danny wished he could have one of them for a brother, or even as his father. (It was his guiltiest secret.) He pictured the two of them alone in the house, his Nan having conveniently moved out. They'd have such fun eating breakfast together and sharing his dad's big bed. The things that were happening underneath his clothes wouldn't matter anymore and neither would his ridiculous size. He'd be friendly but distant with his schoolmates, even when they tried to make up for their past mistakes by calling his name when they were picking teams for football. He wouldn't need them anymore because he'd have a better chum at home: a nice tough brother who'd teach him things he couldn't even guess at.

While waiting for these dreams to come true, he taped pages from *Shoot!* onto his bedroom walls. His Nan said he'd ruin the paintwork but his dad wouldn't tell him off. He said he was a good kid, really. Action shots were Danny's favorites. He liked seeing a couple of bodies in a battle that only one of them could win. That, or a striker heading the ball so hard that his neck was like a racehorse's as it strained towards the finishing post. He hated studio portraits where hardened players got strangled by their kipper ties while Brylcream sank into their collars. Wives and children were worse again. Players were the thing: Their names spoke to him of secret possibilities. And like a map of his attractions, they altered over time.

First and forever after, there was Georgie Best.

Over thirty years later Danny still recalled the day a girlie magazine turned up in his primary school playground. His friend Davey claimed to have bought it, bold as brass, with his pocket money, but Davey was always bragging about that sort of thing and the mag had obviously been blowing round for days. Even so, every boy in Primary Four screamed in jealous disbelief when he produced it.

Was *that* what women looked like?, they wondered.

Like the poses they were stretched in, the models' bodies strained belief. Hair, flesh, teeth. These weren't women like their sisters or their mothers. They were an alien breed calling for shouts of derision and professions of lust. Disturbing though the contortions were, the classmates knew how they were supposed to respond to them. And respond they did, at the tops of their treble voices, until they turned the page and saw Mr. George Best with a towel round his waist.

Years later, when he thought back to how the image had silenced them, Danny wondered whose idea it was to put a footballer in a porno mag. You'd understand it if he'd been loafing in a nightclub showing off his rock-star life with Miss World on one arm and Mother Teresa of Calcutta on the other. But he was alone in the dressing room, his skin wet from a shower and his eyes glancing out, invitingly, to the world beyond the page. What was a bloke supposed to do? Dream of being Georgie, or of fucking the woman on the other side of the page?

Even at the time, Danny marked how the crowing boys who made his life a misery had been frightened into silence by the very person that they most wished to be. For these were their in-between years. Soon they would embrace their changing bodies, revelling in the power that masculinity could bring. But until they reached that point they needed the nervy reassurance of an all-boys gang. As they looked from one to the other, their eyes showed their fear. How could any of them grow to be as big as this, or as frighteningly dark?

Meantime, Danny couldn't take his eyes off the photo. Never had his will been torn from him so forcefully.

Although he didn't have words to describe it he knew, right then, that he was looking at the purest, most dangerous distillation of what it could mean to be a man. Like his friends, he was attracted and repelled by Georgie's arrogance. But unlike the others Danny saw no line between who he wanted to be, and who he wanted to have. *I don't know what this feeling is,* he thought, as he registered the effect that the footballer's cockiness was having on him. *I don't know what it's called.* He just knew that he wanted to be inside this perfect sheath of muscle, skin, and bone.

As soon as it entered Danny's life, the photo summarized and superseded everything that had preoccupied him. His father. His father's friends. His teachers. The players from the local league. And now George Best. Each had something to tell him about who he was and who he might become. When each of them had had their say he was able to look back, as an adult, and laugh that "George Best turned me gay." He meant it as a challenge to the sort of straight men who said their interest in sport had nothing to do with sex. But of course the truth was more complex. Danny couldn't have decided, at nine, that he was gay, for he didn't hear that word until much later. Who knew if he'd chosen the path or had it chosen for him?

And what is choice, anyway? It wasn't true, he decided, that you went through life without alternatives. It was more that you had little say over the options you were given. Whether the subject was dish detergents, politics, or sex, your choices were heavily restricted. Genuinely new paths were hard to come by. And the older he got, the more this depressed him.

(For a moment he stopped chopping carrots and listened more closely to the news. Then he cursed the Prime Minister [or was it the Home Secretary?], threw down his knife, and switched off the radio.)

Other things lapsed when Danny went to London University, but not football.

His straight friends were suspicious when they heard that he went by turns to White Hart Lane and Highbury. ("You can't support them *both*," they protested. "No one likes Arsenal *and* Spurs.") As patiently as possible, he explained that he was simply amusing himself until he could see "a real team" in action. But the truth was, when it came to talent his attention had to roam. Provided his own lot weren't involved, he supported whichever team had the better players on a given day. And if his mates accused him of contaminating the game with queer preoccupations, he just raised a skeptical eyebrow and kept silent, not even saying "I told you so!" when half the men in the TV room jumped up to embrace each other at the full-time whistle.

Of course some of his new gay gang also had problems with his obsessions. ("Don't you think it's, like, such a capitulation to normative masculinity?") But he didn't see why he should give up the ties he'd grown up with. After all, it was thanks to them that he understood desire. Like counting the rings from which a tree was made, he could trace his past selves by rhyming off his heroes.

From adolescence onwards, he'd gone through specialized phases that sometimes clashed and sometimes chimed with the fashions of the time. There was, for example, the hairy period (better not to inquire too closely about *that* one), which had been followed by the age of the sweatband. Perms passed him by, as he was too busy enjoying the early days of Gary Lineker (and what a golden age *that* had been!) but there was no way he, or anyone else, could ignore the cyclical tightening and loosening of the players' shorts. (Like the changing of the tides, that one seemed set to go on and on through history.) But during it all, he still saw matches as theatrical events—the nearest anyone would ever get, these days, to a first night at the Globe. In fact, he'd often boasted to Christian that he'd prefer a local derby, any day, to three and a half hours of *Hamlet*. And he meant it too, for Shakespeare's language was pitifully thin compared to what he heard on the terraces.

Although Christian wasn't averse to watching half-dressed men groping each other while thousands of spectators cheered orgasmically, he wouldn't admit that the game itself was interesting. ("Get real, Dan! It's even more pointless than baseball! It's just their jockey shorts you're into.")

For their first international match, Danny lay on the floor with an only partly ironic England scarf while Christian sat on the sofa—a picture of detachment. "I'm so glad the U.S. isn't playing," he commented. "Otherwise I might have to be patriotic." Although he'd been in England for less than a year, he'd already flattened his New York accent into a curiously robotic mid-Atlantic drawl.

"You could always cheer for the land of your forefathers," suggested Danny. "They *always* go through."

Christian laughed. "Support Germany? Your lot would lynch me."

Was it Christian's appearance that made him so eerily untouchable or the way he spiked his words with irony? From the start, his and Danny's roles had been set by age and class and looks. Christian was younger but more senior: he'd gone straight from Harvard Graduate School to a Philosophy lectureship in UCL while Danny was still finishing his PhD on a diet of baked beans and part-time teaching. Danny wasn't going to complain when the glamorous newcomer took up with an unknown like himself, but even *he* couldn't help wishing, sometimes, that his friend wasn't so cool. Getting through to him about football became a symbol for another kind of breakthrough: it was the greatest incentive Danny had ever had to get his head round game plans and tactics. And sure enough, they were only twenty minutes into the international when he finally grasped what was "really" going on in the game.

The revelation was total and precise.

"Oh you stupid fucker!" he shouted when the manager's face flashed on the screen. "Put someone up the right. Fill the gap! What do they *pay* you for?" He appealed to Christian. "You agree with me, don't you? Their skills are fine but they're not playing as a team. They don't stand a chance!"

Christian smiled enigmatically. "I say," he mocked. "Get a grip, for Blighty's sake!"

"It matters!" muttered Danny. "It's not a joke."

But Christian only laughed and told him he should ring his father. ("Bonding over footie. Isn't that what you English are supposed to do?")

Danny usually forgave these jokes about "the English" but this one hit a nerve. "What's wrong with being patriotic?" he snapped. "Or caring about your family? Just because you couldn't give a shit about yours!"

Christian pulled a mocking face. He loved it when Danny took his bait.

Why bother trying to be cool?, thought Danny as he rushed to ring his dad. "There are more important things in life than that." It was his Englishness that was hurting, and his Northernness. He didn't see why Christian should feel superior just because of the wealth and citizenship his parents had acquired for him.

Once Larry got over the shock of hearing from his son on a day that wasn't the first Saturday of the month, he asked why Danny was calling halfway through a match. Chastened, Danny called back later with a rant about the manager's misguided substitutions. His dad responded with an equally heartfelt attack on the total crapness of the defense. Paradoxically, the more they exchanged disgusted comments the more patriotic they became. As with their hometown side, their devotion was strengthened as much by failure as success—which was just as well given how rarely either team could string three wins together.

When they thought about it later Danny and his father realized, in their separate halves of the country, that a conversation they'd attempted twenty years before had finally taken place. After that, they made more effort to fight back the silence Bravely and stiltedly, they went on talking—though not about everything. Danny, for example, was both guilty and amused that they owed their progress to a man that his father didn't know existed. And although he wished he could tell his dad about his friend, he went on saying nothing.

Comparable gaps cut into his dealings with Christian, for he never did crack The Saturday Problem. If his dreams had come true and they'd lived together, Christian would doubtless have wanted to go to some tiresomely chic restaurant to see and be seen, whereas Danny would have wanted a long night in watching Alan Hansen, Ruud Gullit, and the enduringly attractive Trevor Brooking. He still couldn't solve the puzzle. For, though his memories of Christian were more biddable than his physical presence, they weren't quite biddable enough.

So much joy had left football, and Danny's life, in the years that Christian had been away. Because of his job and his sexuality, Danny got accused of being one of the middle-class Johnny-come-latelies who'd come in with corporate boxes, Sky TV, and multipage fashion shoots. "That's outrageous!" he'd object. "I cried my eyes out when Scunthorpe beat us with two late goals. It was nineteen sixty-five and I was eight years old." But he protested too much. You could say what you liked about his father, but it was certain that Larry Whelan had never let anything but luncheon meat pass his lips, whereas Danny was the sort of person who ate salami on a regular basis.

So was he working class or middle class? Football fan or faggot? He tried to nail himself down. "I'm a gay man," he'd tell himself. "I'm in my early forties. I was raised in the North but I live and work in the Midlands. I'm single. I teach English. I'm from a working-class family. And I'm proud to count myself a friend of Christian Ellis."

Though he couldn't claim it saved him, the mantra brought a certain comfort.

Being alone has only one advantage, but it's a big one: being able to please yourself. Danny reflected on this pleasing truth as he opened a beer and clicked the remote for the opening credits of *Match of the Day*. It was his favorite moment of the week and he needed it all the more after the morning's embarrassments with Freddie in the junkshop. However, the program was unsettling. When he'd taken up his lectureship, it felt as if he and his favorite players were starting out together, equals at the height of their game. But these days he was older than a Third Division goalkeeper, and he didn't even have glory days to look back on. Every season since his teens he'd second-guessed which new players would turn into stars, but this year's lads were already multimedia celebrities with the cars, the houses, and the clothes to prove it. (And the women too.) They were also twenty years too young to be his mates.

Maybe that was why he felt elated, and not indignant as he used to, every time some cute-faced youngster got hacked to pieces. It was more than satisfactory, seeing a cocky youth floored by a grizzled left-back: it gave a body hope. Take the star of the moment. He could have been a "Jamie" or a "Joe" (or maybe even a "Robbie") but let's call him ... "Michael." The trouble with "Michael," as far as Danny was concerned, was that the kid didn't need any tutoring. His speed and guile were already overwhelming. Danny "respected and esteemed" him. And fancied him, too. But he found it hard to *like* him. If the ultra-young like "Michael" (or like Ronan MacIntyre, for that matter) insisted on being so poised, then they only had themselves to blame if people enjoyed seeing them facedown in the mud after an especially nasty tackle.

Sadly, "Michael" and the other infants who appeared in the end-of-match interviews had already mastered the art of personality concealment. Or perhaps they'd had to sign away all attempts at individuality before they could be issued with the blonde sidekick without which no soccer hopeful could call himself well-dressed. However, by turning down the sound, Danny was able to finish his day with a glimpse of perfect beauty. (Keats, he was sure, would approve.)

There was a perverse triumph in his ogling: It was one in the eye for youth, wealth, and beauty. So-bloody-what if some millionaire boyo didn't like being sized up by a poof? At their age, they ought to be able to take it. And God knows they were paid enough for the privilege.

Danny went to bed with "Michael," and Freddie, and Christian. The first two were strangers; he could wish them well without much strain. But Christian was different. Danny would never get to sleep if he didn't flush that image from his mind. One moment he would be remembering a shared joke and the next he'd be weeping in frustration. Scene after scene would pass through his mind. Parties where he could have sworn that signals had been given. Others where he was politely ignored. The old questions would recur. Where had he gone wrong? Why had his friend disappeared? And when, oh when, would he get over this emotional hangover? But what really troubled Danny, as he failed to sleep, was that he'd accepted Christian's actions without inquiry or dissent. And at this he'd feel a violence that he barely understood.

5

Sunday was Barbara Barnes' day for wandering round the house like a fright. Hair unwashed, a mud pack on her face, she ate a Mars Bar with a mug of cold tea. "Yes," she seemed to say as she gulped at her drink. "I don't have to please you every day. I can slob it if I want."

Although it was hours before her fortnightly visit to her mother, she already felt ill. It was like having double Maths followed by double PE: she didn't know where the bodily pain ended and the mental pain began. Cursing her lack of clean clothes, she put on an ancient two-piece, ate two plates of All-Bran, and drove to outer London to catch the tube to Wood Green.

She waited, with rain dripping down her neck, beside the miniature columns that adorned her mother's door. While the adjoining houses were becoming smarter, this one got more unkempt with every visit—and not just on the outside. In her mind's eye she could picture her mother turning this way and that among the mirrors in the mold-encrusted box room. (Or "dressing room" as Mrs. Barnes preferred to call it.) Through long-practiced adjustments Mrs. B could check front and back views, plus both profiles, without moving from her favorite mirror, the one whose surface she most admired. The examination would be repeated exactly three and a half times. Barbara had seen her do it for the doctor and the vicar. Why shouldn't a daughter get the same treatment?

The regulation five-and-three-quarter minute wait was more than usually annoying but Barbara knew better than to shout through the letterbox: there were penalty points for impatience. Instead she noted that the plaster keystone above the door had crumbled so completely that it could almost have been a *real* Greek head. And there were yet more cracks above the narrow bay window.

Mrs. Barnes began her descent at the appointed time.

doi:10.1300/5902_05

Her footsteps were utterly unhurried—a duchess couldn't have been more stately. One stair, two stairs, three stairs: each with a creak, and a halt, and an unseen smile. (If nothing else, she certainly knew how to shape a scene.) There was a much longer pause at the threshold before the door was finally thrown open.

Although she knew what to expect, Barbara still gaped.

The hallway that framed her mother might have been part of a National Trust initiative on lower-middle class décor from the early-twentieth century. But if the passageway was dingily Edwardian, the woman who stood in it resembled a matriarch from a 1940s film: or, better yet, the matriarch's younger sister—a "fast" great-aunt who wasn't entirely respectable. Her cocktail dress was a deeply lustrous purple: it glistened like black mother-of-pearl. However, it was the accessories that made Barbara jump. Her mother's left shoulder carried a brooch that Wallis Simpson might have envied: an abstract spray of diamonds with a square-cut emerald at its base. And pinned to her head was a black pillbox hat as crisply defined as the day it was made.

They looked each other over.

"My *dear*," (Mrs. B always said "my dear") "what *are* you wearing?" And then, not waiting for an answer, "Do you like my outfit?"

"Some people . . . might prefer a less formal look."

Mrs. Barnes whispered a reluctant agreement. "These days, I suppose. But during the War there were women who'd have killed for such a costume." ("Costume" was another of her words.) "It was the first one your father bought me." And she smiled with elaborate wistfulness—memories, no doubt, of the Café Royal.

"Mum, it's pouring. Can I come in? Is your cold better?"

But her mother wasn't ready for a change of subject. In spite of its age, the "costume" was in perfect condition. Here, if she cared to take it, was a lesson for Barbara: "You get the best you can afford—or *more* than you can afford. Then you take care of it." She stared meaningfully at her daughter's crumpled suit. "Shall we have a pot of tea?"

Barbara took the hint.

"The truth is," her mother continued. "I never cared for the nineteen forties. I was too young. It was only when I married that I started to be at *one* with my outfits."

While this was one of their safer conversations, it was also the most boring—especially if her mother started opening boxes. Having filled the kettle to the brim, Barbara let the gas hiss for a dangerously long time before lighting it with an old-fashioned flint. The voice from the front room could have been speaking to a Dictaphone, such was its confidence in being heard and its indifference to the listener's emotions.

Barbara spooned loose tea into a pot. She poured on water. She took out cups. This house had been her grandmother's, yet Barbara hadn't even known that it existed until her mother moved back to it. Nor had she known the grandmother whose home it had been. Although Barbara's mother had been born upstairs, she'd left as quickly as she could. In those days, the address was passable enough but it had never been smart, and smartness mattered to the future Mrs. Barnes.

Sadly, Mrs. B had found Wood Green rather worse when she came back to it in the early 1980s. Unable to view multiethnicity as a bonus, and depressed at the collapse of her finances, she'd let her life close down. These days she rarely went out. As a result, she'd missed the changes that Barbara kept noticing.

Tea made, Barbara joined her mother in the parlor—a cheerless room furnished with a horsehair sofa and a sideboard made of some namelessly heavy wood. Only her mother's chair had any grace. But then it would do: it was the Heppelwhite that Mrs. Barnes had wrested from her husband's creditors. From her manner, you'd never guess that she was back where she had started. These days, the house provoked no childhood stories. Instead, she saw the clothes it contained—chiffons wrapped in tissue, coats on padded hangers. She patrolled her territory many times a day, frightened that some G-man would find what she'd salted away. (The boxes of gloves, the mounds of period jewelry.) Nothing else mattered, least of all the home she'd grown up in. Mold and damp were the real threat to her clothes, but she didn't care to recognize them.

"My *dear*," (her voice was pained) "is *this* your idea of afternoon tea?"

"There was nothing else in the larder."

Mrs. Barnes' look said: "And whose fault is that?"

Barbara's replied: "What am I, the kitchen maid?"

It was bloody typical. Even when she "entered talking," determined to be cheerful, her mother still got the better of her. They should have been discussing her new job, her mother's health, the state of the house—anything but clothes and cake. But the atmosphere was deadeningly polite, and Barbara knew that if she introduced a topic through which thoughts or feelings might actually be communicated her mother wouldn't listen. This determination not to hear was more effective than a direct command for silence. Constrained by the deafness that surrounded her, Barbara wondered if this was why she talked so much—to try to leave some impression on a world that didn't care.

Mrs. Barnes stood up, as if sensing unspoken criticism.

After she brushed a nonexistent crumb from her dress, she gazed at her reflection: it was more a test of the mirror than herself. If anything interrupted the knowledge that she was in her prime, she changed the lights, blamed "the looking glass," or angled her head until a more flattering picture presented itself. *Poor thing,* she thought, glancing at her daughter's suit. *Even when she tries, she never gets it right.* She allowed herself a lady's smile—nothing too vulgar, nothing too broad—and when she returned to the mirror, its judgment was positive. Reality had been reset, like an unwieldy jewel, until it suited her.

"Now *this,*" she said, waving her Art Deco ring, "was another present—"

And off she went about her bracelets, her most-favored hotels, and the maisonette "in the better part of Chelsea" that she and Mr. Barnes had rented after they were married. Barbara let the whispered words pass over her. It was odd how seductive her mother could sound when the subject was real estate.

It's long past its sell-by date, that little-girl whisper, thought Barbara. And who knew how much of it was even true?

Her mother always said there was nothing worse than being "an old lady"—by which she meant the sort of person who wore flowery dresses and went on coach tours to the Isle of Man. Yet letting go might have helped Mrs. Barnes. She had nothing of the bloom, the comfortable bulk, that often comes with age. For decades she'd been forty-one—experienced, serene, and only slightly frozen round the jaw. But in the last few years, lines and sags and liver spots had rushed gleefully towards her. Although she could have relaxed into being a fine-looking woman "for her age," she insisted on the same standards of elegance that she'd used from the start of her career. Except now she couldn't pull it off. Austere and "perfect" though it was, a turban or a cloche would have covered up her hair better than her pillbox. Gray and white strands were showing through the black and its texture was thin, not glossily thick as such a hat, and such a dress, demanded.

Barbara felt like rubbing her mother's nose in whatever it was that was stinking out her sink, but it wouldn't have done any good. One or two Schiaparellis would have sorted out the drains, the gutters, the radiators, and the loo. Throw in the right accessories and she could have retiled the roof. Instead Mrs. B veiled herself in memories that were as airy and unreal as the netting on her best Dior. Above all, she refused to admit what her long-gone "friends" had always known: namely that her husband had married her to spite his family then spent his time fucking other women while wasting his own and other people's money. God knows Barbara had mixed feelings about her dad, but if her mother had let her, they could have helped each other deal with him. Shutting her out had done neither woman any good.

Barbara tried feeling sorry for her. A bankrupt widow—what could be more pathetic? And pity was safe: it produced no guilt. But her mother's behavior didn't always encourage it. ("Of course it broke your father's heart to move out of London," she was saying. "But what could we do? Children cost money.")

Perhaps she saw her daughter pull a face. Or maybe she simply wanted to be difficult. (Life had so few pleasures left.) In any case, Mrs. Barnes turned aside the way mimics do before they adopt a new expression and, when she looked back, her mouth had formed a thin, ungiving line.

Barbara felt herself morphing into a nine-year-old. *Oh Christ!,* she thought, as her power hair grew pigtails. For this look had shaped her childhood.

All those scenes! The farther back she went, the posher the settings became until she found herself in her mother's bedroom—the one that overlooked the rose garden—in the Oxfordshire home that later ruined them. It was hard to tell her crime. Cracking a vase, perhaps, or flattening a shrub. But whatever it was, you could be sure that Barbara would be stuttering excuses while her mother stood beside the wardrobe, a hairbrush in one hand and a chiffon scarf in the other. (She always wore chiffon in the summer.) When Barbara dried up her mother would put down the brush and ask her to leave. She wouldn't make eye contact—not even through the mirror—nor would she raise her voice. If anything, she lowered it.

In the pause that followed Barbara would stare at her mother's back, hoping for a something—*anything*—that acknowledged her existence. A rap on the knuckles or a threat to tell her father. Even a "Well done" when she presented another flawless school report. But nothing came. Nothing ever came. Her mother's back stayed turned. Then she'd lift the brush once more and bring it slowly through her hair.

Barbara ran out crying every time.

She still felt like crying—but this time with rage. Long since a master of the silent treatment, her mother had developed her repertoire since her husband died. Why bother with brave faces? Her humiliated pride needed a more vocal outlet after years of repression. Too bad if the target was her daughter, and not the husband who'd caused her fury. After all, it came to the same in the end.

Barbara smiled from nervousness, not pleasure, while her mother accused her of embezzlement. Not moving was the main thing. If her hand so much as twitched it might smash the teapot against her mother's cheek. Since neither of them could have coped with such a non-U breach of etiquette, she went on listening, her face pinned in place, while her mother told her that if she'd got herself a husband she wouldn't have had to leech from her family. "The way you got round your father! You did me out of what was mine." And she knew all about Barbara's plots: You raise a child—and see how it treats you when it's grown! "But then women are so selfish now. They'd rather wear business suits than be homemakers. No wonder they can't get a man to marry them!"

"Keep calm," Barbara told herself. "Not much more to go."

Although her inheritance had come from a trust fund, not her father's estate, there was no point explaining the difference. And as it happened, she and her mother had had far worse scenes. Like the time the old dear faked a seizure then sprang from the floor, shaking with laughter. Or when she pretended Barbara was a social worker, and told her that her daughter never visited her from one year's end to the next. Was it dementia or spite? Hard to tell when she'd always been so cruel.

But what makes people cruel? That's what Barbara wanted to know. She could be bossy herself, and thoughtless, but only because she was insecure. Her mother had her own excuses—like being presented with a child she'd done her best to avoid. She'd never known what to say or do with children, and it only made it worse that Mr. B was such a charmer. She'd always envied his and Barbara's closeness, and now she was jealous of Barbara's love life, and maybe even of her career.

"It's almost over," repeated Barbara, while her mother's rage approached a pitch that only dogs would understand. "It's almost done."

And slowly the plea became true.

Over the afternoon her mother's voice had risen from a kittenish lisp to blatant shouting. But now it grew hoarse. Little by little, the keening diminished. It wore itself out.

Bit—

by bit—

by bit.

Until eventually it stopped.

The hands twitched. And her eyes sought the mirror—searching, searching for the person that she longed to be. (The elegant hostess, the refined matron.) Barbara wondered which of her mother's voices was the "true" one—or if one of them, at least, was truer than the others. She persuaded herself that she felt some compassion. (What is it about parents and children that makes us so dishonest?) But mostly she wanted out.

She let the silence stretch between them.

Gradually her mother's face came back to the thing we call "sanity"—an approximation of reason that won't scare the neighbors.

Barbara looked away. "Okay?"

Her mother nodded, not owning what had passed between them.

"Good! It's been fun but I really *must* be off. Busy day tomorrow! But then aren't they all?"

As usual when she left her mother's, Barbara's overwhelming feeling was that she had to have a fuck. Too bad Stevie was finishing a commission. Otherwise she'd have nipped to Stoke Newington for a monstrously abandoned sex scene.

It was a terrible thing, hating a parent. Especially if part of what you hated was yourself. Because although she despised them, Barbara hadn't completely disowned her mother's values. Although her politics told her that decorous behavior and impeccable dress were dangerous models for a woman, she couldn't quite reject them. They existed alongside her feminism and her professional ambition, each jostling the other until it felt as if her head would blow off from the pressure.

Tearing off her hated suit, she flitted restlessly around the house. Why had Stevie switched his phone off? She was frantic to speak to someone.

Anyone.

Except her girlfriends were out—they might wonder what was up. And ditto the Oxford gang. But her new colleagues were possibles. A recent recruit could ring to check some boringly worthy detail—like the minutiae of the library cataloging system—without looking sad.

It didn't take long to review the options.

She didn't trust Ronan, and Deirdre was the wrong generation. Danny Whelan was nicely ineffectual; she liked what she had seen of him. But if a girl preferred her seniors, there was only one choice.

She planned her opening remarks while dialing directory inquiries. "I'm looking for a 'Roberts,'" she told the operator. "That's 'Roberts' without an 'e.' 'William Roberts.' R–O–B–E–R–T–S."

The operator punched his keyboard while Barbara chattered on. Already she felt better. "He's a *professor,* you know. A professor of *English Literature*. In fact, he's my *boss*. And he's a *most* distinguished man . . ."

6

Collapsed in his office after back-to-back classes, Danny found an e-mail winking perkily on his computer. "Ciao! Another Monday morning . . . aaagh!!! D'yah fancy sharing a crust circa one? Let's talk soon—Ronan." As invitations go it wasn't exactly Royal Garden Party standard. *But then,* thought Danny as he looked out the window, *this is hardly Buckingham Palace.*

Two minutes before the hour, he stood in the men's room with a comb in one hand and his briefcase in the other. If anyone came in he'd be straight out the door before they knew what he was doing. Thus guarding his reputation he checked his breath while poking wanly at his skin. He felt like one of those doomed volumes that turn up in second-hand bookshops from Aberdeen to Aberystwyth.

Dean Inge's Book of Sermons.
Macramé for Beginners.
Your Hundred Favorite Herring Dishes.

If it weren't for Dirk Bogarde at the end of *Death in Venice,* he'd have been tempted to use a tinted moisturizer.

He felt still dimmer when he faced his colleague across a crowded plastic table. But for his pustules, Ronan could have advertised shampoo. Thick and shiny on the crown, his hair fell in artful tweaks around the neck and ears. Stunned by its abundance, Danny kept tidying his own hair—an unfortunate response in someone who was bald. Even worse, Ronan had started on his least favorite subject.

"Believe me, Dan. These days no one gets published without an agent. Mine's a star; she's got her eyes on Simon Schama. I can give you her number if you like."

Danny smiled with as much enthusiasm as he could fake while the younger man explained that he'd signed the contract for his second book and was negotiating the paperback rights for his first. ("And I

doi:10.1300/5902_06

didn't get a bad deal, either, when you look how the bottom's fallen out of Henry James.")

Danny poked at his salad—an unappealing mixture of brown rice, raisins, and chunked-up sausages. "What's the new one about?"

Ronan grew yet more animated. Teeth flashing and hands flapping, he was like a singer in a boy band showing off his latest dance routine. "It's much sexier than my first book. Putting it bluntly, I'm examining the nexus between post-coloniality and modern queer identities. The main foci will be cyber texts and slasher fiction but I'm also doing a chapter on ethnicity and desire in Hollywood adaptations of the Broadway musical."

Danny brightened. "You like musicals?"

"God, no! But I used to have a boyfriend who was into Rodgers and Hammerstein. You know what some guys are like. Deeply sad."

Danny made a mental note to rearrange his CD collection so that the Madonna albums were at the front. "It sounds exciting."

"Yes, I think so too. But I'm sure you have something up your sleeve as well."

Danny tugged his cuff but there was nothing there. "I've an essay coming out next summer," he lied. "And I'm working on the book of course."

"Remind me what it's about."

"D'you want a drink?" panicked Danny.

"In a minute. But let's talk about your work first."

He felt cornered. "It'saboutBarbaraPym," he murmured.

"Eh?"

"BARBARA PYM!" he shrieked, flying to the opposite extreme. A woman chemist gave him an amused glance as he said more quietly, "It's about Barbara Pym."

Ronan down put his fork. He'd clearly never heard of her.

And why should he have?, thought Danny as he set about the usual explanations. When he'd finished, Ronan asked why he was wasting 100,000 words on a woman who only ever wrote about vicars, spinsters, and anthropologists: "You said it yourself: Her plots are always the same. And they sound so cozy! No one lived like that. Not even in the fifties. I bet she made it all up."

"Isn't that what writers generally do? Make it up, I mean?" Danny hurried on before he could be interrupted. "As it happens, she's fascinated by race. And by deviance too. Her nuns are always gay. And so are half the vicars."

Ronan pouted in polite disbelief. "So that's what you're looking at? The queer stuff?"

Now Danny really *had* been cornered.

"Well ... *No.* I'm looking at her literary borrowings. She echoes some surprising sources. Lots of eighteenth-century poetry. Gray, Thomson, Young. And medieval stuff. Hoccleve and so on ... Of course there's also her kinship with her contemporaries. She and Angus Wilson bear comparison. Then there's Philip Larkin and Kingsley Amis. And later on, Sylvia Plath is influenced by her. Not many people know that she—"

Ronan's eyes grew heavy. How come English lecturers still hunted out these meaningless connections? Queer theory might, as it were, be up its own arse, but at least it *tried* to talk about the outside world.

"I'm including a subsection on Charlotte Brontë," continued Danny. "Pym often defines her heroines against Jane Eyre; it's an index of how Romantic they are. Interestingly she doesn't mention Trollope much. She's more preoccupied by Charlotte M. Yonge. I don't suppose you've read any Charlotte M. Yonge? Few people have, but she's strangely rewarding. Once you get into the mood—"

Perhaps it was the look on Ronan's face, but Danny suddenly became aware of what he was saying. Hearing himself speak—actually *listening* to his words—he grew low and stuttered to a close. For the first time during the meal neither was speaking. Then Ronan shook himself like a dog. It was time to change the subject. "So!" he exclaimed, in his brightest manner. "What about your sex life? I hope you're having fun?"

Danny could have wept. "What about yours?" he countered.

"Oh—can't complain!"

Danny wanted to stick a sausage up his colleague's nose. He'd never cared for Goldilocks—a singularly intrusive sort of person, he had always thought—yet here was her gay half-brother asking questions he didn't want to answer and volunteering information he didn't want to hear. "Don't you have a class to go to?" he asked.

"I've packed my teaching into Thursdays and Fridays so that I can work on my book for the rest of the week. You have to be disciplined about these things ... Now I'm not a great one for supermarket pick-ups, but sometimes you get an offer you'd be mad to turn down ..."

Punched and bloodied as he was, Danny couldn't think how to turn the conversation. There was nothing to do but lower his eyes, fold his hands, and hear his colleague's boasts.

On his journey home, Danny studied his reflection in the bus window. "Misanthrope!" he murmured. "Misanthrope, misanthrope, misanthrope."

Naturally, Ronan had turned out to be in an open relationship—he and his male partner met three times a week "for food, wine, and fucks." (Plus, one assumed, the *occasional* conversation.) The rest of the time they were "free agents" whose only rule was to be "sexy and safe."

Given the rigors of the day, it was just as well that Danny was good at finding humor in unlikely places. One infallible source was his local newspaper's mixture of drug-related crime stories and completely un-reliable restaurant reviews. ("My lady companion plumped for turbot, I for steak tartar. Both were exquisite.") Then there was the lonely-hearts column where a "professional gentleman in later life" boasting a "second-hand car plus occasional use of a caravan" might meet a "slightly older wild rover" who was "seeking someone similar. (Must like children.)" Reluctant to place an ad himself, he read everyone else's with a greedy attention that was halfway between envy and scorn. But his favorite aspect of the paper was the way its advertising placards stated the day's main news followed by the magic word, "PICTURES." Although today's headline was too obvious to be an out-and-out stunner ("Bishop's Boyfriend Was in Porno Film—PICTURES"), it brought back such suggestive classics as "Blood Clot Model's Love Bite Fears—PICTURES" and the all-time-great "Am

Dram Suicide Goes Tragically Wrong—PICTURES." (*Hedda Gabler*
had never seemed quite the same after that.)

Danny wished he could be happier for Ronan. It was shameful, en-
vying someone else's sex life. But even as he smiled at the day's headline, he caught himself resenting the younger man's experiments. He
agreed there ought to be new ways of having a relationship. But it an-
gered him that Ronan had made so much progress down that route
while he himself was stuck at the first set of traffic lights. And Ronan
kept erecting roadblocks. Driven by some peculiar urge towards
openness, Danny had confessed his guilt at not being out to his family: "You must think so badly of me. I mean how can I be proud of being gay when I don't even have the nerve to tell my dad? Of course,
Mum died when I was young so I never had to come out to *her*—in
fact I totally disprove that theory about dominant mothers turning
you gay. But I ought to tell my Auntie Rosie and Uncle Will. And
I've *tons* of cousins—"

Ronan's face remained blank apart from a slight frown at the bit
about dominant mothers turning you gay. "But that's so last year," he
laughed when Danny's flow dried up. "No one bothers coming out
anymore."

Danny dropped his sausage.

"It isn't necessary," went on Ronan. "And it causes more problems
than it cures." Danny gaped while his companion explained that people his age felt constricted by labels. "I mean, where do you go once
you come out? Right into the gay ghetto, that's where. And what's so
special about sleeping with other blokes? Our parents probably do
kinkier things than you or I have ever dreamt of."

Danny pushed his plate away. "You've obviously never met my father."

"I hope I haven't offended you."

"Not at all," lied Danny. He had spent much of his life worrying
that he wasn't gay enough, or that he was gay in the wrong way. Tiresome though they were, these fears had helped define him. But now
Ronan (born in 1973) was boasting that "We've come a long way
from the seventies. I mean if you didn't make a fetish out of labels,

you wouldn't feel so bad about your father. It's your own fault. You're
the one who's laying on the guilt."

"I suppose you can't have told *your* parents," said Danny sulkily,
"since you don't define yourself as gay."

Ronan looked uncomfortable. "When I was fourteen, my mother
asked if I went for guys and I said I did. Then *she* said, 'Don't let anyone put you down for being gay.' But then she used to be a hippie.
And Dad was okay, too. Once she talked him round."

"Lucky you."

"Yes, but that's not the point. She put the words in my mouth and
I accepted them. Who knows what I'd have come up with if she'd left
me alone? Gayness is all very well for middle-aged white blokes. But
there's more to sex than that. What about race and class? What about
gender?"

Danny wondered if Ronan—whose father was a company direc-
tor—was the best person to talk about social inclusion. From where
he was slumped (his dinner gone cold) it seemed that Ronan had spent
their lunch replacing one impossible and tyrannical standard with another. "Everybody's fluid nowadays," Ronan had proclaimed. "Go
right ahead—tell your dad about yourself. But don't tie yourself
down with names. Just be who you are." And he smiled his open smile
as if happiness and self-acceptance were as easy to arrange as the
features on a boyish face.

It was aggravating, getting advice from a kid. And it didn't help
that Danny saw the logic of his argument. *Smug git!,* he thought, not
hearing his own homophobia. *These upper-middle-class buggers are always the same.*

Thinking the day over, he realized that middle age wasn't about
rheumatism or reading glasses. It was about being superseded. Without any change in how you felt about yourself you woke to find that a
new generation had taken your place. Silently, secretly. By the time
you grasped it there was nothing you could do. Already they had won.

Just take his students.

He knew by the look of them, and by what you see in the papers,
that they'd been fucking 'round since they were ten or twelve. In his
day sex had been a guilty riddle rather than a banal obligation. But

this lot took everything for granted. For better or worse, they had nothing left to learn. Instead they pushed Danny and his peers into the background.

Unlike Ronan, Danny had given up prowling The Spread Eagle, the town's only gay pub. (Contrary to many people's hopes, The Free Butt was straight.) He felt sure that Ronan would have laughed at his preference for staying at home and fantasizing about a certain North American philosopher, but then Ronan didn't know what it was like when a cutie half your age looked through you, not even seeing you were there. And nor could he know what it was like to be a Northern boy growing up gay in the sixties.

Danny had been shaped by stories that he couldn't shake off.

He had left home, had affairs, come out at work. He had aged. But he still saw himself sitting beside his father in the pub with two pints of bitter on the table and neither of them talking. It was an unsatisfactory scene yet on some unbiddable level he wanted to re-create it.

Two men having a jar once a week plus a match at the weekends. It wasn't much to ask.

Was it?

7

Barbara Barnes was on fire. Every word she spoke, every gesture she made. She was at her best—in her element—in total control. Pick your favorite of her phrases. Each of them hung around her head as she commented, internally, on her performance. The monologue helped solidify her success: for she only believed in things once she'd commented on them. "You blurred that point," she warned herself. "Try it again. Good. They got it that time. Now ask a question. Check they know where they are. Write that last bit down. Store it for later. God, this is fun. This time it's really come together."

Unlike some of her peers, Barbara was never bored by her day-to-day contact with students. Writing was an agony, shopping a bore, and sex a necessary compromise. Only teaching let her do what she did best: inform, instruct, inspire. And boss people around. (In the nicest possible way.)

"Tony, I want to go back to what you said a moment ago. Do you remember? It was about post-Barthesian reading practices. Remind us of your point." Tony—an amiable if undistinguished youth—looked dazed. What, he wondered, *had* he said? But it didn't matter. Barbara was weaving her web. Asking questions. Producing interpretations. Restating the students' views. Reaching a position, then playing devil's advocate. Pushing the kids further than they wanted but making them know, as they left the classroom, that they'd had their money's worth.

On this occasion, as so often, her mother was with her.

Laughing affectedly, she rounded an argument off by saying, "At least that's what *I* think. But if you asked my *mother,* you'd get a completely different answer!" Her students smiled in recognition; she knew how to get them on her side. Oddly, though, the person she described looked nothing like her mother. Instead of Mrs. B, she offered them a scatterbrain in fingerless mittens, the kind of woman who

doi:10.1300/5902_07

slipped brandy in her cocoa or whisky in her tea. (The details sometimes changed.) She was a humor, this woman, an absolute character.
But she could be a fool, too. Oh, the things she said! How her daughter laughed at them! And how Barbara's students laughed when they
heard about her puce balaclavas. "If you think *I'm* messy," Barbara
would say as she smoothed an immaculate outfit, "you should see
what my mother was wearing the last time I saw her!" Once she got
going, it was a short step from soiled knitwear to hints about weak
hearts. "I like to see a lot of her," she'd murmur, not thinking what
the words might mean, "because I don't know how long she'll be
around. I see her getting frailer every week."

With all this talk of families, it was strange how she never mentioned Stevie to her class. But though she didn't speak his name, she
kept wishing he could see her with the kids. That way he'd know a
different Barbara from the one he had to soothe and reassure. How
proud he'd be, and how safe she'd feel when he praised her teaching
(as praise he surely must). Elated by his approval, she'd have asked
about *his* problems (whatever *they* might be) before they ran upstairs
for an early night, equals at last.

She sighed.

Then, shrugging, she asked the sadly feckless Matthew to recon-
sider his last contribution in the light of Maggie's counterargument
from Lacan. "Or maybe the rest of you would like to come in on this?"
She searched for someone sufficiently handsome to take her mind off
Stevie. "Alan! You're being uncharacteristically quiet. What do *you*
think?"

And so, glowing and relaxed, she went about her job with preci-
sion, skill, and wit—wishing, wishing that the class would never end.

Meanwhile, twelve stories up, Danny Whelan was dying on his
feet.

Although it was his last class of the day, he lacked the energy to
make it work. Faced by students who'd rather stare than speak, jolly
tips from the university's "Teaching Progress Unit" were as ineffectual as his many years of experience.

On a clear day the view across town was lyrical, but all that showed this winter afternoon was Danny's neon-lit face and the backs of his students' heads. What the hell were they thinking? They couldn't just be bored. Had the rest of their year been killed in a drug-fueled motorway pileup? Were they mourning the death of student activism? Or perhaps they'd heard the latest news about the university's finances.

Unlike the heroes of the campus novels to which Barbara was addicted, Danny had no eccentric image to project—he simply gave his classes who he was. While it made his seminars more popular than he knew, his lack of pretension left him unprotected. When teaching went badly it felt as if the kids were rejecting *him,* rather than the course or one another.

His sense of the ridiculous, usually so strong, deserted him.

Surely their silence was aggressive? He could see it exciting them. "Hard luck," they were thinking, "but you're on your own, you sad bastard."

He spoke—but no one replied. He asked a question—and no one answered. He cocked his head to one side, forcing himself to sit still. He restated the problem in another form. Then waited. But still nothing came.

Catching one of them smirking, he wanted to wipe the expression off with a smack.

(Silence.)

His shirt was sticking to his back even though the room was icy cold. He was having a slow-motion fit, a scene from a nightmare. It was like drowning with the soundtrack off.

He posed another teaser but the result was the same.

(Tick. Tick. Tick.)

The gap grew longer.

(Tock. Tock. Tock.)

Then he did what he shouldn't do—he answered the question himself. Trying to recover, he posed another teaser. (Silence.) He reiterated it. (Blankness.) He repeated it again and again. (Oblivion.) It grew longer every time he said it. But still it lay unanswered.

"What *is* it?" He tried to sound calm. "You seem pretty quiet this week."

(Nothing.)

Sweat ran down his armpit and along his chest. He felt like a comic who'd swaggered on stage only to die before the unamused faces of five hundred men and women whose silence couldn't be explained except by saying they'd agreed—through collective telepathy—not to smile at his jokes, no matter how funny they might be.

A sentence formed itself in his memory. *The crowd is like a human being,* he recalled. *The first ten rows are the eyes of the monster.* And then, more desperately: *What the fuck am I going to do?*

Grabbing chalk, he walked to the blackboard. Someone laughed as he turned his back—a dirty, half-stifled sound. Wheeling round, he saw twenty faces staring back. He held their gaze—but not one of them blinked. Standing where he could watch them, his eyes not leaving theirs, he wrote on the board with crazy looping strokes. He didn't recognize his handwriting.

He folded his arms when he had finished.

And then, finally, someone spoke.

An hour later, Barbara bustled into the staff room, as energetic as a Welsh mountain pony, and almost as powerful. Seeking an audience for her exuberance, she rejected a sofa-full of physicists before spotting that nice Dr. Whelan by the coffee machine. Over she went, smiling consolingly at the unwanted scientists, who looked the other way embarrassed by such unprecedented friendliness from a member of the Arts Faculty.

"You don't mind?" she asked, not waiting for an answer. Then she saw Danny's pallor. "Are you okay? You look shattered."

He was too tired to pretend. "I've had the worst day ever."

"Busy?"

"Three two-hour seminars, a lecture, and an office hour."

"That's bad."

"It is when you do it every day. There was a mistake in my course allocations," he added. "So I'm teaching way over the average."

"That's terrible. You ought to complain."

"I suppose. But you can't legislate against cock-ups."

Danny couldn't bring himself to explain that Bill had doubled his teaching load as a punishment for failing to publish his book. In any case, he'd already cornered the market in Brave Resignation.

"What were the classes on?" asked Barbara.

"Two on Katherine Mansfield and one on Ivy Compton-Burnett. The lecture was on postwar women's fiction."

Barbara shifted. "Katherine Mansfield? Do you teach many women writers?"

"A fair number. My research is on Barbara Pym but I take in several of her predecessors." His laugh was nervous; he knew his colleague had much the better grasp of feminist history. "I'm interested in concepts of the 'minor' writer. Mansfield is one of the better-known people on my course."

Though piqued at the idea that women writers might be minor, Barbara sensed he wouldn't be a rival. "You're not teaching any modern women?"

"I stop at Iris Murdoch."

"Nothing on Angela Carter or Jeanette Winterson?"

"Not a sentence."

"Good!" she laughed. "I'm sure we'll have lots to talk about."

"Yes," he said, doubtfully. He wasn't sure that Barbara (or anyone else) would be able to follow his muddled attempt to reclaim "minor" writing as a viable and self-conscious form of literature. "And you?" he asked. "What have you been teaching?"

"An introductory class on French feminist theory. Terribly basic— I won't bore you." Instead she took a bundle of photocopied sheets from the coffee table. "What's this?" she asked.

"Give it over," laughed Danny. "It's my favorite mag—the university newsletter." He found what he was searching for, then handed it back. "It's so hilariously amateurish. The new editor's threatening changes but the only thing he's done so far is write some weird articles. I mean, look at that."

He pointed to a feature on the hundredth birthday of the university's founder. Under the headline HAPPY BIRTHDAY, TOM the piece congratulated "Tom Baxter, our very own éminence grise" for reaching "his first century" in a nursing home beside "his beloved Blackpool beach." Though suffering "(alas!)" from advanced dementia, "Tom" had had a rousing day. In attendance along with "a veritable rugby squad of grandchildren" were "Professor Simon Simonssen (representing the Sciences) and Professor Bill Roberts (representing the Arts)." Following a "slap-up feast of jelly and cake," speakers paid tribute to the 1933 funding drive that led to Tom's establishment of "a range of unpretentious evening classes for the unemployed." After Tom moved to "pastures new" his "humble acorn" became, by turns, a Technical College, a College of Further Education, and a Polytechnic before "finally turning into the path-breaking University you see before you now."

Closing the article was a quote from Bill Roberts: "He's still a grand old man. There's nothing he likes more than a sing-song or a good old-fashioned cream tea. And the nurses say he never causes any trouble. We at the university could learn from that sort of simplicity."

At no point was "Tom" granted his full title: Lord Baxter of the Wirral.

Barbara pushed the paper away. "Poor old sod."

"It's tragic," he agreed. "No one would guess he used to be a leading trades unionist. It's like Senior Management want to punish him for being more principled than *they* are. And now they've got this new bloke in to do their propaganda. God, I'm tired," he yawned, forgetting to be scared of her. "And I could murder our students sometimes."

"It's rough when they don't cooperate."

"You're not kidding! I saw my whole life flash before me. *Not,*" he added in an undertone, "that *that* took very long."

Still relishing the heat of her seminar, Barbara reached out to her less successful colleague. "Why don't we have lunch sometime? What's the point of having exciting new colleagues if you never get to see them?"

It was good of her to class him with the lively ones even if neither of them entirely believed it. "That would be nice," he said. Then he roused himself. "That would be so nice," he repeated, trying to sound more enthusiastic.

"Excellent!" She was all shimmers and smiles. "I know next Monday and Thursday are out but I'm not sure what I'm doing after that. Let's diarize this evening. I'll ring you when I've had a chance to check my schedule for the next three weeks."

"That would be so—nice." He felt like a child bride accepting a proposal of marriage. "Very nice indeed." He wished he could find a different adjective.

"Good! But now I have to fly. I'm speaking at Reading next week and I have to finalize my talk." And off she went, leaving Danny sunk a fraction deeper in his seat.

"Diarize," he murmured.

It was a word he had never heard before.

8

That evening Danny paid a rare visit to his study. How *did* his theory go—the one about minor art?

Lines swam up from the first file he opened:

"How might we account for Mildred Lathbury's perplexing reticence about her father? Coming from the heroine-narrator of *Excellent Women* the gap cannot be accidental. Is Pym satirizing Western kinship models? Or might there be a less obvious rationale?"

"It is crucial to note that the symbolic consumption of human flesh is integral, not merely to the 'primitive' tribes that Alaric Lydgate studies in *Less Than Angels,* but also to the Anglicanism professed by most of Pym's characters—and, indeed, by Pym herself. What—we might ask—does this *mean?*"

"With humorous overstatement, Pym suggests that university life has more to do with obfuscation than ideas. Rather than depicting the intellectual exchanges that structure higher education, she crams academia with arcane ceremonies, pointless debates, and eccentric social misfits whose communications are undermined by the utterly impenetrable idioms in which they are couched."

Danny had no recollection of writing these words let alone any memory of how they advanced his argument. (Whatever *that* might be.) And he despaired of getting them into print.

When he'd started his research, Virginia Woolf was the only twentieth-century women writer that academics worked on. But now that you could write PhDs on anyone, male or female, who'd produced so much as a shopping list, he guessed that even Barbara Pym must be provoking scholarly analysis. It surely wouldn't be long before his book was pipped by others taking sexier angles. Their covers would taunt him in the university bookshop:

Spinsters, Nuns and WRENS: Barbara Pym's Reluctant Feminists
Barbara Pym—A Lesbian Reassessment (One for Ronan, that.)

   doi:10.1300/5902_08

Two Tribes Go to War: Barbara Pym on Africa and England
From Esher to Eternity: Barbara Pym's Suburban Muse
Or Danny's favorite, *Incensed by Acolytes—Barbara Pym and the Politics of the Pulpit.*

For a moment he was tempted to swap his study of literary influences for a more political approach. Then he realized that the sentences he'd just been reading were from an earlier attempt to be adventurous. More characteristic of his work were the countless pages of literary cross-references that lay on the pages underneath. "*The Prelude*," ran one note, "but there's something older there as well. Percy's *Reliques?* Too bad she's paraphrasing, not quoting directly. Otherwise it would be a cinch."

Dry though they were, these glosses delighted him; they were the way he read books. Caught between the pleasure of spotting allusions and the realization that such connections were wholly irrelevant to "the real world," he envied the ease with which Ronan and Barbara followed a more socially engaged agenda. Yet their work disheartened him: he found it too unflinching. And they could be snobbish, those two. Although Ronan claimed to reject "the fallacy of inherent literary value," that didn't stop him from scoffing at Charlotte M. Yonge.

Where was he . . . ?

Ah yes—minor writing.

As he'd suspected, there was nothing helpful in his notes. His thoughts were too meandering to have formed a proper theory. But maybe that was the point. He was intrigued by unfinished gestures and open-ended sentences. Formal perfection was a fetish these days. It was killing writing off by making language bloodless. He wanted a more casual style—one that could accommodate clutter, mess, and chaos. (And failure, too.)

Given his own obscurity, it wasn't surprising that Danny identified with minor writing. But he believed he had an honest point. Mightn't imperfect writing—by its very muddle—be truer to life than those books where every intercepted look was related, with exquisite finesse, to a developing plot? Life, he thought, is not like that. It's full of chance, absurdity, bad taste, irrelevance, triviality, coincidence, small domestic scenes, loose ends, bathos, clichés, plotlessness, sentimentality, casualness, flatness, inconsequentiality, clunkiness, and farce—things that critics usually condemned. He wanted a form of writing that could include such unfashionable richness in its loose and bulky folds.

And while he was on the subject, he wished everyone would stop mucking things around just when he was getting used to them. He wasn't sure how much novelty people welcomed in their daily lives, yet they were supposed to adore it in fiction, along with equally dubious concepts like "greatness" and "sublimity." But Danny had no desire to be "great." He simply wanted to be happy.

He sighed.

Did he really have a theory here?

Ramblings like this wouldn't survive long under Barbara's eyes. God knows they hadn't fared well under Christian's. (Danny's next sigh was deeper than his first.) *Still,* he thought, *I might as well put something down while I'm in the mood.* So he dug out a scrap of paper and started to write, a little hesitantly, in the margin of his page.

In the end, a mutual suspicion of Ronan MacIntyre provided a sounder foundation for Barbara and Danny's friendship than Danny's theories would have done. With a spark that surprised them both, their weekly lunches covered sex, showbiz gossip, university politics, and Britain's ever-disappointing government—but never Eng Lit. Being with each other was like taking a holiday from their usual anxieties. Barbara didn't have to put on the sort of show she'd have mounted for a straight man. And though Danny got exasperated when she tried to fix him up with one of her many gay friends, he relished her humorous directness. Indeed he'd always liked strong women.

This unexpected kinship lightened Danny's term. As the autumn darkened and grew chill, football provided further cheer. With three away wins in a row, his home side looked as if it might avoid relegation for another year. Meanwhile—in another stratosphere—"Michael" was knocking goals in faster than his PlayStation double. It was *his* season—the year he became a star—and Danny watched the elevation with resentment and desire. It was the same with Posh Freddie from the Junkshop. Too embarrassed to go in, Danny dashed past the shop every Saturday, craning his head towards the window for a furtive glimpse of JOY.

These imperfect pleasures weren't the wisest backdrop to the forty-second winter of his life. And what a winter it was! So much rain fell on Bonfire Night that it was as well it wasn't a single evening any-more but an entire fortnight of crashes, bangs, and flashes. "A Penny for the Guy" had become similarly inflated: Round his way, the going rate for institutionalized anti-Catholicism was at least one pound fifty. On the other side of town, hail scraped the concrete towers of the uni-versity. Trees came down in the park. There was the misery of dark af-ternoons and flooding gutters without the ancient thrill of overnight snow.

It was intolerable getting up before seven with the sky a curtain of black and the wind wheezing through his windows. *And for what?*, he wondered. *Thirty bleary faces and not enough pay?* But he did it as best he could. *That's me,* he thought. *Solid as a cart horse and almost as exciting.* At such times it was hard not to dwell on Christian—a circus horse if there ever was one, all fancy footsteps and a plaited mane. Reading Virginia Woolf's diary on the loo one morning, he came across a par-ticularly terrifying text for the day—or, damn it, for the decade: "The middle age of buggers is not to be contemplated without horror." He slammed the book shut. "Thank you, Virginia, for that vote of confi-dence in my future." (A motion shortly followed.) But while he wanted to prove her wrong, he still spent the trip into work thinking about love's impossibility.

"What's the perfect relationship?" Christian had asked him once, smiling enigmatically and playing with the stem of his glass. Al-though they were into the early hours of the morning and the other partygoers had left, Danny knew what to say: "The perfect relation-ship is where you can stay up talking—like this—or stay up having sex, and where both things are completely natural." Christian's agree-ment was so immediate that Danny closed his eyes, expecting more. But when he opened them, no hand had touched his knee, no lips had brushed his cheek. And if Christian was looking at him differently, Danny was too busy sending telepathic messages pleading "Please seduce me" to notice. Twenty minutes later Christian went, with the curtest of goodbyes, to the room where his lover of the week had been asleep since 2:00 a.m. Before the door banged shut Danny heard, "Where the hell have you been?" followed by "None of *your* damned business!"—at which he'd dug himself from his beanbag and picked his way home, alone yet again.

Six years on he wondered if he shouldn't have been more daring. But at other times he'd been alive with confidence and decision until Christian gave a look that said: "Try me if you dare; I refuse to be charmed." At moments like that Danny's self-belief shriveled to a hollow stalk—cow parsley at the end of August. The climax of these maddening occasions was the picnic they took, one Indian-summer day, just before Christian disappeared. Although his latest "friend" was driving, Christian ignored the passenger seat and jumped in the back beside Danny. It was a delicious torture being so close and so divided. Danny barely noticed the Cotswolds. Instead he had a self-defeating wish to know where Christian had picked up his new chum—whose neck was hard as stone as he turned each country bend.

After they escaped the M40, Christian rejected half a dozen stopping points as too hot, too exposed, too obvious, or too ugly. Bad tempered from the wait, they ended up in a lay-by where Danny snapped pictures of them as they ate. The photos summed up that classic summer: Christian as photogenic as a 1940s film star, Danny's hands shaking on the viewfinder, and Christian's screw somewhere in the background. It was typical of Christian not to bother with the smiles that normal people use in their desperate attempts to charm the camera. Instead, his level gaze was a definition of arrogance: he dared you to look away while knowing that you wouldn't.

Years later Danny was still poring over the image like a child peering into a shuttered house. However much he cupped his hands together he couldn't pick out the shapes on the other side of the glass; he just found himself reflected back. It made him sad that he didn't even have a photo of the two of them together. A celluloid pairing was more modest than the other unions he had dreamed of, but perhaps it would also have been more enduring. For in photographs, if nowhere else, the ones we love must stay with us forever.

Danny could trace his loss via a cardboard folder locked inside his desk. "The Christian Archive," as he called it, consisted of book reviews, interviews, gossip items, and cuttings from the best-sellers lists—it mapped the staging posts of his friend's career. Powered by his intense conference appearances, Christian's profile had moved in less than a decade from small philosophy mags to a double-page spread in *The New York Times Sunday Book Review*. According to the latter, *Silence and Remorse* was "the most original contribution to philosophy since Derrida's early writings. ... A book that Kierkegaard might have been proud of."

Even so, it was Christian's disappearance that truly made him famous. (Up, up, up went the sales—an amazing showing for philosophy.) There were hints of foul play until his agent announced that Professor Ellis had neither perpetrated, nor fallen victim to, a crime. While it was true that he had resigned his post and left the country, he was merely withdrawing—for the foreseeable future—from the academic, philosophical, and publishing worlds. And though he was in good spirits, he didn't want to be contacted—not even by his friends. Thankful though he was for the public's support, if they valued his work they should leave him alone.

For a time, Danny couldn't pick up a paper without his friend's stark face looking back at him (for Christian's beauty had always been austere). Would the press have been interested if Christian looked like the average philosophy lecturer, a breed not noted for their dress sense? And would *Silence and Remorse* have sold so well if the dust jacket hadn't carried an oversized close-up in which he looked to one side with half-parted lips? That photograph also headed the many articles in which journalists warned, triumphantly, of the pressures of fame. Up he stared—as unreachable as a murder victim, or as inscrutable as the murderer.

Danny fantasized about storming the BBC to make an appeal over the airwaves: Would Christian Ellis please come back? More modestly, he wrote letters which he couldn't send and drafted eulogies that he chose not to publish. He felt a weird delight in being pointed out on campus as "the man who knew Christian Ellis." And he shuffled ceaselessly through his photos.

This was when he learned to like *Silence and Remorse*. Deconstructive philosophy had never been his thing and he'd been jealous of the book's reception. "Why isn't this happening to *me?*" he'd asked when it first came out. "Why is his work more successful than mine?" Granted, Danny hadn't actually *published* a book, but if he did he couldn't see it being "a free-form meditation on selfhood, loss, and the impossibility of narrative closure." Nor was he a fan of abstract titles. Faced with "the modern subject's doomed desire for a meaningful personal trajectory," Danny would have tried something homelier, like *Losing the Plot*. (Which, come to think of it, was a pretty apt assessment of his life, his place of work, and the country he was living in.) But whatever else he might be, Christian wasn't a charlatan: he couldn't help having produced such a seductive mixture of insight and obscurity. Indeed for Danny, *Silence and Remorse* was an echo of Christian's personality. Like its author, the book combined come-ons and brush-offs to delicious, though unreadable, effect.

Once Christian was out of the way, *Silence and Remorse* became Danny's through the utter force of his attention. Month by month, he studied its place on the best-sellers list as if he was following his own career. There was comfort in this appropriation. And there was solace, too, in his drafts of Christian's obituary. ("Just in case" was how he thought of it.) Coming across these notes was like seeing Christian in the street: it brought back all his need. But another part of him felt jubilant. Failure though he was, he was still in the game. Unlike his friend, he hadn't given up.

While Danny waited for the second coming, he took comfort from men who were even more untouchable than Christian. Unless *Match of the Day* changed its "Goal of the Month" prize to a postmatch shower with a Premiership player of your choice (and what a prize *that* would be), Danny's footballing frolics would have to be imaginary. But despite their money and their straightness, his favorite players weren't any further off than Christian. In fact, maybe they were closer. Because the love existed in another world he could propose what he wanted and never be rejected. Whereas each time he fanta-sized about Christian he was reminded, eventually, of his friend's am-bivalence, his failure to cooperate.

By keeping these things secret, Danny limited the terms on which he and his friends related to one another. How could they help when they'd no idea of the scale of his mourning? But although he indulged his fantasies when he had nothing more pressing to do, he pushed them off when shame or duty got in the way. The result was a con-stant self-division. While they were on him, his early-morning rever-ies shot him through with nostalgia and regret. But when his bus stopped beside the Arts Tower he'd put up his umbrella and run for shelter. In doing so he let in such different preoccupations that by the evening Christian would be far from his thoughts. Indeed there were large stretches of time when Christian was entirely absent from his mind. It was only the habit of waking up early and alone that brought him back so clearly and so often.

9

Barbara Barnes was pleased with Danny. A good, clean, harmless man who laughed at her jokes and listened when she spoke—what more did she need? She wouldn't have wanted him as a lover but he was an ideal friend. And the time had come for a new step. "I want you to meet my little Stevie," she proclaimed one hurried lunchtime. "Why don't you come round next week? Nothing fancy. Just supper after work."

And so it was that Danny found himself outside her door with a bunch of tiger lilies and what he thought of as "the inevitable bottle of Jacobs Creek." Repressing his desire for a can of beer and the latest Ryan Giggs video, he tried to persuade himself of the benefits of a quiet meal with a favorite colleague. Meanwhile, on the other side of the threshold, Barbara was producing enough nervous energy to give anyone who touched her an electric shock. Unable, by some quirk of personality, to stick to small-scale entertaining, she was using Danny's coming to bring together her and Stevie's friends. ("I'll be doing him a favor," she reasoned. "I bet he hardly sees a soul.") Their different expectations became clear when she opened the door. Danny had dropped his briefcase at home but hadn't bothered changing, whereas Barbara was in a black sheath dress with politically incorrect ivory accessories and strenuously discreet makeup.

"What an outfit! It really suits you."

"Yes," she replied, her eyes traveling over his shirt. "I suppose it does."

Snapping into focus, she led him to the drawing room. "Now come on in and don't be shy. My little one's on his best behavior." She addressed a figure on the other side of the door. "Aren't you, darling?"

To her great satisfaction, and his own embarrassment, Danny gaped. "G-good to m-meet you," he managed, marveling at Stevie's height. "Barbara's told me so much about you."

      doi:10.1300/5902_09

"I bet she has!"

"Mind you, she didn't mention how tall you were."

"No." Stevie smiled in Barbara's direction. "It's odd how she leaves that part out."

Knowing that Stevie was a management consultant, Danny had been prepared for a loud-voiced, stripy-shirted stereotype. It was disconcerting being faced, instead, by soft brown eyes, broad shoulders, and the sort of moleskin suit that cried out to be stroked. "Oh good," teased Barbara, noting his appreciation. "You *will* get on!" And she returned to the kitchen in a bustle of knowing chuckles.

Danny picked at his shirt, hoping that his lunchtime soup hadn't stained it. And he prayed that Barbara's man wouldn't expect him to talk about anything controversial like politics, or cricket. (For he was obviously as posh as hell.) However, Stevie liked to put guests at their ease. Having established, in words of more than one syllable, that he could be a wicked fast bowler, he acknowledged that he "greatly preferred" soccer. ("As a spectacle, that is.") He was also a "keen environmentalist" and a recent, and enthusiastic, convert to the "new" Labour Party. It was true that he stared when he learned that Danny's membership of "the Party" had lapsed at pretty much the point when his own had taken force, but it didn't take long before they reached the safer ground of academia. Thanks to Barbara, Stevie knew the university inside out. (And, oh yeah, his public school was pretty minor.)

While Stevie drew out their guest with shrewd and careful questions, Barbara flitted in and out with placemats and cutlery. Though she kept up a continuous stream of talk her topics were different from Stevie's. While "the men" (as she coyly called them) were discussing the death throes of the Tories she entered saying, "I do still miss her. I know it's wrong but I can't help identifying with her." Several moments passed before Danny realized she was talking about Princess Diana, not Mrs. Thatcher, although perhaps Diana was bad enough.

His head grew sore from the embarrassment of producing two separate sets of platitudes. Stevie—who was more experienced in these matters—obeyed Barbara's commands ("Oh, *do* use the coasters, dear—the black slate ones we got in Snowdonia") without trying to follow her conversation. Although Danny thought this rather mean, he did see Stevie's point. And he had a better grasp of Barbara's mood when he realized, with horror, that she'd been laying *twelve* settings.

Thirty minutes later he looked back on the party's first phase with a wondering nostalgia. Ungrateful though it seemed, he couldn't help thinking that Stevie and Barbara knew some of the pushiest people on the planet—or in London, anyhow, which was where most of them lived. He assumed, at first, that they were forever socializing with each other like one big self-assured sitcom cast. However, closer study showed a split between Barbara's friends, whose boasts were mostly cultural, and Stevie's business chums, who were richer and more openly brash: they had less need to keep up liberal appearances.

Despite bonding about the trauma of getting to the provinces at that time of night, the atmosphere between the two groups resembled a wedding reception where one family examines the other, each wondering how long they can stay polite. The other thing that was like a wedding was the food. For this—when it finally arrived—was of a standard that Danny had never encountered outside of restaurants. Barbara did not subscribe to the spag bol and chili con carne school of dinner party catering that he and most of the people he knew had been following since they left university. For her, entertaining was like giving a conference paper: carrying it off with flair mattered more than the conversation it was supposed to produce.

Lamb, roast potatoes, and honey-glazed carrots occupied one layer of her thoughts. Different anxieties took over when she moved from the kitchen to the dining room. Was her dress all right? What did her friends think of Danny? What did Danny think of her friends? Why were they drinking such horrible wine? (Oops—it was Danny's.) She wished that everyone would disappear so that she and Stevie could start discussing them. If only things would go well. Otherwise she'd lie awake, blaming herself for the things that she should or shouldn't have said, or served.

Brisk in her front-of-house duties, she reorganized the conversation while clearing away the starters. But she returned to the kitchen with a sense of failure. Because she'd forgotten to drain the excess fat from the roasting tin, her "gravy" consisted of an oil slick suspended on a pool of stock. Her stomach turned and she was reminded, uncontrollably, of jokes that hadn't worked and conversations where she might have seemed too loud. Not being blessed with the domestic divinity that *some* cooks can boast, she poured the gunge down the sink, not caring if it blocked tomorrow's drain, and started afresh with a stock cube. "Be careful," she murmured as she wiped her forehead with some kitchen roll. "Be careful and be steady."

She was calmer when she served the main course.

It was hard to say whether Stevie or the roast looked more splendid as he carried it through on an antique plate. She shrugged noncommittally when her friends acclaimed the garlic-scented flesh and crispy roast potatoes, but inwardly she was pleased. Then a girlish voice rang out, all innocence, from a far corner of the table: "It's so brave of you, Barbara. Cooking this sort of meal." The doll shook its ringlets at the company. "Roast red meat and root vegetables! It must be so handy. Getting your recipes out of Delia." And it pushed its plate away as if it couldn't eat such solid fare.

There was a pause during which Barbara thought, *That Cassie is a bitch.* Then Danny cut loyally in: "But it's right back in fashion. Except now they call it Modern British Food. And you can't deny it's good."

Cassie seemed perfectly capable of denying it. However she contented herself with a partial change of subject: "Has anyone been to the Dovecot yet?"

"Isn't it wonderful?" someone replied. "The chef's a genius. He used to work at Alistair Little's."

"Really?" laughed Cassie. It was extraordinary how much pleasure she could get from opposing people. "I thought it was completely overrated. Nondescript food and atrocious service. Too many prettyboy waiters for *my* liking! They'd spend the whole night chattering to each other if they thought they'd get away with it." Stevie looked rather foolish, as well he might, given that he and Cassie worked side by side at the office. But there was no stopping her. Instead she gave a flounce in Danny's direction as if to say, "Though I bet *he'd* like it well enough."

Barbara dropped her fork. The contents of her plate disgusted her. What was it but a lump of dead sheep? She'd spent an entire day planning and executing this charade. And for what? The night was a disaster and she had been punished, yet again, for her ambition.

Meanwhile the conversation moved to art.

Here money and appearances were everything. Talking of a recently acquired piece Guest A would ask, "Do you want to know how much I paid for it?" to which Guest B would reply, "That means you want to *tell* us how much you paid for it!" Damien Hirst was agreed to be "overhyped" but as someone pointed out, "That just means we can't afford him!" Others were described as "promising little artists" whose work could be picked up "for two or three grand" provided "you knew where to look for it."

Danny watched Barbara emphasize a point: she'd gone back to stylish self-assertion. He knew her well enough to guess at the nerves she hoped to hide. (She was laughing now, with her entire head lifted back, and he could almost believe that she was happy.) But where did she fit into her party? For all of her poise, she looked strangely lonely: you'd think it was Stevie's place, not hers, from the way his friends had made themselves at home.

Danny worked his way through a second helping of meat while considering the scene. Unfortunately Barbara was too agitated to take his silence as a compliment to her cooking. Instead she decided on a Major Conversational Initiative. Pushing the roast potatoes at him as if to encourage participation, she asked how often he went home.

"Danny is from Yorkshire," she explained in a theatrical whisper.

"Lancashire," he murmured but she didn't seem to hear.

"Whereabouts exactly? Don't tell me, I remember. Doncaster, isn't it? I used to know someone from Doncaster—"

Danny cut some gristle from his meat.

"Of course, the poverty is terrible." She had come over all soft and slow and serious. (Stevie thought of it as her *Newsnight* voice.) "What *should* we do about social deprivation? You know better than the rest of us. Tell us what the government should do about the North-South divide."

Danny bit his lip and reached for the salt shaker. "First there has to be a change in the larger political culture. We need to rethink our attitude to public spending. Take Salford Council—"

Barbara nodded furiously; her eyes were on stalks. Seeing her lips part, Danny wondered what was coming next. But she only called out Stevie's name. "Go on," she told Danny. "I'm listening." Then, to Stevie: "The salt shaker's empty. Look at poor Danny. He can't get a grain out! Quick, get the other one."

Danny said he didn't mind but Barbara silenced him with a gesture.

"We're listening, aren't we?" She swept her gaze around the other guests. "Isn't it fascinating?" But her glance returned to the kitchen: "Not that one! The one your sister gave us. I filled it this morning." Her attention swung back to the table. "Now what were you saying? The thing about public spending—as far as *I* can make out—is that it never goes where it should. Of course, you must have thought about it more than we have. Doesn't your father still live up there?"

Danny considered sliding his body onto the floor then scraping his nails across the parquet. Everyone was watching him, their mouths open in primitive awe. Was it the sight of a working-class infiltrator that stilled them, or were they wondering how he'd extricate himself from Barbara's gushing?

"What does your father think of where we're at? Politically, I mean?" Her expression was expectant. "He must have seen so much. The miners' strike. All that! And what do *you* think? It's not often we have an expert in our midst."

Danny's shirt got smellier and smellier until Stevie rescued him: "But darling! Haven't you heard? According to Our Beloved Leader *everybody's* middle class these days." He winked encouragingly at Danny. "I'm sure you and your dad like nothing better than cracking open the chardonnay after he gets back from the pit."

"Yeah," deadpanned Danny. "We drink it by the pigeon loft in our clogs." And everybody laughed, some of them not unkindly.

As soon as she could, Barbara slipped into the kitchen, murmuring something about dessert.

She'd hardly started banging spoons onto a tray when a voice crept up behind her. With studied gentleness, it asked if she was okay. "I'm absolutely fine," she snapped, not bothering to turn. Though she was glad that Stevie had saved the conversation, she resented how he never lost his timing. "I know what this is about," he continued. "But she can't touch you anymore." His voice was invasively sensitive. "Why don't you relax? I mean, *she* had a cook and a housekeeper. You don't have to do it all. Not when everyone loves you already."

Why, wondered Barbara, did he always have to be right? It was so un-endearing. For sure enough, her mother's voice was sounding in her head. ("Not *quite* the menu I would have chosen, my dear. And *do* try to remember: A good hostess must never force the conversation.") But long before she'd met him, she'd condemned herself to rush, servant-less, between kitchen and dining room, trying to do everything her mother had done while having a love life and a career on top. She was damned if she was stopping now. Especially when Stevie had his own reasons for wanting her to let up.

Meanwhile—back in the dining room—Danny was tipping back his chair and peering through the open door.

It was as good as a silent movie. As far as he could tell, Stevie had made a bad move, for Barbara was hissing the sort of words that really wanted to be shouted. (No wonder she was tearful!) Stevie tried to hug her but she pushed him off. Then he bent his lips towards her. Who knew what he was saying? But whatever it was it worked.

For he put his arm around her while shutting the door with a kick.

After he'd settled back into his seat, Stevie winked at Danny as if to say: *I know what you've been looking at.*

"Women!" He rolled his eyes. "Believe me, Dan, you're better off without them."

But his words were contradicted by a self-satisfied smile.

Barbara, too, was beaming when she carried out her tray of rame-kins. With élan she dropped the individual pots of crème brûlée onto the table moments after blowtorching them in the kitchen. Not a hair was singed. No fingers had been burned. Her mother couldn't have done it better. She smiled delightedly when Danny told her his was perfect. He repeated the compliment—and she instantly disbelieved him. Needing to reassert herself, she was about to launch another Conversational Gambit when Stevie gestured towards the company. She cleared her throat, smoothed her dress, and listened. (And so did Danny.)

This is what they heard:

"Come on! It's one of the most important books of the century. The quality's stamped on every page."

"His photo's stamped on every page, you mean. That's the only reason anyone bought the damned thing."

"*I* wouldn't have minded if his photo *was* on every page. He's absolutely gorgeous. It's his style I can't bear. I thought it was a bad translation until I realized he was from the States. Though maybe that explains it."

"With all due respect, that's total shite! I mean, it's not *his* fault you can't follow what he's saying. And the chapter on Jewishness is masterly."

Danny frowned. He hadn't been expecting this. But Barbara grabbed her cue: "Are you talking about Christian Ellis? Because if you are, you ought to speak to Danny. You knew him, didn't you?"

"Didn't everybody know him?" drawled Cassie. "He was never off the box."

"But Danny *really* knew him. Weren't you friends at UCL?"

Although he hesitated, his correction, when it came, was only partial. "*Best* friends, actually. In fact, I was one of the last people to see him before he—"

Eleven faces looked at him expectantly but he hardly needed to finish the sentence. Leaving it hanging sounded more portentous. Letting his voice take control, he told them how he'd known, at their first meeting, that his friend would be famous. He had an aura, you see.

An aura and a presence—

"Oh God!" screamed Barbara laughingly when the door had closed on the last of her guests. "Weren't they awful?"

Stevie grinned down at her before slipping off his moleskin jacket—she called it his "laborer's chic look"—and joining her on the sofa. She leaned against his chest and closed her eyes. "Poor old sod!" she murmured, meaning Danny. "He takes everything so seriously." Stevie stroked her hair and bitched about his friends. Big, scared Danny was a star, he said, compared with Cassie.

Barbara smiled.

Despite her tiredness she had better things in mind than sleep. The best way to deal with post-party tension was to blast it into orbit at the soonest opportunity. And Barbara knew the finest way of all. For though it brought its own complications, a good fuck seemed preferable—as self-annihilations go—to the ones wrought by her perfectionism. However, before she could make her move she caught Stevie looking furtively around him.

"Where did I put my jacket?"

"Beside the coffee table. But it won't crease. What a funny thing to worry about."

"It isn't that." He looked defensive. "I should have told you sooner but I'm seeing a client first thing tomorrow morning. I'll have to stay at my place."

Somewhere in Barbara, a door closed. She wanted to shout "Why are you *doing* this?" but she wouldn't give him the satisfaction. It was too old an argument. Since he wouldn't move in with her, the only thing she could do was not show her need. And she was getting better at it. In fact, by the time he left, she not only matched his detachment, she exceeded it.

"Drive carefully," she called, not troubling to rise.

"I'm sorry about this. But I'll be thinking of you."

"Of course you will," she managed.

His voice went up as though he was asking a question: "Love you lots?"

"Yeah," she whispered, as consolingly as she could. "I know you do, I know you do."

10

If nothing else, Stevie's absences stopped Barbara from becoming one of those abjectly clingy women who clutched and leaned on their men in public. (She thought, particularly, of certain lawyers who ought to have known better.) She was reminded of this type a week or so later when she found Ed and Susan Upshaw canoodling by the whiteboard before the English department's termly meeting. It was nauseating seeing Susan toy seductively with a felt-tipped marker while Ed gazed lustfully at her cleavage and said things like, "We must action this immediately." But then, Susan used to be his student—they'd fallen in love over Ezra Pound. And even now she was liable to stare at him in awe while complaining, breathily, that his book on imagism had been shamefully neglected. Oddly enough neither of them mentioned *her* work on Gertrude Stein.

A more positive role model was Lisa Lewis, their departmental administrator. Bill was lecturing her with his customary slowness but Lisa, who needed instructions from no one, least of all Bill, met his commands with polite professionalism. Without being indiscreet her expression warned that he was in one of his moods. Barbara winked her an acknowledgment before waving at Deirdre Waugh, whose caftan was bearing down in a merciless assault.

"Barbara! I've been hearing wonderful things about your feminism class. My girls are simply *raving* about it."

Yes, thought Barbara. *After years of you and Rachel, I should think they would be.* But her better side smiled, for she was fond of Deirdre and valued her kindness. The grin diminished with Rachel Glover's approach. Although Rachel was as gloriously and unapologetically large as Deirdre, there was something pinched about her personality. And as usual, she was annoyed. "Guess what?" she exclaimed in the sort of whisper that is meant to convey horrified disbelief. "Ronan MacIntyre

doi:10.1300/5902_10

wants Shakespeare removed from the first-year syllabus. And he's only been here five minutes!" She waved her agenda, too shocked to continue.

"If Ronan's only just arrived," smiled Barbara, "where does that leave *me?*"

Rachel was dumb.

"There you are!" laughed Barbara. "I ought to support his motion out of newcomers' solidarity."

"You aren't serious?"

"I might be. What's he want to replace it with?"

" 'An Introduction to Cultural Studies.' Whatever *that* might be! Of course, Bill won't stand for it."

Naturally there'd been none of "that sort of thing" at Oxford, but Barbara *had* taught Cultural Studies in North East London; she decided to hear the discussion before deciding how to vote. Meanwhile the room was filling up. Marcus Cranborne was treating Lisa to his thoughts on Virgil. Far from recoiling, Lisa smiled approvingly while making notes on her agenda. Barbara felt that such exquisite tact didn't deserve to be interrupted. Then came fragments of a different conversation: "Quite apart from the ethnicity book, I'm miles behind with my latest article for *Postmodernity Today*. The trouble is, I've started something even more exciting. But I mustn't talk about it yet."

Sucking in the corners of her lips, she skipped to Danny's relief. "I've been hearing about you," she said, tapping Ronan's shoulder. "Rachel Glover is out for your blood."

It took a second for Ronan to change gears. "In that case, I hope you'll support my motion." Then he returned to the previous subject. "I was telling Dan about my new project. The only thing is, I don't want to jinx it while it's still at the development stage. Otherwise I'd tell all."

Although Danny would have taken him at his word, Barbara wasn't one to let a hint go by, especially if there were amusing revelations to be had. "Come on," she coaxed. "You know you want to tell us."

The youngster pouted and primped and patted his hair. (*Come the revolution,* thought Danny, as he studied his bright red CCCP T-shirt, *I wonder how* your *parents will fare.*)

"Okay, already!" He was obviously longing to spill the beans. "But you'll have to keep it secret. I don't want anyone beating me to it." He took a luxurious breath after Barbara nodded her agreement. It felt good prolonging the moment. But he regretted the words as soon as they were out of his mouth.

"Writing a film script?" Barbara's laughter was shockingly loud. "You can't count *that* as academic research, Mr. Spielberg!"

"We shouldn't let research rule our lives!" insisted Danny, as well he might.

Ronan nodded his thanks before giving a passionate defense of his all-black, all-male remake of *Hello, Dolly!* ("with rap versions of those icky songs"). By going backstage at a community production in riot-torn Los Angeles the film would combine "a frank portrayal of the drugs scene" with the inevitable "cross-dressed homo love story."

Danny suddenly understood Ronan's vocabulary.

Enough, already!

It was, like, such a kiss-off.

That's real icky, man.

Thanks to an infatuation with the LA punk scene, the poor lad didn't realize that Keanu Reeves was the one person on earth who could get away with words like "gnarly."

Danny drifted to the window. In another hour everything would be dark but for now the town lay clear before him. *Time was,* he thought, *that everyone in academia was writing a novel. Now they're doing movie treatments.*

Ronan's voice cut in and out. "The shooting-up scenes are *bound* to be controversial but they're crucial to the storyline ... And the sex will be completely up front."

You couldn't make it up, thought Danny.

If anything, his irritation was increased by knowing that Ronan wasn't the only one with a screenplay in his filing cabinet. The bottom drawer of his own desk contained a mysteriously named file that came out once a month for rereading and enlargement. His "MEAT" folder was the hidden shadow of his thesis. It was where he laughed at his pretensions, pandered to his darker desires, and revenged himself on the unwitting subject of his research, Miss Barbara Mary Crampton

PYM. She, poor woman, would have been appalled to find her characters slotted into a "subversively pornographic fantasia" in which "unusually attractive vicars, nuns, and academics" were filmed "revealingly" in low-budget mock-ups of "a Cotswolds village, a London suburb, and a new university."

Most of Danny's actors resembled leading sportsmen but a few of the younger parts had been assigned, somewhat against his better judgment, to fondly remembered ex-students. The genre was compulsive. It wasn't just erotica, he felt, but a form of literary criticism. It took an expert close reader to load familiar settings with unexpected yet strangely apposite events. The film—which he'd provisionally titled *A Man Must Have His Meat*—included all the obvious scenes: the village fete with the unconventional lucky dip, the spate of mystifying noises during Evensong, and the lads' club evening where darts and ping-pong were not the only games played. Equally satisfying were the faculty talk with the unusual handouts, the office party that went with an unanticipated bang, and the seaside hotel that offered a fuller-than-expected service. The dialogue might still be rudimentary but the mise-en-scène was highly promising. (And oh yes, he also liked the title.)

Many casting choices remained unresolved. The pleasures of screen-testing made it hard to fix on a definitive cast. Danny preferred to keep his options open. Take that impudent charmer, Mr. Rockingham Napier—

As usual, Danny's musings were interrupted just as they got interesting: "Dr. Whelan, are you *almost* ready?"

"I'm sorry. Are we starting?"

He squeezed beside Marcus—it was the last free place—and flicked at his agenda with an air of forced calm.

First up was Ronan's modest proposal.

Shakespeare was considered from every possible cultural, historical, ideological, dramatic, aesthetic, linguistic, poetic, and financial perspective. Ronan argued that removing his work from the syllabus would challenge "retrogressive ideas of inherent literary value." Rachel fought back against "the kind of postmodernist charlatanism that happens to be destroying our profession." Their supporters heckled, mocked, and even reasoned while Bill Roberts looked blankly at the door. Having let the factions wear themselves out in pointless debate, he asked Lisa to minute their "frank and invigorating discussion" before proposing the establishment of a working party—its composition to be decided later—which would report "after a comprehensive consideration of the issues in, say, ten months."

Rachel smiled, Ronan frowned, and Bill said time was pressing.

The matters to which they then turned included the university's ever-falling recruitment figures, the intolerable burden that tuition fees placed on students, the administration's short-sighted decision to double faculty teaching loads, the exceptionally large number of faculty members currently on sick leave, the latest swingeing cuts to the library budget, and the Vice-Chancellor's inability to produce a policy document that did not contain at least one split infinitive per page.

Although each topic was discussed with passionate articulacy, Danny felt disheartened. Was this what their jobs had been reduced to? He pictured similar debates in scores of other universities. Then— fanning out—he heard echoes from the rest of the public sector. In ill-equipped rooms proceeded angry discussions lit by gallows humor and righteous indignation. Worthy, well-informed sentences came from teachers, nurses, librarians, transport workers, ambulance drivers, the police, civil servants, firefighters, and social workers—each of them under-resourced. It was enough to make you weep.

"What was that?" asked Marcus.

"Oh, nothing!"

Worried that he might actually *be* crying, Danny twisted his face into an intelligent aspect. But instead of following the conversation, he traced the web that underlay their official business. This was a not-so-delicate counter-melody of hums, sniffs, groans, and indirect speech. He could tell Bill was enjoying himself by the way he licked his lips before he spoke then smacked them when he finished. The longer his sentence, the louder the smack. Then there was Barbara's habit of moving her head back and forth while listening to an argument. Caught between political caution and the overwhelming need to put her oar in, she jiggled and squeaked during other people's pronouncements. These decorous sounds—too ladylike to be grunts—were pitched between demurral and acceptance: indeterminate signals that spoke, more than anything else, of her need to be heard even when she had nothing much to say.

By contrast, Ronan was surprisingly reticent, especially after the shelving of his Shakespeare motion. He rarely spoke, and when he did his voice went even deeper than usual before jumping an octave as he completed each sentence. He'd blush at this like a boy soprano whose voice was on the turn then clear his throat with a high-pitched cough. These punctuated the meeting along with Barbara's "*UH*-hums" and "mm-*HMMs*" and Deirdre Waugh's shrewdly skeptical laughs. Marcus Cranborne gave endearingly large yawns while the student reps looked unimpressed by the whole display. And every time Ronan dared to speak, Rachel Glover made the sort of scornful noise that eighteenth-century playwrights would have represented with the word "HUMPH!" Recognizing this for the aggressive intervention that it was, Ronan would flush and do another cough.

Danny was smiling at this unsuspected vulnerability when a voice cut through his reverie:

". . . Is that not so, Dr. Whelan?"

"Excuse me, Mr. Chair?"

"We were talking, Dr. Whelan, of our proposed new post in twentieth-century fiction."

Bill preened himself discreetly while explaining how he'd wrested the job from the Forward Motion Group. "Because of their gross mismanagement of the budget, we will be unable to fund another new post for at least three years. The current opening is therefore of the highest importance." He stopped for some licks. Like the lip-smacking that followed, these were gestures of mastery. Both scary and absurd, they were the nearest he got to public indulgence. (It was almost sexual, the pleasure he got from controlling meetings.) In his own good time, he continued. "While your thoughts were elsewhere, Dr. Whelan, I was remarking that it would be kinder to excuse you from participating in the appointments procedure."

"But I'm an expert in the field!" blurted Danny. "I don't see why I should be—*removed*." He stopped, not sure why such a trivial thing should rile him. Speaking slowly and trying not to stutter, he asked why he'd been pushed out.

Professor Roberts examined the agenda with elaborate care. "I'm not sure that it's appropriate to discuss these things in public."

"What things?"

Danny realized his mistake when Bill's mouth curled upwards in a parody of smiling.

"This isn't something I would ordinarily canvas at a committee meeting, Dr. Whelan. However, since you press me, I am obliged to point out that you have published exactly *one* scholarly article in the last five years. Your only other contributions to knowledge have been *two* book reviews which appeared more than six years ago in *The Barbara Pym Biennial*. Since then you've published nothing." Bill allowed himself a smack; things were going as he liked them to. But it wouldn't do to get excited. Wetting his lips, he slowed still further. "Given your failure to produce any worthwhile research, not to mention the unpromising state of your so-called book, I'm not sure how the department could benefit from your advice. As I know only too well, appointment committees are time-consuming. In my view, that time would be better spent on your writing. Do forgive me, though, if I've missed any reviews. Perhaps you've been busier of late. Maybe the number has zoomed up to four. And all in *The Barbara Pym Biennial*. What *would* they do without you?"

It's over, Danny told himself. *It's almost over.*

But Bill hadn't finished. "Tell us, Dr. Whelan. How many reviews *have* you published? Is it three or four?"

Danny made a choking noise. Marcus hid it with a cough.

"I can't hear you, Dr. Whelan. Would you please tell the meeting how many reviews you've published?"

Danny looked him in the eyes. "Three."

"Thank you. I think we've discussed the matter in sufficient detail. If you've no further objections let's progress to more important issues." And on he swept—not with a smile but with the loudest SMACK of the meeting.

11

It's true, thought Danny, *that a little quiet reading lifts the spirits:*

Enrique is a Spanish lad who stands twelve inches long in his bare feet. Call him now and you won't be disappointed. Unless you like small dicks.

Whatever their other flaws, at least universities produced unusually cosmopolitan graffiti. Before him were messages from Sergio, Nicolas, Boris, Miguel, and Jacques. Then there were the mysteriously terse *LB.132.a.Hbt.1* and *LB.147.b.Hct.56.* When he first got his job he'd assumed these were prison serial numbers. It took him the best part of a month to realize they were just library shelf marks.

Having heaved his rectum free of obstructions, he zipped his pants with a despairing moan. It was Monday morning and he'd passed the weekend in shock. His dressing-down had been like a rebuke from a medieval prince. There was nothing to do but turn his back on court or beg for a suitably vicious form of penance, like being flagellated in the library courtyard, or having his dickhead stapled to the departmental photocopier.

Meanwhile he was stuck with waking nightmares about the obscene motions of Bill's mouth. It was like a 1950s movie.
Attack of the Killer Academic
The Tongue That Licked the World
Another dream replayed the scene in which Ronan had confessed that it was *he* who had taken Danny's place on the interview panel. ("Bill asked me last week. I didn't think about the implications.") Finding nothing to say, Danny had glared at him until he looked away.

doi:10.1300/5902_11

The only thing that stopped the flashbacks was clasping his hands over his ears and crying "No, No, No!"—a policy that was scarcely suitable for public use. Dragged from the house by his teaching duties, he edged along the Arts Tower corridors, terrified of being trapped with a sympathetic colleague.

Naturally, the first person he met was Barbara.

At the meeting she'd whispered rebelliously about votes of no confidence. Now she peered at him inquisitively while recommending the union. "There's no such thing as democracy round here," she complained. "I think it's appalling that Bill never consults us in advance."

She was overdoing the concern, he thought, when she told him how ill he was looking. "I'm fine," he replied, trying not to sound defensive. "Why shouldn't I be?"

"But I called you yesterday. I know you don't go out, so it was worrying not getting an answer."

Thinking fast, he told her he'd been away.

Was it his imagination or did her face fall? "Oh," she managed after a pause. "Where did you go?"

"Paris, actually."

Blocking all memories of ripping the telephone cord from his wall on Friday evening, he extemporized brilliantly on the Hotel Charles de Gaulle (where the service had been highly efficient though a *touch* impersonal) and the bliss of a weekend break in the off-season. ("It's so transgressive. Treating yourself in term time.")

Discomfited by his unexpected bravery, Barbara said she had to run. ("I've tons of photocopying to do. And if the machine's not working at half past eight on a Monday morning, when *will* it be working?") When she was gone, Danny's glib words crawled back to him—signs of his abjection. "You know what?" they lisped. "It's so refreshing being able to *move* in the Louvre. And the Marais nightlife couldn't be better, even at *this* time of year!" Despising the flimsy veils he'd drawn around his humiliation, he sat at his desk with the computer not on until it was time to teach. Then he burst into the seminar room snapping "What can you tell me about Enid Bagnold that I don't already know?" If he'd been carrying a carrot he'd have bitten off the top like a venomous Bugs Bunny. Roused from Monday morning stupor, the students gave their best performance in weeks.

But Danny still despaired.

He'd never write his book, he'd never make his name. He would feed the grass when he was dead—and that would be that. No one would visit, no one would cry.

Not surprisingly, he couldn't finish his packed lunch.

Then it was time, once more, to face a hostile world. (Or rather, yet another class on neglected woman writers.) Unable to sustain the morning's air of not giving a damn, he faltered under the paranoid delusion that news of his humiliation had spread among the student body. He lost his thread, repeated himself, and gazed out the window. (The days were getting longer.) It was then that he wondered about throwing himself out. *This is mad,* he thought. *A total overreaction.* But Bill's words had traveled, with despicable brilliance, to the center of his insecurity. He couldn't defend himself because Bill had merely uncovered his self-hatred. Contemptible though it was, the attack deserved a proper acknowledgment—like a single hand-clap, bitter and sarcastic in an empty theater.

At four a cup of tea helped. ("I'm turning into my father," he laughed.) Then he taught a sweet-natured bunch who always did the reading. Their warmhearted concern almost made him weep. One asked how he was. Another said he looked ill. "You should take better care of yourself," ventured a third as she looked at him with gray, respectful eyes.

Shaking his head, he taught a solid class.

Although he was touched to be recognized as a fellow human being, the students who haunted Danny's journey home were the two who'd looked away, not the ones who'd asked after his health. Was it a coincidence, on either count, that these were also the only men in the group?

Gerry had mild blue eyes and an expanding waistline. Scott had a V-shaped fringe and thick black eyebrows—he looked like something with horns in a Robert Mapplethorpe photograph. They were in

Danny's nervous system, those two. He had eyed them all term—coolly, professionally. But now he felt rage and curiosity, and a certain mad desire. Gerry probably had a girl who baked bread while he was boozing with his mates. Although Scott wasn't so handsome, he was infinitely sexier. No faithful girl for him but screws where he could get them and nothing for keeps. And, unlike Gerry, he was bright.

Although Danny was the teacher, Gerry and Scott owned the earth. Round and round they trampled, one of them taut, the other slouching, as they beat the bounds of his consciousness. They guarded the Land of the Big Straight Lad—a country that Danny would never know. Things seemed simpler there, and safer, but faced with such ambassadors Danny could only stare like Jack when he first saw the beanstalk. If he lived a hundred years he'd never have their confidence.

I hate myself, I hate myself.

The words ran through him so loud and fast that he wondered why no one else could hear them. Getting on the bus, he opened his mouth to shout "I HATE MYSELF" before he realized that that was the wrong destination. "Moore Street," he murmured while heading for the back.

His fellow passengers were an unsavory bunch. He would usually have laughed at the woman whose glossy folder from the National Financial College turned out, on second glance, to be from the National Funeral College. As it was, he only managed a quick smile at her black-bordered article on "The Dead Citizen's Charter."

Descending meekly, he trudged through side streets to his house.

More clearly than ever he saw his dreams pass out of reach. He'd never be an academic superstar with groupies fighting for his favors. He'd have to renounce such hopes and desires along with the tensions they provoked. Instead he'd smile benignly on Ronan MacIntyre and Barbara Barnes—frenetic worker bees to his lazy queen, drowsing on the roses. Rather than struggling to be a Name he'd embrace the warm and limited world of The Retired. Without giving up his job he'd abandon his hustling ambitions in favor of a shambling life of carpet slippers, warm fires, and bone-dry sherry. (Tío Pepe, of *course*.)

He could read Charlotte M. Yonge and "Miss Read" and endless Barbara Pym. He would live his life through books. Not in the tiresome way that "scholars" do—he'd give up *that* for good—but in the way that elderly matrons are said to do, burying themselves in paperback romances then trawling round Waitrose making eyes at the doctor and the dentist, and fantasizing that the checkout boys were in thrall to their fatal beauty. It would be a brand-new career for him. He'd get a ribbon for his glasses and a harsh shade of blusher. (The walker could wait.) The shop lads would come running after him and he'd tip them extravagantly for their pains. And if they laughed behind his back, he simply wouldn't see it.

When he got in, the answering machine was winking at him. He examined it warily before pressing the button.

This is what he heard:

"Hey there . . . This is your number, right? They gave me it at the university. I hope you recognize me! . . . Dan, it's Christian here . . . I haven't seen you in ages. Well—that's an understatement. Anyhow . . . Could we meet sometime? . . . I've found a great new restaurant near Soho Square . . . It would be wonderful to see you. After all this time—"

PART TWO

1

As usual at the start of December, Barbara was wondering where she and Stevie should take their winter break. Although they wanted heat, a beach holiday would be vulgar. There had to be a twist, like their literary tour of Algeria, or their archaeological trip around the Occupied Territories.

Since their dinner party, Stevie had been staying with her almost every night. But attentive though he was, the dear boy could still be difficult.

Take the night before.

There they'd been, curled in front of the box with a bottle of wine and every appearance of a romantic night ahead. It recalled the early days of their affair: Barbara could hardly keep herself from touching him. But although Stevie held her hand he wouldn't take her hints. She'd shifted this way and that while he went on watching the screen. Incapable of long periods of silence, she scrabbled on the floor with *The Guardian,* humphing and pshawing at every other sentence.

"Anything interesting?" he'd asked, his concentration fixed on *Newsnight.*

Rather than replying, she had half-stifled a laugh as if something had amused her in the paper. Then she snorted affectedly, put her hand to her nose, and told him not to take any notice of her. (So he didn't.)

He felt pleased with himself. For how could he control other people if he couldn't control himself?

Barbara studied his profile. Why did he have to go distant at the precise moment when she was prepared to lower her defenses? *Very well,* she'd thought. *Two can play at that game.* Having swept herself up, she'd paused in the doorway like Bette Davis with a pearl-handled pistol: "I'm going upstairs."

"Oh." He was vague. "I'll see you in a bit."

doi:10.1300/5902_12

She slammed the door, knowing that he'd trot up ten minutes later like an errant Saint Bernard. He'd wag his tail and offer the usual range of reviving fluids—but he could forget it. No longer was she in the mood for his woolly coat and overactive tongue. (Being licked on the face had *never* turned her on.) Instead she turned in fury to *Speculum of the Other Woman*. Luce Irigaray was bound to keep him at a distance.

They had performed this scene many times before, each wanting to make love but getting caught, before they could do so, in a tangle of ego. Though the dumb show had a power of its own it wasn't clear what it communicated. It was as if the avoidance of sex was as meaningful as the act itself. The notion was curiously pleasing. How special their relationship must be that it should find its ideal expression in a delicate dance of longing and denial, of silence and speech. It was more comforting to think of it like that, she thought, than to see it as a territorial war in which their pride had to be protected above everything else—even their desire.

They hadn't made love that night but soon they would—and the sex would be better for the delay. This thought warmed Barbara as she rejected Florida (too common) and Amsterdam (too wet). Then "poor Danny" came to mind. Was he okay? She hadn't heard from him in weeks. He must find it hard, being alone. And she looked at Stevie with renewed satisfaction.

Surely the time was near?

Not considering what she was doing, she pinched the back of his neck. He looked up, startled, from his laptop. *Let* him *take the initiative,* her instinct warned. So she waited for the arm that pulled her down. (So much for their exquisite evasions!) *This is not what I want,* she thought, but they went on kissing. (Meanwhile, Stevie tried to forget about work.) *In books,* she reasoned, *there's that discreet sentence "Afterwards they lay exhausted on the bed." But that doesn't tell you much.* She gasped as Stevie dug his nails into her arm. If only she could know whether other people felt it too—the pulling close when you wanted to break away, the breaking away when you wanted to go on.

She let him lead her upstairs where they undressed with separate efficiency. And before she knew it, he was crouching over her. He revolted her. His bulk, his unexpected hair. The smell of him. She pushed him off. He lay on his back and laughed. *You disgust me,* she thought as she crawled under the sheets, spat on his dick, and took it in her mouth. Up and down she went. (*You disgust me, you disgust me.*) Down, down, down until his cock hit the back of her throat. Then up to lick his dickhead. (Stevie was no longer thinking about his laptop.)

She stopped before he got too excited.

He did his best to thank her. He knelt above her, kissing her neck and breasts. But she couldn't relax. He was too young. There wasn't a fold on his skin. She wanted to cover her face, her chest, her stomach. She grasped his shoulders and pushed him further down.

Does he feel what I feel?, she wondered as a wire of heat passed from her hairline to the back of her knees. *He'd fucking better do.* Unless they cost him something, his attentions weren't worth having. He, too, had to need and dislike the body that was tangled in his own. He, too, must feel the mad ambivalence of wanting to stop yet always going on.

At this, a clench of pleasure convulsed her and the next she knew they were shoulder to shoulder. It was a transitional scene. Props were being shifted while the actors looked at the ceiling. There were no words here: their breath made the only noise. She wanted the silence to go on. But she also wanted more. They might toy with leaving before the second act but they knew it wouldn't do. Having come this far, they'd have to continue.

Given this, she might as well take charge.

Take this, she thought as she climbed on top of him, scoring her nails against his thigh. He tried to lift her off but she wouldn't budge. So he bit her on the neck. (It was another of their rituals.) But would it always be like this, she wondered, as she pressed her fingers round his skull, pulling him close while kissing him as deeply as she could. Why this struggle between pride and desire? There was the joy of abandonment. (She let him pull her down again.) But there was also the need to be in charge. (She didn't like seeing him above her.) And she hated what was coming next.

It was ludicrous—the idea of "being entered." The words were absurd, and the concept, and the act most of all. There ought to be a
new approach. Something that would cut out this tiresome playact-
ing. What was Stevie thinking as he drew himself up? He didn't seem
frightened. But he might be, he might be. Perhaps he'd like a change.
It would be a release—not having to do *that* every time. (She studied
the side of his head but it gave no clues.)

He was fumbling with a rubber. (Contempt overtook her.) But it
wasn't too late to stop. (The idea excited her.) They needn't always
fuck. (But she couldn't bear looking weak.) He massaged the top of
her thighs. (And turning away would look so cowardly.) So when he
pushed his way too sharply she lifted up a guiding hand.

[————]

The moment always shocked her. His hairiness and weight! (He
was a sack of something big.) But much as she wanted to, it was too
late to push him off.

He was in her and she didn't know what was happening.

He was in her and there was no continuity of thoughts or emotions.

He was in her and—

She closed her eyes. He was kicking up inside her. She had another
limb. It was hers and not hers: both foreign and familiar. She found
herself responding. Her back arched as he drove further in. And all
the while she was hot—dry—cold—sore—deaf—

(There were no words for what she felt.)

She opened her eyes to find him moving in and out of focus. He
went faster now. One moment he was ahead of her, his face screwed
up in concentration. Then she had a chin in her eyes and a nose in her
hair. He crashed up and down, hurting her as he went. And he was
completely out of scale. (She wanted to laugh—it was the proper
thing to do.) His eyes were squinting and his mouth hung open. She
wondered if he even saw her. (His whining got louder.) She almost felt
sorry for him: he was only partly in control. She pulled him closer and
he groaned. Thinking *This will soon be over,* she opened her mouth to
mime her pleasure. He lifted himself above her then pushed much
harder than before. She cried out—not miming.

And then—

And then—
And then—
A wave began to rise. (There was no other way to put it.)
She wanted to call out "This is a scene from a movie. Everything's
in clichés." But her mouth was dry. Sweat covered their bodies. His
face turned from her in pain. Then she felt another wave. But it was
weak—it failed to gather pace. It wouldn't carry her. And Stevie was
in his own world. He was scrunching up inside her. She felt a clench-
ing of hands, a gasping for air. A leg twitched—an arm shook. Someone called out—she didn't know who. She just knew that she was
cold. She was cold and wet and Stevie was lying across her, too spent
to move.

His weight oppressed her. Why was he still there? She wanted him
out. But defeat came down on her when he reached for the top of the
rubber and lifted up his hips. Another union had been broken. Another phase of aloneness was about to begin.

She hadn't come.

She rarely did, like that. But there had been pleasure in this rising
up of blood. And there was more, for Stevie was careful that way. He
wouldn't roll over; he took too much pride in his reputation. Prop-
ping himself up before his eyes could close, he gave her what he hoped
was a seductive look. But she didn't even blink.

Instead of striking her, as he almost wished to, he got on his hands
and knees—ungainly now—and nuzzled her belly. He put his finger
in her. Then he bent down his head.

Dear boy, she thought. *This isn't necessary.*

But she let him go on.

She tried not to think about what was happening. In fact, she tried
not to think about anything. She studied the blue-black spots on the
back of her eyelids. Off, off, off—she wanted him away from her. But
almost unwillingly her body quickened and her eyelids shifted. The
spots were going purple, scarlet, gold. Her heart beat faster. He had
knotted his hands around her waist. She gaped and breathed hard.
She gasped. It was red on black, black on orange. Deep, deep orange.
She was crying out. She was itching—prickling—burning—freezing—

(There were still no words for this.)
And she saw red—black—purple—green—

They lay side by side when it was over, their hands loosely gripped.
"Good?"

"Mmmm."

They had crossed the barrier. Once more they had taken the risk. It was odd how it got harder over time. Odd how they found excuses for deferral—demurral—refusal. But she was glad they'd done it. She could feel him inside her. It was a memory in her blood—better than his actual presence.

Yes—she was happy they had done it, happy they were still together.

"Stevie?"

"Yeah?"

"Love you."

He turned his head towards her. "Love you too."

A long silence.

And then she thought: *I* really *must see Danny Whelan before we go to Crete.*

2

For his part, Danny was confronting the remains of his supper. Despite eating hours ago, he hadn't bothered clearing up or moving to the sofa. Instead he reviewed a day which had begun with Emily Brontë on the toilet seat before progressing to dreary classes on the usual dreary subjects. Lunch had been followed by what sport commentators had learned to call a bathroom break, where he had read a graffito from "Ten-Inch Eric" and one from a European visitor who gave his measurements in centimeters (a disturbing trend that ought to be discouraged).

Although the youth of the university managed to seem alert, if not ecstatic, at his neoformalist readings of Nancy Mitford, Danny hadn't believed a word that came out of his mouth. When he finished he felt so low, and so edgily desperate, that he went creeping around the university library with a list of shelf-marks culled from the lavatory walls. He didn't ask what mixture of danger and excitement he hoped to find; he simply nudged along the stacks without looking left or right, and trying not to hurry. The notes in the loo had promised "Complete Satisfaction" but all he discovered, despite mounting excitement, was Delia Smith's *One Is Fun* and a book about crabs.

Cursing his gullibility, he wondered why his fellow travelers did their cruising in the cookery section. Couldn't they at least have chosen woodwork? Finding no one near, he'd stomped home and flung himself on the sofa, where he had a dream in which Sexy Scott sodomized Good-Natured Gerry in a library carrel. Their goings-on were so vigorous that Elizabeth David's *English Bread and Yeast Cookery* fell off their table, causing Danny to jolt awake with a stiff neck and a bad conscience. He couldn't face cooking after that. So he rang for Chinese takeout.

It was bizarre, given last week's news, that he felt depressed.

doi:10.1300/5902_13

Rather than phoning Christian he'd paused, that first evening, to replay the unimaginable, pulse-arresting message. But twelve playings later, having memorized each rise and catch in his beloved's voice, Danny's pleasure had turned to fear. When he reached for the receiver, he saw the small cold smile that Christian used on the unattractive, and he knew he couldn't ring—at least, not yet.

But he'd do it the next day.

Without fail.

For that wouldn't look too desperate.

Except when daybreak came he couldn't even *look* at the phone. It was always the same. The more he wanted something, the more he short-circuited his desires. Then delay, the disease of his life, took over. Every evening, he put the call off until the morning. Every morning, he put it off until the evening. Desire, shame, and uncertainty canceled one another out, letting stasis run in, day after day, until five nights had passed and he was sitting at his table feeling sick from too many prawn crackers.

Irritated, unreasonably, that Christian hadn't rung him again, he dug out his draft obituaries. "Christian Ellis is dead," ran his favorite. "The giant has departed! And we who are left behind must follow feebly in his wake with only his work to guide us." The nineteenth-century phrases pleased him: they were a love offering to someone who could never read them. But now that Christian had returned, they were merely embarrassing. And as so often happens, embarrassment turned to anger. Midway through yet another replay of the message, he felt like smashing his answering machine against the wall.

"I'm independent," he told the empty room. "I don't need him messing me about!"

Pleased with this tack, he ticked Christian off for being an arrogant little fucker. (Well, it made a change from vowing eternal love.) But he was alarmed when his fighting talk melted into thoughts of rough and sweaty sex. And when he grabbed the phone—to tell Christian to piss off, once and for all—he realized he had his biggest hard-on in weeks.

Down went the receiver. (It would have been like doing the shopping on an empty stomach.) Instead he thought about the day he'd
had, and the week, and the whole damned year. Who was he fooling?
If independence equaled loneliness, then he was pretty cool. If earning
more than the minimum wage was success, he must be quite a character. But apart from once or twice with Barbara, when was the last
time he'd screamed with joy? Or wept with laughter?

The truth was, he'd been lost without an Object.

Unlike Ronan or Barbara, he couldn't be bothered pursuing professional success. Instead he'd landed himself with Awful Old Love—a
treacherous path that he couldn't bring himself to bypass. It was more
a way of being than an emotion. And it made him feel alive.

Like Christian, it drove him crazy.

But it also gave him purpose—meaning—identity.

The jangling of the phone made him jump.

He waited—four seconds, five seconds—before hurling himself at
the receiver, impatient for whatever pain or hope the call might bring.
He nearly dropped it, though, when he heard his father's voice.
"There's no need to panic," Larry kept saying once they got through
the preliminaries. "But I hope you'll be coming home for Christmas."

"I always do, don't I?"

"Yes, but I needed to check."

Since it didn't occur to him that there might be something perverse
about a middle-aged man taking satisfaction from his power over an
elderly parent, Danny felt renewed when he put down the receiver: If
he wanted, he could disappoint his father's hopes. (Even though he
knew he wouldn't.) In fact, the conversation was so cheering that he
was able, when the phone rang a moment later, to pick it up immediately. This time he heard, as he somehow knew he would, the strange,
cold, maddening voice of his great beloved, his object, his Christian:

"Dan! Did you get my message? Is everything okay? Say something—!"

"Yes," he squeaked, sounding like a man whose lungs were full of water. Choking back salt, he felt his body drop through carpet tiles and floorboards. The balls of his feet hit sewer walls then bounced him to the roof. "Yeah," he grinned. "I'm here, I'm here." And he laughed and laughed, intoxicated by the sound of his own happiness.

3

As a self-declared feminist, Stevie often worried about his wish to fuck Barbara senseless. He praised. He listened. He advised. No one could be more attentive. And yet still he had these lapses! It was more than he could credit.

With the confidence of the tall, the handsome, the straight, and the conspicuously well-paid, Stevie liked telling off his laddish colleagues for their "outmoded and thoroughly reprehensible sexual politics." It was odd how his friends winked at this and raised their eyebrows as if the whole thing was a joke they had between them. However, Stevie knew better. Unlike *them,* he'd picked himself a career girl, and a feminist, not some bimbo in five-inch spikes. And hadn't he always been interested in "the irresistible effects of crude male power"? It must have been guilt, then, that made him linger in the typing pool explaining gender studies to the secretaries. And they must have learned so much about it, too, as he bent forward on his long, long legs while they crouched before their VDUs.

Not that he ever would have played away from home.

Why go elsewhere, with the thrills that Barbara gave him? He loved her social poise, and the way his mates eyed her up. But her vulnerability was the real appeal. It was so sexy, the way she acted tough for everybody else but showed her neediness to him. What a joy to haggle on the phone, bag a difficult commission, be rude to his secretary, and still have the patience to soothe a troubled partner. He reveled in keeping his temper, and even liked her to be unreasonable: it gave him a chance to be calmly understanding.

For sympathy was his lifeblood. He got high on it. Giving and receiving it. Dealing in it. How warm it made him feel! How warm, and how needed! And all for a hidden fee. "Don't keep anything from me," he warned. "I want to help you because you're much more important than *I* am."

doi:10.1300/5902_14

Holding Barbara together confirmed his feminism. "For men *can* be feminists," he claimed, and Barbara, who had always been skeptical on that point, found her doubts worn down by his attentions. Yet it was curious, given his empathy, that there wasn't a single ex with whom he was on speaking terms. Earlier loves had snapped at him when he got too close. They resisted him (which he couldn't understand) or even—God forbid!—prodded into *his* psyche. But girls were the ones needing comfort, not him. Never him.

And nor did he believe in forgiving goodbyes. Quite the reverse. For despite his loving words, he saw no call to waste his time on people who didn't know what was best for them. If they wouldn't let him help them, they could go right off and fuck themselves.

Happily, Barbara wasn't like that.

Instead of brooding on his motives, she let him pry as deeply as he wished. She was like an old-time star poring over stills from a forthcoming movie and needing reassurance. Which images to print and which to kill? A woman like that was warm, imperious, and insecure. She needed a man she could trust: someone who'd forget himself in her. Stevie—at last!—was such a man, and the more she responded, the more she depended.

Stevie felt her grip, and knew its meaning. It wouldn't have occurred to him to be offended when she failed to thank him for his help. On the contrary, her obliviousness was pleasing. It made him certain that she'd fall to pieces on her own. (Which gave *great* satisfaction.)

For her part, Barbara thought that anyone who put up with her must be soft. Was it helplessness or strength that made her needle her boyfriends until they lost their cool? Who could tell? But Stevie guessed, correctly, that she'd dump anyone who was weak enough to lose control. With this in mind he'd stay in London now and then, not to "finish a report" but to loll around with his PlayStation and a little light pornography. ("A restorative," he called it, as if she really *had* done something to offend him.) He wasn't bothered when she huffed about his absence. In fact, he liked her to be angry: for he knew he'd win the fight. And when the time seemed right (that is, when she'd stopped taking him for granted) he returned with all the sex that she could take. (And all the sympathy, too.)

Dysfunctional though their relationship might sound, it worked. Each answered needs that other lovers hadn't touched. And God knows they turned each other on. If there was a danger, it wasn't that their affair was built on power struggles—for few relationships are free of *that* tendency. No, denial was the real problem. Rather than admitting his selfishness, Stevie saw himself as humble, altruistic, and progressive. Meanwhile Barbara disguised the ambition, and the wish to dominate, that underlay her neediness. In doing so she concealed, even from herself, how she resented his support. As a result, she grew dependent on the very things that made her edgy.

Such matters were far from her mind, however, when she bustled up to Danny in the photocopying room one bright, cold, mid-December morning. Having her own needs seen to always made her want to sort other people's out, and she had felt so much closer to Danny since Bill Roberts had publicly humiliated him. "What are you doing for Christmas?" she asked, adding "Stevie and I are going to Crete" before he could reply.

Smiling at such a typical opening, Danny told her about his dad.

"We've wanted to go there for ages," she continued. "It's our sixties thing. Hippies used to live in the caves, you know."

Danny tried to picture her in a cave. "Won't it be cold at this time of year?"

"Oh no! It's quite far down. Virtually North Africa."

He didn't press the point, and in any case she wouldn't have heard. "What have you been up to?" she swept on. "I've hardly seen you since we had you over. I can't have my friends deserting me when I'm looking out for them."

"Oh yeah?"

"Yes. I've been sniffing out essays you could do. My friend Rosie's editing a volume on femme fatales but she's an article short. She'd slip you in if I tipped her the wink."

Danny muttered that there weren't many femmes fatales in Barbara Pym but his other Barbara was already somewhere else. "Talking of fixing things up, I met *the* most gorgeous guy at Hermione's launch party. What *is* it about me and gay men? We couldn't stop flirting! But I was very good: I told him all about you. He's an agent, so he'd be marvelous for your career. And he looks like a cross between Tom Cruise and F. Scott Fitzgerald."

"Oh great—a stumpy alcoholic."

"And another thing! You'd never know he was gay. Stevie said he was the most straight-acting bloke he'd ever met."

Barbara caught, but did not understand, Danny's look.

"You don't mind me matchmaking?" she went on. "I mean, I'd have snapped him up myself if he'd been interested."

Danny bit his lip. It was one thing for him to spend his Saturday evenings watching millionaire lads in muddy shorts. It was quite another for straight friends to tell him who he should be going out with. But he shrugged away her homophobic agent. And for once he wasn't fibbing, for he had resources Barbara didn't know of.

These came to the fore a few days later when he waited on a pale, bare platform for the London train. Barbara and his colleagues were suddenly irrelevant. Instead he was taken up with Christian. On looped his memories like a home movie filled with close-ups, blurs, and unexpected cuts. But this wasn't the unnatural clarity of digitalized video; it was old-fashioned cine film that you projected onto walls with a light-box that fluttered on and off until you got high on the past.

Naturally, his train was late.

While the other passengers rustled *The Daily Telegraph* in an openly rebellious manner, Danny contemplated a matron on the opposite platform (tweed suit, wicker basket, personal CD player), and tried to calm his heart. He wished he could run away. Instead he visited the toilet—a dark and stinking pit—to check on his appearance. "Due to improvements," read a notice, "there are fewer WCs on this side of the station." He was reminded of a sign announcing alterations in the town's traffic system. CHANGED PRIORITIES AHEAD, it said, as if something more than pedestrian crossings were at stake.

Without consciously intending it, he had put on one of Christian's old uniforms. ("Lesbian chic," Danny used to call it.) Black jeans, socks, and boots, plus a black T-shirt, and a leather jacket. (Black.) It must have suited him, for he sensed an appreciative glance as he staggered down the carriage on yet another visit to the loo, but that didn't

stop him longing for Hush Puppies and a woolly jumper. He felt ridiculous clunking round in such heavy gear. He couldn't fold his legs.
Instead he had to sit with his knees far apart and his eyes staring
carelessly ahead.

The underground was its usual heaving self. In England, he reflected, cattle are carried with more compassion than people. "I am a
forty-something professional," he whispered as the Covent Garden
lifts tipped him into daylight. "It's not a blind date. I don't have to
run away." Desire, though, is a terrible thing, for he felt like puking
while he scanned the crowds, as nervy as a handheld camera. Then he
saw him! He was waiting, his back turned, beside the Opera House.
That's my friend, thought Danny. *My Christian.* He considered this for
a moment before realizing he was happy.

Christian turned, as if sensing he was being watched.

Danny wanted to morph into the man with the fingerboard advertising West End tickets. It was a lifetime's gift, being able to follow
Christian's eyes as they searched, uncertainly, for their target. But
why wasn't there a crowd around him? He was so much better value
than those maniacs on unicycles.

Danny waved, unable to take the suspense. Christian looked panicked, as if he'd been clapped on the shoulder by an undercover cop,
then smiled his famous smile when he recognized his friend.

"H-hey!" he said, with an endearing catch. "How's this for old
times?" Like Danny, he brushed the corner of his eye. "By the way,"
he added in a brisker tone, "you're looking great."

Although Danny mumbled a reply, neither man could have said
what it was. They started moving, quickly but without aim, and with
neither looking at the other. "You look pretty good yourself!" managed Danny, who was regretting that he'd missed his chance to give a
hug. But his words were automatic. It was only when they'd walked
down Bow Street that he could take a sidewise look and wonder, *Is he
really the same? Is this going to work?*

He asked where Christian had been, only to have the question
waved away.

"Later, later! First we'll have lunch."

Danny giggled at his tone. (*Yes,* he thought, *it's really him.*)

As always, he was surprised that Christian was so much shorter than him; maybe that was why he always looked boyish. But he was paler than Danny remembered, and the winter light had lined his face. His beauty seemed more human, somehow, for those pencil strokes around the eyes. Studying them, Danny wondered if he might be in trouble.

Something registered through the elder man's reverie. "Isn't Soho Square over there?"

"Eh?"

"You said there was a restaurant near Soho Square?"

Christian pulled a face—"I don't go *there* anymore"—and quickened his pace until they came to a plate-glass window which he announced as "Conran's latest." After pushing through the heavy doors, he plonked himself on a metal seat while Danny looked around uneasily. It wasn't the sort of place he'd have gone to on his own.

His eyes narrowed. "So when did you get back?"

Christian waved at the waiter. "Get back?"

"To London."

He hesitated. "About a month ago." He hurried on before Danny could speak. "There was tons to do before I got in touch. But I had to come back. I'd had enough of being away."

Danny could have wept at such a melancholy smile. "What was it like? Were you okay?"

Christian looked away. "Oh, sure. Now, what'll you have? The scallops are fantastic."

Danny thought, *You're hiding something.* But out loud he said: "You're looking fantastic, you know."

Christian wouldn't meet his gaze. "No," he said. "I'm not. But *you* are."

And they smiled on the beat, their eyes moving towards each other at exactly the same moment.

"It's like a sign," murmured Danny, though of what he wasn't sure.

4

By the time he went to his father's, Danny had several London trips to look back on. They already had a nostalgic charge reminiscent of the journey north for Christmas. In both cases, the traveling to and fro was as loaded with significance as the conversations he would have at either end.

The villages on the way to London had gained a romance by association. "Hopton, Monksfield, Weeping Cross and Mellford. Downhill, Pelham, Broken Bridge and Redmill." He wove their names into a song and peopled their platforms with retired majors and Church of England nuns—although drug dealers and computer programmers might have been closer to the mark. Watching two middle-aged men getting off at Larkswood, their shoulders almost touching as they shared a cigarette, he realized that there were more things in the world than the *Daily Mail* would ever dream of.

The journey to his father's drew out conflicting loyalties. Working class by birth and middle class by training, he fitted neither world completely. Despite loving the landscape of his birth, he longed for the click of his heels on Soho streets and the taste of imported beer drunk straight from the bottle. ("Waste of bloody money," his dad would have muttered—right as always.) Transit brought his lives together, but only for a time and only in his head. And though he wanted to be faithful to both locations, only one of them filled him with an adolescent joy that was all the stronger for having been unknown during his *real* teenage years.

Since Christian had come back, transfiguring visions had been slanting through Danny's life the way the early afternoon sun was slanting through his carriage window. Two weeks earlier, when the London train stopped beside a village green, he'd seen Christian's face everywhere he looked. "There he is," he'd murmured as the December light went raking over a silver-gray pond. "The man I love." He

doi:10.1300/5902_15

spoke the words aloud like a spell to summon up his friend or—better still—to make his friend love him. And though he'd heard no answering declaration, it had almost been enough to see Christian's face among the winter trees.

That same vision had returned during the next day's lecture on female suicides. Suddenly everything was shimmering. A smile played on his lips as he talked of Sylvia Plath and "the real tin thing," a smile so palpable that even the deeply dopey Gerry noticed.

"They probably think I'm having a breakdown," he'd reflected, somewhat smugly, as he went back to *Mrs. Dalloway*.

The closer he got to "home," the more he was possessed by excitement, fear, and boredom. Old landmarks had vanished, changed, or stayed the same. He could only see so much from his window but, if anything, he slouched a little lower in his seat. Why sit up straight when he'd see it all soon enough?

He felt the same about his father but didn't get the luxury of waiting. For Larry was pacing the platform. This annoyed Danny. "It's cold," he grumped, wishing the journey could have continued indefinitely. "You shouldn't have come out." He dashed towards the taxi rank but Larry, unperturbed, walked through puddles to the bus stop.

"You'll want to be alone," said his dad when they got in. "To unpack."

Danny didn't argue. Given that you can only fit so much football into a day's talking, the two of them would have to develop some new conversations—and fast. And he had enough to do coping with the pathos of his childhood room. It wasn't just the narrow bed. There were also the patches on the wall where his pinups had been, and the half-painted Airfix model hanging from the ceiling. (Aircraft carriers weren't so cool after he discovered CND.) Instead of literary criticism his bookcase held Rosemary Sutcliff, Alan Garner, and a pile of magazines. Although these were mostly *Shoot!*, he also glimpsed the *Gay News* he'd bought on a school trip to York and had never dared throw away in case the bin men saw it. He'd no idea why he'd left it sandwiched between Glenn Hoddle and Chris Waddle, where anyone might find it. He simply knew that every time he returned, he reread it nostalgically, thought about bringing it south, but always replaced it where he'd found it.

What would Christian make of the room, and of the life it had contained?

As if in answer, his friend took shape so clearly that Danny could have touched him. The face smiled with open acceptance but when Danny grinned back its expression changed. Without becoming any less attractive, it formed its lips into an ironic pout. Realizing too well what Christian would have said, Danny threw down his holdall and went in search of the inevitable.

"Hey, Dad! Where's that tea you promised? I hope it's good and strong. I need it after the journey I've had!"

It was bracing, over the next few days, to walk through streets that had never heard of Ronan MacIntyre or Bill Roberts. Old women in what used to be NHS glasses would wave him over, telling him they knew him when he was small. "And how's your father?" they'd leer. "Is he keeping well?" It was an odd question, he felt, considering they saw far more of him than *he* did. When he answered that he supposed so, they'd wink back, saying they supposed so too. Then a middle-aged man would brush past with a penetrating look, and Danny—his nose well-trained for the smell of queens—would hold the stare before realizing it was some long-forgotten friend edging up with pointed words about his desertion. Knowing he was single, they boasted of their families and asked after his until he wanted to shake them off as he had shaken off their town twenty years before.

The best and worst of these was Davey Mitchell, once the class know-all and now something in computers. After comparing their salaries, Davey dwelled on how their hometown had improved since Danny left. Danny recognized, but didn't like, the images that this evoked. Had they and their families sided with the miners so that Davey could live in a disused loft with "Katie and the kids"? Apart from upsetting Danny's nostalgia for urban deprivation, the conversation showed the shrinking distance between the town he'd made his home in and the one he'd left behind. Though he sniggered at his friend's talk of "laying down a cellar" with his pickings from *The Sunday Times* wine club, he himself liked Mexican beer with a slice of lime and always tried the more obscure cheeses from the deli counter. The difference was that Danny had gone south for his lifestyle props while Davey got his without leaving home.

Now that "exclusive consumer goods" were available in every other converted factory from Nottingham to Glasgow, Danny found it harder to feel superior. Fortunately, the likes of Davey still lagged behind the truly fashionable. "His problem," reflected Danny, "is that he's too predictable." Though he didn't live in London himself, he was closer than Davey to the power source. He often went to "the Serpentine" and "the Almeida" and he felt utterly comfortable navigating the tube in a pair of "Fuck Off" boots. (Or were they only "Fuck Me" boots? He wasn't sure.) He'd even seen Madonna, once, in a Soho restaurant—at which he'd studied the menu for a *very* long time before not going in.

Thoughts of London led inevitably to Christian. (For wasn't Danny a personal friend of "Christian Ellis, the well-known deconstructive philosopher"?) Even now his friend was everywhere he looked. In town, on television, and at the pub. He was the face on a giant billboard, the voice on a supermarket Tannoy. When the phone rang and went dead halfway through the Christmas lunch, Danny was sure who'd been on the other end.

"I'll ring back."

"But you don't know who it was," objected Larry.

"I think it was a mate of mine. I'll do 1471."

"No," snapped Larry. "It's Christmas. Leave it."

When Danny frowned his annoyance, his friend's face superimposed itself upon his father's. Instantly, he softened. "You're right," he smiled. "Now—d'you fancy the Queen's speech? Just for a laugh?"

"Not bloody likely."

"No change there, then."

They agreed that the Bond film was more promising. "Class enemy," muttered Larry in a comfortable way as he settled down to sleep. (He always made a point of cheering for the Russians.)

Unwilling to waste a chance for silent contemplation, Danny meditated on the loneliness that had driven Christian to phone him, and the nervousness that had made him ring off. Then he considered his father's profile. (He was handsome in his way: tall and bald, like his son.) Danny wondered what his dreams were—as if a child could ever know! A question came from nowhere: "Has he had sex since Mum died?" But the thought carried too many taboos. So he coughed and asked about the next day's match.

When they'd finished slamming the pathetic delusions of their cross-town rivals, he and Larry disparaged their home side with more affection. No eavesdropper could have doubted they were discussing one of the loves of their lives. (Standing in a muddy field—what strange settings we make for romance!) Realizing that they hadn't yet discussed "Michael," Danny gave a comprehensive list of the lad's precocious skills. When he finally noticed his father's face, he admitted that maybe the kid *had* been overrated, but he was already rather good, and his best days were still ahead of him, even if they'd never be as exciting as this special season, his first as a star.

Mr. Whelan listened restlessly before cutting his son short. "You'll feel better after this," he said, making a cup of tea.

"Or at least," he added under his breath, "I hope you will."

After months of instant replays it was strange, on Boxing Day, to watch a real match. Not that much of it merited being replayed, either instantly or at any other time. But it was nonetheless a worthy battle with a logic of its own. Not the ballet of the Brazilian game, or the operatic excess of Italy, but a wonderfully physical display marred, only occasionally, by lunges from behind, strikers tripping over the ball, and free kicks wafting high above the stand. (Flaws that any Premiership match might have suffered.) It was true that the mid-fielders started clutching their sides after thirty minutes, but what could you expect from people who looked more like rugby players than soccer stars? Such guys weren't anything like "Michael," let alone Christian.

Danny and his father shared a flask of tea at halftime. Larry produced sandwiches wrapped in the waxy paper that loaves used to come in, and that some evidently still did.

"You make a mean packed lunch, Dad."

His father looked at him as if he might speak but in the end he only smiled.

Two days later Danny traveled south.

5

Danny went shopping as soon as he got home; he felt an urgent need to stock up on middle-class food.

As usual, much time was spent looking at other people's groceries. A slim youth went by with a loaf of sliced white, a tub of marge, and a jumbo packet of crisps. Another man's basket had ten extra-strong condoms and a hemorrhoid preparation, at which an entire world seemed to rise before Danny's eyes.

Having picked the checkout line purely on aesthetic grounds, he had no one to blame but himself at having to wait for an obscenely long time. (In this case, as in many others, male beauty failed to go hand in hand with outstanding intellect.) Happily, he returned to a twinkling answering machine. Feeling the stirrings of an erection, he pressed the play button, only to get Barbara Barnes in schoolteacher mode. He was so flustered at not hearing the metallic tones of his beloved that he had to play the message twice to get the sense of it. This seemed to be: dinner at eight if he was free, and sorry about the short notice. He did nothing for an hour and then, depressed, told Barbara's machine that he'd be more than happy to come.

As soon as they'd not kissed ("Don't touch me; I'm infectious"), Danny knew something was up. Barbara was in sweatpants and a baggy jumper. Stevie was nowhere to be seen.

"I hope you haven't been extravagant," she sniffed, taking his bottle. "The food's nothing special."

"How was Crete? Nice weather, I trust?"

"Torrential rain the entire time."

"And your cave?" He almost laughed—it was such an absurd question. But Barbara answered with fierce concentration. The caves, it seemed, were not at *all* what they'd been promised.

doi:10.1300/5902_16

Once they finished the topic, her attention wandered. And the food—a steak which she cooked in front of him—was pulled at random from her fridge. She kept sneezing into the frying pan while apologizing endlessly, and somehow aggressively, for her failure to put on a good show.

It was a mark of friendship, he suggested, when people stopped hiding behind a front. ("It's like breaking wind in public, or admitting you like ABBA.") Her incredulous expression made him wonder if his words were true: perhaps friendships thrived on pretense? Meanwhile she was tossing the salad with such ferocity that he sank into a chair feeling even more bachelorish than usual.

The mood wasn't improved by an unexpected phone call.

"Stevie?" he asked, when she banged down the phone.

"My mother, actually. Trying to make me feel guilty."

"What about?"

"I don't know. The usual. Giving you a fry-up and not dressing for dinner."

"But no one does that anymore!"

"My mother does. Even when she's not having anything to eat."

Danny pictured his father handing out sandwiches on a football terrace. The comparison made him smile.

Barbara caught the look. "You wouldn't find it funny if you'd grown up with her."

"I don't suppose I would," he agreed, and the conversation lapsed.

He wondered how much time they'd have to kill before he could go home. Why invite him if she was going to snap and be sullen? Then he noticed she was shaking. Before he could ask what was wrong, she turned to him with gaping eyes.

For the first time in their friendship she spoke without knowing in advance what her words would be. "You'll have to help me, Danny. There's no one I can talk to. I've got myself into the most terrible state and I haven't a clue what to do." She clutched at her hair and evaded his embrace. "It's Stevie!" she exclaimed. "I've tried to keep it to myself but I can't, I just can't." And she burst into tears, horrified by what she thought of as the spectacle of her neediness.

An hour later they were still talking.

Or rather, Barbara was. (Her reserve, once broken, was slow to re-assert itself.) And she'd been saying pretty much the same thing all evening: "He's so fucking passive! It makes me want to yell. He sits round, waiting for something to happen. Lying there on the flat of his back, as if the world owes him a living, and not even a hint that he'll make the first move."

An eavesdropper might have leaned closer, expecting juicy revelations, but Barbara was thrashing something different out. "If it were me I'd *do* something, but he's like a great big crab hiding under a stone. He acts like I'm going to hurt him but I only want to help."

She paused to offer coffee but kept her elbows planted on the table. Her nose was fluey and red. *What would your mother say if she could see you now?* was Danny's unworthy thought. Then he roused himself: "So is London his shell? The place he hides out?"

"I don't know. Who cares?" Abruptly, she put the kettle on. "And we heard in the worst possible way." Once more she described how they'd gone straight from the airport to Stevie's office, only to discover that he'd been "downsized" in his absence. "It was horrible. They were all so bloody shifty. They assumed he'd already heard, but how could he have? Then someone told him what was up, and everybody sniggered. No one else got shafted. I'm sure it was personal."

The kettle boiled and grew still.

"I've always loved his patience. You've seen him; you know what he's like. But I can't stand him giving in. He'd get damages, but he won't hear a word about tribunals."

She stopped for breath.

"Did I ever tell you about my ideal man? I always say: 'I want a man worth fighting with.' I don't want a yes-man. You might think I do, but I don't. I want someone who'll stand up to me. I mean, like Stevie does. We have the most amazing battles, and they really turn me on, even when he winds me up. But I'm terrified he's going soft."

As usual, Danny was caught between exasperation and affection. So much palaver because some posh geezer had been given his cards. "Why is this happening to *me*?" Barbara was asking, as if she was the one with a London mortgage and no job. In Danny's world such fuss would have been self-indulgent. Things happened and you dealt with them as best you could.

"Middle-class affectation," was his verdict as he eyed the unopened coffee beans, wondering where she had bought them, and when, or if, he would ever get to taste them.

It was as if she'd read his mind. "The coffee! I never made your coffee."

She splashed her hand as she poured the water into her *cafetière*. Tears of pain, and of irritation, wet her eyes but she mastered them without a sound, rearranging her expression so that by the time she sat down her face was transfixed, as if through martyrdom.

"What is it?" asked Danny. The beatific vision was faintly sinister after so many tears.

She laid her head on her hands and spoke in tiny gasps. "Right now it's terrible. But we'll be happier in the end."

"Oh, really?"

Danny was alarmed by the skepticism in his voice but Barbara's reply was breathlessly warm: it allowed no contradiction. "Of course we will. No doubt about it."

"How come?"

She paused from pouring the drinks. "I love him; you know I do. Except I've never really shown it. It's always been me, me, me. But now I can help him. I'll look up his rights, and listen out for freelance work, and be the best advertisement that he's ever had. It won't be long before those fuckers will be groveling to have him back, but he can tell them where to go. He won't need them anymore. Not when I've finished with him." Her smile, as she continued, was oddly scary. "And if the worst comes to the worst, I'm happy to support him. In fact, I'd love to. It would be so cool, being able to pay him back for all his help." She searched out Danny's gaze. "So I can't imagine why this wouldn't bring us closer." Her stare was like a challenge. "Can you?"

He shook his head immediately. "No," he said. "I can't."

But even so, he thought, as he sipped her delicious coffee, *I bet you wonder what he's up to. In London on his own, with nothing to do all day—*

Picturing the worst was one of Danny's favorite leisure-time activities. No wonder he envisaged disasters for Barbara. However, the events that he'd foreseen were stolen from a drama in which it was Christian, not Stevie, who misbehaved in town. Danny's script included cruisy afternoons in Tate Modern, dinner at Nobu, and clubbing at Trade. The storyboards showed Christian eating up the location scenes, his eyes staring wide as he looked out, out, out at everything that the capital could offer.

Danny's unease increased every time they met, for Christian rarely brought him to the same place twice. Instead, sexy new discoveries were constantly produced. It was as if the younger man was declaring his ease in the city. By contrast, Danny was forever one step behind. And though Christian could be uncomfortable if things didn't go as planned (for example, he hated being late), he usually found ways of recovering.

Danny was amused, one time, to watch him pushing fretfully through briefcases and Burberry raincoats to get to the counter of Selfridges' Oyster Bar. You'd think he was late for his own funeral, judging from his pallor, and the moisture he was rubbing off his forehead. Yet it wasn't heat that made Christian sweat—it was anxiety.

He gasped a "Sorry" before asking why to God they'd decided to meet in what might as well have been the middle of Oxford Street.

It crossed Danny's mind that it could have been something to do with *GQ*'s recent article on "London's Ten Best Power Breakfasts," a piece that he himself had come across at the barber's. However, he couldn't be bothered pointing out the similarity between the journalist's account of the Oyster Bar and Christian's. Instead he stared, even more frankly than usual, at his friend's chest.

"What is it?"

"Oh, nothing!"

Poor Danny. He didn't feel up to explaining how astonishing it was to see his friend wearing an AIDS ribbon. Nor could he describe the amusement and annoyance with which he'd realized, after a second glance, that the dash of red over Christian's breast was actually the Yves Saint Laurent logo on his shirt. "So how are you, anyway?"

"Pretty good. The same. All right." Christian's voice was careless as he grinned towards a passing face. "And you?"

"Fine. Though it's murder at work—"

"I'm sorry. What was that?" (He made an elaborate mime of bringing his attention back.) "Something about your house—?"

Danny didn't know how to respond. Should he, too, greet total strangers? Although he wouldn't have let Ronan MacIntyre get away with such childish maneuvers, he couldn't be hard on Christian. *He pulls you in,* he thought. *He's like a black hole. Or a blond one. If there's any such thing*—

Deciding that his best bet was amused indifference, he adopted a would-be superior air and started prodding for info. "I suppose it must have been difficult," he hazarded. "Getting good food."

"Good food?"

He gestured with his napkin. "When you were away, I mean."

Christian raised an eyebrow. "Are you trying to ask me something?"

"You must admit it's weird. You ring me out of the blue, and we see each other loads of times, and you drop lots of hints about how great it is to be back in London—and all the time you hardly say a word about what you got up to, or where you were. You know I never push. But it would be nice if you volunteered something. For a change."

"You must have some theories. Why don't you tell me what they are?"

"How the fuck should I know? I wasn't the one who pissed off without a word."

Christian laughed delightedly; he loved it when his friend got riled.

Was it glamour that made Christian untouchable, or was it untouchability that made him glamorous? Either way, he seemed unable or unwilling to understand that an old friend might have hesitated to ask about his disappearance. Faced with his delightfully inhuman charm, Danny didn't know whether to slap him or kiss him. "Just tell me where you went," he asked, too weary to raise the bigger question of whether his friend had had a breakdown, and what had caused it.

Christian adopted an ostentatiously innocent expression. "You should have asked me sooner. I'd no idea you'd been brooding on it. Not that I did anything exciting. I went to Berlin to photograph some street names and see what was left of the old buildings. The usual sort of thing. I snapped lots of empty spaces. Then I did some galleries, and I went to Marrakech for a tan. And I've been to the States a few times, but apart from that I've mostly been in Margate."

"*Margate?*" Danny made it sound like Beirut. "I thought you'd gone abroad."

Christian waved at a woman carrying a Liberty scarf and a tin of foie gras. (It seemed an odd gesture for someone who'd recently come out of hiding.) "I did consider it." (The woman looked at him as if he were insane.) "But it wasn't necessary. Academics are so short-sighted. Once you stop going to conferences they assume you've gone to Mars."

"But Margate! I mean—*Margate*! What's the average age of people who live in Margate?"

"Don't be silly. If I'd gone to North London I'd have known half the people on the tube."

Not for the first time, Danny wondered what it would be like to move through a world like Christian's. People would respond to you in a special way. It was in your bone structure, or the way you walked. Some indefinable combination of qualities would make people gush at you, and defer. Everyone from shop assistants to interview panels would be yours before you even opened your mouth. A power like that could change a person's life. It was almost as good as being rich.

For how many years had he been missing Christian, and loving him, and writing his obituary? And all that time they'd been a couple of train journeys apart! When Danny thought of these things—and when he saw that glamorous face—he felt a wordless fury that was as old as their friendship. But when he led himself to look more closely he saw the lighting fall harshly on his friend's skin. There was a mark beside his mouth. And though they were as young as ever, his eyes seemed pale and lost.

When Danny spoke his voice was gentle. It was a contest he played with himself: How softly could he speak? "But you haven't told me everything. You haven't said why you left."

Silence.

Then reluctant speech.

"I couldn't follow *Silence and Remorse*." (Christian bit off the name as if he hated it.) "The publicity was driving me mad."

Danny paused like a therapist. "But there was more?"

"Yes," laughed Christian. "Isn't there always?"

But he refused to say what. Instead he gave a bittersweet smile that never failed to conquer.

Danny longed to lift his friend's dejection. And for once he might be able to. "Look," he said, pulling out a yellow package. "This is for your new flat. A welcome-back present."

Christian gave one of his special grins before pulling fastidiously at the wrapping. ("Nice paper!") Too late, Danny remembered what a mutual friend had said after ending her acquaintance with Christian: "The trouble is, he's not the sort of person who'll like something just because you've given it to him. It has to be perfect in its own right or he won't touch it." At the time Danny had said that Christian wasn't really rude, it was only his manner, but his woman friend wasn't convinced. "Who could love such a person?" she had asked, to which Danny had silently replied: "I could." Indeed his devotion grew stronger the more Christian was dropped by other people. But now he wondered if she hadn't had a point. From the way Christian held it, Danny's pot might have been full of Semtex.

"You don't like it! Won't it go with your stuff?"

"It's not that," said Christian. Perhaps he realized that someone who hadn't seen his flat could hardly be expected to make the right aesthetic choice. "I was just wondering where to put it. Everything's still so messy that it's hard to know. You know how bad I am at having people round. But I might have a housewarming, and I'll make sure it goes up before then."

Danny guessed that he was lying, but he didn't care. The lie was almost better than the truth would have been. His shout of laughter made Christian jump. "You *do* deserve it," his joy seemed to say. "You *do* deserve my love."

As he'd hurried across town Danny had seen a distant cherry tree in early blossom. Its boughs were spread behind the railings of a communal garden in a square he didn't recognize. He'd been too eager to see his friend to stop for a proper look. Now he dawdled, hoping for a second sighting. Had they been delicate or vulgar, he wondered— those fists of pink? He pictured them, great wads of bubble gum hanging in the breeze, but couldn't make up his mind. And nor could he find the square again.

This peeved him, for lunch hadn't ended well.

As if compensating for his earlier rudeness, Christian had turned on the charm as soon as they started eating. No longer waving at the other diners, he kept his eyes on Danny's face while asking flatteringly personal questions. But it couldn't last. After beguiling him through three extra coffees, Christian said he couldn't stay another second as he had tons to do that afternoon, and had tickets for the English National Opera, and would have to go back home to get changed, and that frankly he ought to have gone hours ago. So off he went, leaving Danny with half a cheese Danish and an obscure sense of guilt. The way he'd put it, you'd think someone had been forcing him to stay against his will. And though Danny stood at the window to wave him off, Christian didn't look back.

But at least the day had a solid outcome. Rummaging in a WH Smith bargain bin during the customary thirty-minute train delay, Danny found "Michael's" official calendar with "twelve full-color pinups" plus "room for noting Life's Big Fixtures." The excitement was almost enough to distract him from what was playing at the ENO and whether or not Christian was going on his own.

"What the hell," he decided, after beating back embarrassment. "It's only one pound fifty!" He'd hang it by his bed, he decided, for old time's sake. After all, it wasn't as if anyone would ever see it there.

The purchase made, he stuffed the calendar into a totally inadequate plastic bag, hoping he wouldn't meet anyone he knew. But on second thought, why be ashamed? Standing defiantly on the concourse, he removed the cellophane wrap and flicked over the pages until he discovered "Michael" standing by a bedroom door with his shirt undone. (For April was the sexiest month.) At this, the train arrived and Danny stepped from the platform with his head held high, warmed by good fortune.

6

At first Stevie hadn't believed the news.

Someone had blundered and the firm would beg forgiveness. Then he remembered the atmosphere before he went on holiday—the eyes that looked away, the overly hearty voices—and he knew they wanted him out.

He could guess why, too.

In spite of his charm, he'd never been that popular. Overconfidence is rarely welcome, even in professions where it's a prerequisite of success, and his colleagues had more reason than Barbara to see him as destructively ambitious. Even so, his pride was hurt when he thought about the sheeplike pea-brains who'd felt too threatened to let him do his job.

For all his famous empathy, life hadn't given Stevie many chances to "feel the pain." Like any other attractive and assured young man, he usually got what he wanted without even showing his arrogance. And if he had some minor reverse—a snub from a secretary, or an unsuccessful tender—he still had Barbara to make him feel important. But now, for the first time in his adult life, he'd been kicked in the balls for no other reason than that someone more powerful had taken against him.

Fuck them, he thought. *Fuck them all.*

You see, he wasn't meant to hurt like this. This was how other people felt. Smaller people. Ugly people. People too weak or too stupid to look after themselves. And he'd no patience with such people. He might pretend he did, but only because they made him feel superior. In any case, kindness comes easily to winners: it gets harder if you're thwarted. Maybe that was why he wanted everyone he knew to rot in hell, and Barbara most of all.

doi:10.1300/5902_17

For being sacked wasn't the worst of it. Left to himself, he felt he could have coped. Had other things been equal, he'd have nailed the bastards for unfair dismissal. However, he hadn't been prepared for Barbara's response. In the past, her mixture of sexiness and neediness had excited him more than he thought possible. There seemed no limit to her dependence, or his own strength. But as soon as they'd heard his news, she had taken the aggressive stance that should, by rights, have been his. "What's your boss's number?" she'd demanded. "I want to tell him what I think of them." And she would have, too, if he'd let her.

In some ways, it was bracing. After all, it was her grittiness that made their fights exciting. Except now her energy was besting him. Down she'd sit him, like he was one of her students, while she told him to believe in himself.

"You have to show them you're not ashamed," she insisted.

"Do I?" he'd reply, as coolly as he could.

Who did she think she was, his grandmother? Soon she'd be telling him that time healed everything and that he had to find the hero inside. And meanwhile he was sure that her brain was whirring behind her concerned expression.

Take her crying. Was he so abject that she could produce glycerine-free tears every time she looked at him? Or was she putting them on to humiliate him? He wouldn't put it past her. Not when every droplet shifted the seesaw in her favor.

She'd taken to announcing that "If the worst comes to the worst, I can always support you." But he'd have had more respect for her if she'd said "If the best comes to the best," because they both knew that that was what she wanted. Nothing would suit her more than having him in *her* house with his apron on and a ring through his nose.

And even that might have been okay, in moderation—for flirting with passivity was the essence of being a New Man. But this sobbing, and commiserating, and telling him what to do was different. Faced with it, he started to mass his forces.

Although he'd never admitted it, he hated Barbara's name for him. Objecting would show that she'd got to him. And he could always get his own back in bed. But as far as he was concerned, he was a Stephen, not a Stevie. And "Stephen" had had enough of being small. Even his feminist self agreed that control had to be applied. For didn't feminists believe in self-assertion?

These things had been growing since he lost his job, but they only crystallized on the day that Barbara had Danny round to dinner. That afternoon she'd called at Stevie's unannounced and found him naked and unshaven. And his flat was a mess. When she told him they could fight his depression together, he had to clutch his arms to stop himself from hitting her. He said he needed his solitude and would be in touch when it suited him. When she burst into tears, he let her cry on.

It was the first time he hadn't comforted her.

Mind you, it was okay for her. She could get weepy with one of her tame men. (That sad Danny, probably.) But Stevie couldn't do anything so wet. Instead he had to recover the initiative. It wouldn't be hard finding a consultancy post. (Telling other people how to do their jobs was the safest career in the country.) But first he had to boost his morale.

Barbara said you had to attack your problems, you shouldn't just give up. Fine: He'd take her at her word. But she didn't have to know the kind of fight back he was planning. And nor need it change their love. Indeed he owed it to her. For if he couldn't regain his confidence they'd surely break up. And then where would she be?

The more he thought about it, the less he could resist.

As the day went on, excitement turned to calm: He knew what he had to do.

When it was late enough, he opened his wardrobe to examine a row of clothes that changed, almost imperceptibly, from cream to black as you moved from right to left. After an appropriate degree of thought, he took out a slate-gray suit with an Italian label. The cut would have been severe but for the way the silk clung to his shoulders and arse, showing the shapes underneath. It was the sort of suit that you couldn't help but touch. That and a plain shirt were all he needed.

An hour later—just as Barbara waved off Danny—Stevie was heading for one of the better West End clubs, sure of his success.

Over the next four days Barbara left six messages on his answering machine.

Only one was returned.

As spring and winter slugged it out for control of the year, Danny became ever more fixated on the number fourteen bus. Some innovative executive—who ought to have been sacked—had tried bringing the service upmarket by naming the buses after people. There you'd be at the bus stop when Dame Judi Dench would come bearing down on you, bigger than a house and dirtier than an oil tanker. But then Dame Judi was a double-decker: Zoë Ball and Jamie Theakston had to deal with the humiliation of being Park-n-Ride minibuses. That said, he *did* feel sorry for the famously battered Duchess of Windsor. ("I married the goddamned King of England," he could hear poor Wallis saying, "and all I got was a lousy double-decker.")

Once onboard he studied the human and mechanical traffic. There were always details to be observed, clues to be uncovered. Cute pedestrians and harassed cyclists. Lesbian bus drivers. Sweaty joggers in pale blue Lycra. One time he couldn't take his eyes off a lorry driver's arm. Muscular and brown, it was covered with yard upon yard of snaky tattoos. (*Were they sexy or repulsive,* he wondered, *or both at the same time?*) But when his bus lurched past, and he peered into the cab, he found that the driver was flicking through a sheaf of photographs in which every snap was of a tiny newborn baby resting its head in those same scaly arms. This image stayed with Danny for a long, long time. (Longer, by far, than the span of this book.)

He loved these signs of everyday life: the stuff that rarely makes it into print. But how could he communicate what he saw? He had his personal shorthand—a raised eyebrow, an amused smile. But no one knew him well enough to read his gestures. And the moments passed so quickly. Capturing them would require a new form of writing. Something that could include his visions of Christian as well as his twice-daily bus rides. Something that could bring together fiction, and poetry, and criticism, and speech, and—everything, everything. And something, also, that could explain the unease with which he sat in the staff-room one afternoon, trying to place a melody that ran through his mind in broken sentences.

It was then that Ronan tapped his shoulder.

"What's on your mind, Dan?" His voice was joltingly brisk.

Danny returned his smile uncertainly. "Oh—something odd."

When the youngster grinned encouragingly, Danny saw he'd have to finish his thought. "I keep waking up early, so this morning I watched the sunrise. The air was pinky-gold. It could have been alive. But by seven everything was gray. That's what I was thinking of. Why does the photocopier break down exactly when you need it, and why does the dawn have to lose its color? And why can't I finish this song I'm humming?"

"I knew you wouldn't understand," he added, seeing Ronan's incredulous expression. "But the more I think about it, the less I understand why we push ourselves. I mean, what's it all for? This place. Our jobs. The lot."

"That's weird," stared Ronan. "Because I often ask myself the same."

It was Danny's turn to look disconcerted. "I don't believe you."

"Why not?"

He hesitated. "Because you're so—focused. Your work's about something. Mine isn't."

"But that only adds to the pressure. You never know if it's helping people. I mean, with the bits of their lives that won't come right."

"Like the photocopier breaking down?"

"Yeah. Or the way the dawn turns gray. I couldn't sleep this morning, so I know what you mean about that."

For the first time in their acquaintance, Danny felt that he and Ronan might have something in common. However, his next speech broke their understanding. "I thought you were going to say I was mad," he laughed. "I mean, I was sure you'd say I was bonkers!"

It was as if a razor blade had sliced through a theater backdrop. "I wouldn't say any such thing," claimed Ronan, his face sharpening to an ugly point. "It would be morally untenable."

"But—"

"I'd never sit judgment on someone else's sanity. And I don't know how you could think it of me!"

"I only—"

Ronan's voice was threateningly low. "It isn't funny. Or fair."

"But—"

"It's not good enough." He snatched his briefcase in a comical huff. "I'm sorry; you'll have to forgive me. But I can't continue this conversation."

Riding home in Dame Margot Fonteyn, Danny tried not to dwell on Ronan's snub. Removing his eyes from the deeply unattractive man on whom they'd been resting, he studied the signs splattered round the bus. One showed an orange-colored actor saying THANK YOU FOR TRAVELING WITH US. In another, two saintly seniors were gleefully turned back with the words *No Pass? Then FULL FARE!* Elsewhere a shifty-looking character in an ill-fitting suit was smiling insincerely over the message PLAINCLOTHES DETECTIVES MAY BE CIRCULATING IN THIS BUS. Danny looked in panic at his ugly co-traveler. Perhaps he was a private eye, and not the ax murderer he so clearly resembled. Or maybe the detective and the serial killer were one and the same. Edging closer to the window, he felt suddenly exhausted. What with disappointed pensioners, actors pretending to be bus drivers, and ex-jailbirds mingling freely in dogtooth jackets, it might have been safer to get a taxi.

Once home, he took to his study with a glass of sherry and a packet of digestive biscuits. Ignoring his research, he searched the file marked "MEAT" for something soothing. The style made him blush. Triple subjunctives had no place in a porn movie. It was time he cured himself of such bookish defenses. But first he'd block out the incident on the clergy-house stairs. Piers Longridge came easily but Marius Ransome was elusive. And Danny was old-fashioned when it came to sex: he felt you needed a face. After some tantalizingly inconclusive activity, he tried a new location. The long and tense exchange at the Women's Institute meeting was central to the film's structure but it wasn't the sort of thing that he, personally, could get excited about.

Then Sexy Scott from his Thursday class fell from nowhere into the boys' club segment. The casting was inspired! Scott would be perfect as a borstal boy with an unflattering, yet oddly provocative, haircut. The new curate (who was tall and balding) could make friends over darts before taking him swimming. And in the changing rooms—
No!

Neither Danny nor the curate could countenance such unprofessional behavior. So he buried that unworthy fantasy deep in his mind, from where it would doubtless pop, to torture him, during some long and sleepless night in the near future.

But if you can't dream, what *can* you do? Happy to embrace a less loaded scenario, he unhooked the calendar that dangled by his bed. Almost imperceptibly he began to hum "You'll Never Walk Alone."

Some scenes were just too rich to resist.

7

"What does it mean," Danny asked himself, "when Jewish parents call their son Christian?"

The question was far from new. Indeed it had appeared in each of the obituaries he'd drafted while his friend had been away. And it returned to him, now, as he watched a familiar shape disappearing into the crowds round Charing Cross.

He associated the problem with an image from his student days.

He'd been looking for his friend in the British Library—("the old one, the *real* one")—but when he found him, he didn't dare to interrupt. Christian's left hand was resting on an open book. The other held his pen but he was staring outwards, his face barely recognizable. Danny walked past without speaking. Although the light from the dome was as thin as skimmed milk, Christian's hair and skin were a fiery gold. Later on Danny wondered if *Silence and Remorse* had been born at such moments. And he wondered, too, what traumas lived in his friend's gaze.

Although the Jewish section of *Silence and Remorse* cited everyone from Sigmund Freud to Woody Allen, it said little about the author's family. "Fill the gaps yourself," Christian seemed to taunt, "for you'll get no help from me." Taking up the challenge, Danny mused obsessively on Christian's parents. With what irony, or desperation, or satisfaction had they acted? They were safe: they'd got out in time. But why convert? And why pick *that* name for the son of their old age—their Isaac, their Joseph, the one whom God had given them against their expectations?

Without such puzzles he'd have long since lost interest in his friend: for secrets, as much as beauty, powered Danny's need. They were part of the great unanswered problem of what made Christian act the way he did. This was someone who'd left a successful life to

doi:10.1300/5902_18

photograph places that no longer existed. For what would he have found in Berlin but air-conditioned lift shafts? Gone would be the alleyways where his parents had played and in their places would be car parks and shopping centers. Yet he'd still wanted the image.

If Christian's character remained an unfathomable mystery, at least his return produced some new lines of inquiry. That very day, over another of their lunches, an oddly tipsy Christian had reminisced about his ex-boyfriends. ("Not that you can call them boyfriends, really, when you think how long they stuck around.") It was thanks to one of them, he claimed, that he'd gone into hiding. ("He was absolutely shameless. He must have had four other men in the week I knew him.")

Danny noted, but did not pursue, the reference to Christian's disappearance. "I can never keep track of your blokes," he remarked, dreamily. "In fact, I often wonder how many you've had."

Christian took another sip of wine. "God knows."

"D'you miss any of them?"

At first, he seemed not to understand the question. Then he smiled. "Maybe one. He wasn't that cute. But he did this thing I liked."

"Oh yeah?" said Danny, feeling sick.

"He called me Chris. No one *ever* calls me Chris. But *he* did."

"So what happened?"

Christian pushed his glass away. "I wasn't after that kind of relationship."

"No," Danny started to say. "I don't suppose you were."

But his friend wasn't listening. "Tarts," said Christian suddenly. His voice was louder than usual. "Tarts they were. The lot of them. And no, I don't miss them. Not one of them. They were just cheap little fucks."

Danny gaped, but already Christian was grinning and waving for the bill. "Well, Dan! We can't have you getting old and bitter like me." His voice was bumptious as he flicked on his jacket. "In fact, I'd do anything to make you happy."

"In that case—"

"But first I'll walk you to the tube."

"Tarts and fucks," marveled Danny, when his friend was lost from view. Christian's language was usually so buttoned up! But the outburst fit Danny's theory, for surely Christian was projecting his self-hatred onto his partners. And where did the loathing come from, if not from his parents? They'd named him to betray their past, and then they'd scarred him with their guilt. (It must be true, thought Danny, for that's what he'd said in his obituaries.)

Having marshaled this new chunk of evidence, he directed his pity on the poor dim loser who'd dared to call Christian "Chris." For all his faults, he himself would never have been so casual. Instead he turned his friend's name around in his mouth, savoring, yet again, the elegance of it, and the fitness of each syllable. "Christian Ellis," he repeated. "Christian Ellis—my friend!" And he looked forward, already, to their next meeting.

These, by now, were frequent—at least twice a week.

He'd never have guessed, before this compulsive period of his life, that London had so many fashionable bars. He told himself that he wouldn't have braved their glass-and-aluminium counters without Christian, but he was shocked to realize, one afternoon, that he himself was indistinguishable from the other shaven-headed men in the room. Indeed one or two of them might even have been naturally bald: you simply couldn't tell these days. However much he tried not to feel alienated from them, their rings and suits got in the way. To Danny, they were the sort of sharp-dressed guys, both gay and straight, who liked laughing their dicks off at other people's misfortunes.

He loathed them.

And he loathed himself for being with them.

Nevertheless it was in one such bar, later in the spring, that Danny spotted an instantly recognizable figure. He was about to call a greeting—for the enormous guy could be no one but Stevie Myerson—when he saw that the man's hand was resting on a woman's shoulder. And the woman wasn't Barbara.

Stevie looked round, as if sensing he'd been spotted. Danny had no time to turn away. Instead they faced each other square, neither hail-ing the other. After a moment they returned, as if by mutual arrangement, to their companions.

Shortly afterwards, Danny lunched with Barbara.

"It's not like you to arrange something," she told him. "I'm usually the one who suggests getting together."

Danny told her she was looking well.

"Oh—*you!*" she laughed. "I hope Stevie never finds out what a charmer you are."

"So how's he getting on?" he ventured.

A second's pause.

"He's been in London. Calling up his contacts. One of them's bound to come through."

Yes, thought Danny, *almost certainly*. But try as he might, he couldn't tell her what he knew.

Don't get involved, he told himself. *Keep yourself separate.* Instead he wept for her misplaced confidence, and for himself. For his veils were even more fragile than hers. He had no lover, no book, no hope of promotion. He only had pity for his friends, and the smile of the falsely brave with which he started every day. Guessing nothing of their kinship, Barbara went on ringing him, her moods flashing between high spirits and gloom. She bridled when he asked if Stevie was around, from which Danny guessed he was stopping by less often. If she didn't know the truth, surely he should tell her? But every time he resolved to do so, she called up in a voice that was crisp with self-belief, a voice lit by an odd, partly suppressed joy, and he found he could not break her.

Time was passing.

Wet black buds unfolded their wrinkled surfaces, as hopeful and untried as a baby's foot, while day by day the light grew stronger. Standing at the bus stop one morning Danny saw fine green leaves pushing through the flagstones of a paved-over garden. ("Sorrel?" he asked himself, not sure what sorrel was.) The shoots were already sooted-over. "Is this the freedom that I've chosen?" he wondered as he looked at the blank, untidy face of the multi-occupation house that rose above the garden. But then he heard echoes of the odd, lyric voices that can sound, in the middle of the night, in any town that's not the one you grew up in. Things like kids passing outside his bedroom window, their laughter loud and unselfconscious after hours of drugged-up dancing, or the unknown citizen who had scrawled "I am queer, I am queer, I am queer" in the late frost on his next-door neighbor's People Carrier.

Meanwhile, for reasons that he could only partly trace, Danny grew obsessed with Stevie's "mystery companion." Unable to share what he knew, he pieced her together in intricate detail until his memory of her was more accurate than anything the man himself could have offered. For although Stevie claimed that fidelity was the one of the duties of a male feminist, he also felt that a man had to be a man. He assured himself that when he went back to being faithful, Barbara would be overwhelmed by the force of his attentions. But for now he put political correctness aside in favor of the redhead, the blonde, the brunette, the local councillor, the junior doctor, the typist, the chemist, and the modestly glamorous librarian. As far as he was concerned, they were interchangeable: nameless and characterless. They served a purpose. Then on he moved, leaving ethical dilemmas for those who had a taste for such things.

Stevie had an instinct for other people's weaknesses: he knew Danny would keep quiet. But he couldn't have guessed how fully he had entered Danny's mind. However much Danny hated what was happening to Barbara, a part of him responded to the banal arrogance of Stevie's actions, and to the potency and contempt that they revealed. Fancying Stevie as he did, he sometimes fantasized about having, and using, that sort of strength.

Danny didn't know if his desires should be censored or acknowledged.

The problem was power. Not having it was humiliating but using it badly was dangerous. And what counted as a proper use? It was one thing to hang on Christian's every word, it was quite another to dream of fucking him with cold, slow thoroughness. Being on the receiving end seemed, somehow, to be more politically acceptable but it wasn't clear why this should be. And in any case, Danny's psyche had long since decided his preferred position, and there was little he could do to change it.

Of course in some respects his fantasies pleased him.

Apart from the obvious ones—like stripping Christian at knife-point before forcing him to take part in *A Man Must Have His Meat*—there were more obscure pleasures, such as his wish to piss over the heads of all the teenage couples who sat in buses with their tongues down each other's throats and their fingers clamped around their shoulders. Was it affection that made them clutch so hard, he wondered, or the terror that one of them might escape?

Half-scary and half-welcome, these stabbing images made him smile sarcastically. ("You're not as predictable as everybody thinks," he laughed.) It was tricky, though, the relationship between aggression, eroticism, and revenge. How much sex was there in his need to plunge Bill Roberts' head into a boiling hot jug of typing correction fluid? Not much, he assumed. But there was still a blur between sexiness and cruelty. It wasn't that violence, in itself, turned him on. He just found it hard thinking up scenarios that didn't involve domination. And even where sex wasn't an issue, he felt increasingly afraid of his anger. So many things were penned in him. Who knew what they might do to him?

These things were sharp in his mind when he arrived home, one evening, to find that he had nothing for supper. Forcing his face into a resigned expression, he headed for the supermarket, hoping his migraine wouldn't get any worse. The store was too hot and bad-tempered for him to linger, as he liked, over such important decisions as whether to have dead cow or dead sheep. Worse, the place was more than usually stuffed with old men, his latest phobic objects. (It was odd but the women didn't seem to bother him.)

Oh the horror, the futility, of plastic-wrapped animal parts and "family" packs of toilet paper. How could such things be cheerful? You might as well paint smiles on a Francis Bacon. But they became yet more unbearable when retired traffic wardens blocked up the aisles while deciding between butter beans and sago. They haunted

Danny. Their clothes, their smell. Their elongated figures. (For tall ones disturbed him more than short ones.) He hated when they poked for change and failed to get their shopping into their bags before his own went whizzing down the chute. But it was worse again if they were behind you, gagging for the "Next Customer" bar as if their life depended on it. Yes: they were the *real* culprits. Repressed old men with a mania for birching.

"I won't look at them," he murmured as he opted for the dead pig. "I'll just pretend they aren't there." Yet it was uncanny how they tracked him; they were like aliens trying to make contact. For example, he knew, when he saw a splash of blood dropping on the eerie white of the refrigeration unit, that the bloke behind had snatched a leaky tray of offal. He veered to the side as if he'd touched an open wire. "No, nein, non," he promised as he dashed towards the eggs. "I'm not going to let you ruin my evening."

The rest of the visit was a game of chess.

Danny walked the aisles with exaggerated care: he refused to show his fear. But it was strange, this shadowy closeness. Behind him, a wheezing presence reached for the same pint of milk only to withdraw as quickly as it could, too timid or too grumpy to press its right to the carton. Danny couldn't turn. (Who *would* if they were being stalked by their future?) But it also felt as if a plea for company had been offered, and rejected. He couldn't stop picturing the bloke's appearance—sick and alone, he expected, with worn-out clothes and a desperate stare. The image might turn his stomach but who could blame a guy for letting go when he hadn't had a human touch for years, and years, and years.

(And years.)

As usual, the obscenely bloated checkouts were full of office workers buying oven-ready meals and bottles of plonk. Danny despised them all the more for being one of them himself. Resigned, yet again, to having chosen the wrong checkout he amused himself by studying other people's misguided purchases. Digestive biscuits he could understand but not "fondant fancies." And simply looking at the "Swan Lake Meringue Nests" would rot your teeth. The mere idea of them disgusted him. They were almost as bad as the six-pack of Mars Bars he had hidden underneath his Bran Flakes.

And still his ghostly friend pressed near.

As he started putting his things on the belt, Danny felt the bloke behind him pushing closer. His instinctive response was to shrink forward. For the man's only concern was getting his purchases onto the belt. And without turning, Danny knew what they would be. (A lamb's heart, waxy with fat. A loaf of sliced white bread. A block of sweating cheese. And half a dozen tins of cat food.)

Danny had barely scrambled out his items when he sensed this rival stack nudging at his own. He pictured the groceries being molded into geometric perfection. For that's what the old boys did. They made Aztec temples out of Kitekat and pigs' livers, or calves' kidneys, or whatever other delicacies they'd chosen for their Sunday lunch. They let nothing stand too tall or overhang the conveyer belt. Instead every purchase had to be balanced, meticulously, with another.

The truth, however, was worse. For no sooner had the hand honed its own territory than it started straying into Danny's. After shifting his eggs from the edge it moved his olives closer to the pesto. Then it straightened up his orange juice.

Danny felt contaminated by Brylcream and cat litter. ("Now with ultra-clumping.")

Oh Lord, he prayed. *Let me not turn out like this.*

It was pathetic, this rush to get past. (For the drooling idiot was all but breathing on his hair.) And why? To forge some human connection? Or to save five seconds of his wasted life by taking Danny's place? It was rude, that's what it was. Rude, and inconsiderate, and typical of pensioner boyos who swore by cold showers and National Service. Danny felt helpless. It was like watching someone light a fag in the nonsmoking section of a train: though filled with indignation he couldn't bring himself to speak. Yet the longer he stayed silent, the more furious he became.

No wonder he started singing when the hand finally withdrew. Unfortunately, his mood encouraged a similar levity in the man behind, for Danny had hardly got through the first verse of "Happy Days Are Here Again" before he saw four surprisingly soft fingers landing on his tinned tomatoes. Intending to twist that scraggy neck until it broke in two, he swung around to shout, "Would you take your fucking hands off my shopping, *please?*" But all that came out was: "You?" For standing behind him—almost touching him—was Ronan MacIntyre.

Ronan opened his mouth but Danny didn't wait for him to speak. Responding to a deeper instinct, he did what he'd wanted to do from the start. Leaving his groceries on the conveyer belt, he pushed past the other shoppers and left the store—his back straight up, his head erect—not looking left or right, and not replying to any of the people who were calling out to him. He walked on, not speaking, his expression set, until he reached his house for a cold and supperless evening with the curtains closed and the lights turned off.

8

It was around this time, or maybe slightly later, that Danny began to wonder if he wasn't going mad.

There had been hints in the past. Some sleeplessness. A touch of paranoia. But nothing too worrying. Nothing he couldn't cope with. Except they seemed to be getting worse as he got older. His passions and ambitions were piling up in front of him, like great snowdrifts of unfulfilled desires, with the forward path growing dimmer every year. In fact, he didn't know what to make of his trips to London, let alone the larger journeys that he faced.

As he returned from one such visit on the last day of term, he felt the Midlands air thicken into soup: it was as if God had clamped a lid over the university to watch it grow moldy and damp. And sure enough, the vapor he inhaled was far from fresh: it seemed to combine Marcus Cranborne's boozy odor, Bill's sharply disinfected air, and Barbara's imperialistic perfume. Each of them declared their presence whole corridors away. As, in his different way, did Christian, whose hilariously bitchy comments on mutual friends often resurfaced in the night, making Danny feel queasy.

It was almost a relief, spending Easter at "home," even though it involved pondering why his father started so many sentences he didn't finish.

"Dan, you should—"

"What's that—?"

"Oh, nothing—"

It was so marked he began to fear the worst. Would caring for an aged P be the making of him or would it drive him further round the twist? He pictured himself with a bedpan in one hand and his pen in the other as he wrote his best-selling guide to coping with an Alzheimer's patient. ("That was my *first* book," he told Radio 4. "The one that enabled me to retire from teaching.")

doi:10.1300/5902_19

Not surprisingly, he resented breaking this compelling scene to return, before the start of the new term, for what Bill called an "extraaaooordinary" meeting of the English department. The stretched vowels seemed to promise exceptional events.

"You *are* coming?" his boss had oozed on the phone. "I'd really value your contribution."

Two-faced git, thought Danny, who begrudged giving up the last Friday of the holiday for an event at which Ronan MacIntyre would probably throw his own "extraaaooordinary" behavior back at him. But when the day came, the youngster was absent.

"That's a first," murmured Danny. "Ronan skipping a chance to suck up to Bill."

"He has the flu," explained Barbara, who made it her business to know Ronan's movements.

"A spring flu!" exclaimed Marcus. "Who knows where that may lead?"

"Ah!" said Bill. "Our guests."

Taking no notice of the uncomprehending gaze of their hosts, these two—a man and a woman—produced two flip charts, a pack of felt-tipped pens, and a box of flash cards. Their preparations done, they tugged their sleeves in a business-like way and turned, with frightening smiles, to their audience. It seemed as if they spoke in unison, but probably they did not. "Well," they said. "And are you sitting comfortably?"

Taking the hint, the department fell upon whatever chairs they could find.

And for what?, thought Danny—for two less-hopeful specimens he had never seen. When one of them spoke, the other scanned the room, head cocked on one side, like a bird examining a lawn. Although the gesture was meant to indicate an interested attention, it carried sinister overtones, as if they were ready to bite the head off any worm foolish enough to show itself above the ground. Despite speaking of "inclusivity" and "progress management"—buzzwords of the moment—their "mode of delivery" (to use another favorite phrase) "carried an alternative signification." And while their "informal oral presentation" was dazzlingly professional it was hard to know what they were actually *saying.*

"We want to know what *you* think!" said one.

"We're here to *listen!*" finished the other.

But on they rattled, too fast for anyone else to speak.

Half an hour in, the woman drew a chart with modest self-satisfaction. *"This,"* she exclaimed, "should summarize our position." She stood back to evaluate her handiwork before nodding as if to say, "Yes, I *am* worth my salary!" Meanwhile the department gazed in silent wonder. The diagram was a tangle of words, arrows, and circles. Some were in bold. Others were italicized. Others still were underlined. Several of the arrows had two points; others had one. And the words themselves! "Fast-Track Self-Assessment Strategies"—"Task Force Management"—"Self-Reflexive Teaching Modules"—"Target Maintenance (Aims and Objectives)"—"Gross Product Streamlining"—and most gnomically of all—"Downsize Development (Hints for Future Progress)." Even Bill seemed unsure of what this great web might mean.

"We only received the university commission six months ago," she continued. "So this represents our initial Goal Assessment Survey. We're looking to *you*" (her companion surveyed the room) "to provide feedback. After hearing your comments we'll spend the next fortnight drafting a fully streamlined Resource Management Scheme. And when *that's* done—!" (They grinned in unison.) "It's over to you for implementation. Now!" (A businesslike nod.) "Any questions?"

Danny felt that questions were neither welcome nor expected.

He longed to say something that would plug the duo's smirks, but there wasn't so much as a crag on which he could balance his understanding. Even their features had been buffed free of expression. Not for them the comfy cardies of the academic world. Instead they were be-blazered and be-buttoned with cuff links and earrings and countless other accessories that tried, but failed, to make them look older than their twenty-something years.

Danny grew bitter thinking of their salaries. They were like a pretty weed that flourishes unchecked, crawling from victim to victim until every tree in the park is a hollow column wreathed by flowers.

What hope did the university have? The same plant was at work in newspapers and TV, in the health service, in schools and local government, in publishing, in Radios 1, 2, 3, 4, and 5, in the Football Association, in politics, in retailing, in tourism, industry, and business. The only safe professions were the ones that had already folded.

At least they had one redeeming oddity. At five-foot-very-little, the man barely reached the woman's chin. (And to make matters worse, *she* was Amazonian.) His height had evidently shaped his personality: He kept jutting his head from his immaculate collar as if to achieve an extra half-inch. And when he went to the whiteboard (which was often) he pushed his forehead up, up, up in case his audience gazed over him to the cityscape beyond. (For you could see more of it now that the afternoons were getting longer.)

No queries being forthcoming, the pair announced a Mutual Exploration Session. Promising though this sounded, it merely consisted of their holding up flash cards for an instant response.

"Here's an example," said the woman.

"When I hold *this* up," the man continued, "I want you to tell me what springs to mind."

He raised a card marked "Product Placement"—but no one spoke.

"Nothing much there," said the woman as evenly as possible. The man looked around encouragingly.

"Let's put it another way!"

"Where do you place your products?"

"Are there ways of improving the delivery rate?"

"Ways of streamlining your resourcement policy?"

"Ways of exploring different markets?"

"Or even—"

"And this is an important one—"

"Ways of *servicing new requirements*?"

"*Now,*" (a reproving glare), "*now* do you understand what we mean?"

Danny giggled and Bill looked worried. Barbara cleared her throat. "Our products?" She was oddly tentative. "I'm not sure I follow you. What do you actually *mean*?"

The man and woman raised their eyebrows simultaneously. Clothes dummies though they were, they managed to convey an unmistakable contempt for such a stupid remark.

"Excellent," said the woman, "I'm *so* glad you asked that."

The ensuing "explanation" brought little illumination. It was still unclear whether "product" referred to the department's research writings (which might possibly make sense) or their students (which made no sense whatsoever). "In conclusion," (the woman made a flourish) "it's up to *you* to investigate a variety of fora for your product management. That way you'll maximize the personnel uptake on your teaching modules."

"You mean we'll increase student numbers?" tried Bill.

"That's right. Your uptake/downtake ratio will improve."

Despite much practice, Bill had trouble formulating a vote of thanks. The speakers' time was precious, he explained, because they were engaged in "a root and branch audit" of the university's academic policies. "Yes," he repeated, clutching at the phrase. "Root and branch, root and branch." And he fiddled with his pen until the top flew off and he had to scramble on the floor to get it back. Sadly, by the time he got up he had gathered himself together again. Avoiding the sarcasm that he used on visiting academics, he told the newcomers that it was marvelous having a clear set of eyes about the place. And those eyes glittered as they listened: for part of their job, as Bill well knew, was to inform the Senior Management Group of any departments that dared to obstruct the university's re-organization.

Bill's collaboration disgusted Danny. Thanks to this lot, you didn't teach your students, you gave them "personal growth opportunities." Like all consultants, they spent their energy spinning a language that only they could understand: and never mind if it was full of contradictions. For how could "non-hierarchical teaching strategies" be squared with "course delivery" when the latter sounded like something you'd do with a sack of coal?

Danny wondered why academics were so craven. *We're all to blame,* he thought, *unless we stand up for our principles.* But there was the rub: they each had different values. Bill used his classes to bully "the kids" into seeing how sensitive he was. Ronan wanted his students to resist heterosexism. Although Barbara and Deirdre were feminists only one of them thought that "French theory" had been sent by the devil to undermine good old-fashioned literature. Marcus was a classicist: he believed in ancient Romans. And Danny, poor Danny, dithered from position to position, too uncomplaining to be as political as Ronan, but not so complacent as to wallow, like Bill, in a world where the "intuitive" understanding of Great Poetry absolved you of the most atrocious acts of incivility and ego.

Meanwhile, his boss made mingling noises. ("These bright young professionals have agreed to stay for coffee. Let's use their expertise while we can.") In response, the Honored Guests simpered that they'd be delighted to hear what people "on the ground" made of the university.

"What d'you think?" whispered Danny. "Time for a Twix?"

Barbara grimaced. "Better show my face," she said, making for the automata. *Fast work,* thought Danny as he watched the astonishingly convincing reaction shots she was throwing at the Amazon. Feeling left out, he twiddled his cup and examined the airbrushed male of the species. There ought to be a club for such people—a Society for the Smooth where like-minded folk could rub their oozing shoulders while swapping Personal Advancement Strategies.

Bill interrupted with a nudge. "I'm glad to see you, Dr. Whelan. I feared you might not come."

"I wouldn't have missed it for the world."

"Most invigorating," agreed Bill, taking something from his bag. "But of course these two are only advising us on teaching. They're a smallish part of a much larger process. And the re-branding is already bearing fruit. Look at this!"

Danny assumed that Bill was handing him a university prospectus—the brochure was glossily expensive. Then he saw it was his favorite publication, the university newsletter.

"But they've—"

"Yes," said Bill, in an obscurely gloating tone. "It's been entirely redesigned. We can't have it looking like a third-rate parish magazine."

Danny turned the pages without comment. The blurred pictures that he loved had been replaced by well-defined smiles under snappy headlines. "Of course the center-spread is the best," said Bill. "It's pure genius."

Taking the hint, Danny found twelve caricatures beneath the tag line "Your Management Team Exposed." Each drawing featured an enormous head attached to a scrawny naked body—fig leaves were prominent. All the subjects were male.

"Pure genius?" he echoed.

"It's going to be a series," explained Bill. "They'll each have a column where they describe their work for the university."

Sure enough, speech bubbles rose from the cartoon heads.

"Hello," said one. "Tired of teaching boring subjects in a boring way? My name's Mike and I'm your E-Text Leader. Next week I'll be telling you about WEB-SHELF. WEB-SHELF is a Virtual Library designed for long-distance learners and students who are living with dust allergies. If it's successful, WEB-SHELF will be applied across the board, thus freeing the current library for redevelopment. So join now and get ahead of the game!" The accompanying caricature showed a fresh-faced boy with a manic grin and hair that stuck up in clumps. Like the rest of them, he resembled a loveable eccentric—a little crazed, perhaps, but only with enthusiasm for his subject.

Danny looked up. "There's no one from the secretarial staff here. Or the union."

Bill was unimpressed by this line of analysis until Danny added that there wasn't even anyone from the Arts faculty. "Yes," concurred Bill. "That *is* an omission. I'd better tell the Vice-Chancellor." And he leaned his head on one side as if posing, already, for his caricature.

"Oh, the Arts!" said a voice. "Whatever we do, we mustn't leave them behind!"

It was the homunculus.

"Yes," he continued. "I'm devoted to the Arts. You mightn't believe it but my first degree was in Comparative Literature."

For once Bill and Danny were united by the same emotion.

"Oh?" said Danny after a short pause. "That *is* a surprise." He peered down while the consultant pushed himself up on desperate toes. (*Forget it,* thought Danny. *Not even double platforms will get you high enough.*) "So have they helped?" he asked. "The classics and so on? In your management career, I mean."

"Oh, yes." The man was nothing if not eager to please. "We never forget the lessons of the masters. Dante, Flaubert, Shakespeare. They stay with us forever."

Bill smiled a patronizing agreement. "And do your colleagues share your enthusiasm?"

"Alas, no. But then I specialize in academic restructuring. Universities, primary schools, and nurseries. If it's educational, I can improve it! But most consultants work in the commercial sector. For example, our subcontract comes from Richards, Hill, and Kelly and I doubt that many of *them* will have heard of—"

"Franz Kafka" he was going to say, but the words were never spoken.

On hearing the main contractor's name, Barbara did a one hundred and eighty-degree turn. "Richards, Hill, and Kelly!" she exclaimed before she could stop herself. "But that's Stevie's firm!"

"Or rather," she corrected herself. "It *was* Stevie's firm." Glancing back to the Amazon she explained, "Stephen Myerson, that is. I expect you came across him before he left?"

The woman looked confused.

"Don't worry," said Barbara. "You can talk about his work situation. I know him rather well. In fact, he's my partner."

The woman's embarrassment took another turn. Blush fading, her features settled into blankness. She might have been a supermodel: her air of boredom was positively professional. "Really?" she said in a voice that was as calm as it was decided. "That's not what I've heard."

"Excuse me?"

"I said—that's not what he told me last weekend."

"What do you mean?"

The woman allowed herself a smile. "How far do I have to spell it out?"

Barbara's voice was louder than it should have been. "What the hell do you mean?"

Everybody looked at her.

The Amazon shook her head. "I mean, my dear, that he's been fucking me for weeks."

And off she swept, with her briefcase in one hand and a flash card in the other.

9

"You and I are even now," said Barbara as she staggered to her car. "We've both had public humiliations."

"Yes," agreed Danny. "And at faculty meetings, too." Tactfully, he laid his bag over a pair of male tennis shoes lurking on the backseat. "What'll you do? Will you phone him?"

"I wouldn't give him the satisfaction. If he wants me, he knows where I am."

She veered into the cycle lane (all six inches of it), swore, then checked her reflection. The effect was of a somewhat flustered Medusa. "But I won't have him back," she continued, trying to be icy. "Not even if he begs forgiveness." ("Think Dietrich," she told herself.) "And first thing tomorrow, his stuff's going to Oxfam."

In her position, Danny would have saved every pencil stub and plaster (indeed he already had). But despite the signs she sent out, one instinct was much stronger in her than neediness: and that was pride. A man who sneaked round town was too much like her father. She couldn't respect such a person. And Barbara was damned if she was going to force her anger underground the way her mother had. The Marlene act was okay if you could put up with a two-note range like Mrs. B's. But Barbara wanted more than that. She wanted to sing long flowing songs with operatic endings that triggered love, and applause, and weighty bouquets containing thousand-pound necklaces from wealthy admirers. She could do it too—she knew she could! But God help the man too weak or stupid to enjoy her performance. The best a loser like that could hope for would be a painless death when the rest of the audience hurled him from the gods.

So with one thing and another it wasn't very likely that Stevie would be hoarded, regretfully, in her memory the way Christian was

doi:10.1300/5902_20

in Danny's. True, she took a day to "consider her position." But by Sunday morning she knew what she would do.

Looks from other passengers enlivened Barbara's journey. In her blood-red dress and fake-fur stole, she felt like a murderess going to the stake. (Either that or the executioner.) "I'm a big girl now," she told herself. "And I'm going to have my fucking scene."

Having headed there with no plans but to take him by surprise, she was disconcerted, as she turned into Stevie's street, to see him locking his door and walking off in the opposite direction. Going home again would have been tempting if it hadn't been for the hateful confidence with which he was disappearing out of sight. (Her mouth went dry at the thought of what he might be up to.) And if things were as they looked, she had a chance to embarrass him even more than *he* had embarrassed *her*. So she turned up the collar of a metaphorical dirty raincoat and set off after him like the Gender Studies special agent she had always longed to be.

And Stevie, too, was full of furtive anticipation.

With time on his hands and money in his pockets, a handsome man could find adventures behind every other window blind in London. Stevie's line of attack was more deliberate than that, but who knew what might happen between the setting out and the getting back? That's what his tiresome consultant friend had learned when he dumped her. (Career women were such a bore, he found, when they didn't ask for reassurance.) Today's date was more promising. What could be fitter, on such a sunny day, than a light lunch and a Sloaney graduate who could almost have passed as a teenager? And even there, he had no commitments if a better option cropped up.

Yes, he thought, quickening his walk. *I like this freedom.*

It was only slightly alarming that he couldn't remember exactly how his date looked. That's what happened with PR parties: you flirted, you texted, you arranged to meet. Then came a mixture of efficient sex and casual abandonment. It had been quite a time since he'd had such pleasures but, if he was honest, even well-practiced pick-ups couldn't really compare with Barbara's insecurity.

God, he missed her!

It was tragic, the way she'd turned herself back into a school-teacher. Like so many women, she'd no idea that vulnerability was her strongest suit. In fact, he wouldn't have had to cheat on her if she hadn't gone all bossy on him.

Of course, he'd be back with her once he'd gotten even. And in the meantime he could have lunch with this girl—and with someone else, no doubt, by the middle of the week.

However, his tactics depended on Barbara not having a clue what was going on. If he'd known that he'd been exposed, he'd have crawled through tar to get her back. (He couldn't bear people thinking ill of him, especially if he deserved it.) And with charm like his, he might even have succeeded. But as it was, he was humming his way to her favorite bistro, unaware that the woman herself was sharpening her stiletto two lampposts away. And all because another of his lays had seen a chance to get her own back when he had ditched her!

As she followed him, Barbara flashed backwards and forwards between hatred and desire. She loved the breadth of his shoulders. And hated the firmness of his stride. She wanted to have him; and to punch him. To kiss him; and to kill him.

"Oh God," she moaned, as she had on so many other occasions but for rather different reasons. She'd tasted his strength in bed, and when other women had looked at her with envy. She needed a different power now, a toughness that had nothing to do with bullying. But she didn't know where to find it or what it would look like.

Stevie, meanwhile, was alive in his youthfulness.

And London, too, seemed renewed. Pedestrians picked through the light Sunday traffic, looking for adventure, or brunch, or some air after the night before. Tuning into the mood, Stevie's bistro had rolled down its awnings and opened its windows to the weather. Looking in, he found his girl sipping, by turns, at a glass of Ballygowan and a bitter-black espresso. The coffee was a grownup touch but try though she might, she couldn't fool him. He was determined that she should be virginal.

Peeking more cautiously through the same window, Barbara was astonished to see him with a blonde-haired waif in a floating dress.

She'd readied herself for an epic confrontation with a ten-foot giantess bearing flash cards and whiteboards. Yet the switch made sense. She'd never really seen him with the crisp consultant. But these two were more like it—a *jeune fille* from a novel and her dark seducer.

She wondered how many others there had been and if he'd taken all of them to "her" restaurant.

Not wanting to give her hand away—indeed not knowing what her hand was going to be—she dropped into a chair outside the neighboring café. Right away, a handsome Latin pounced on her with a notepad and pencil. *Might as well see it out,* she thought, the waiter's smile having done her no good. *But it's not the same as it was.*

Sipping perfunctorily on a spritzer, she watched couples walking up and down. Most were young, some were middle-aged. (She touched her face without thinking.) They gathered under awnings similar to her own or passed out of sight, too tense or self-absorbed to worry where they went. A young South Asian man parked his BMW then walked round to open the passenger door. Out stepped a pretty red-haired woman. They neither spoke nor touched as he led her to the mansion block on the corner. When she'd passed inside, he took a last look down the street before closing the door behind them.

Barbara stared at the brasses on the blank red entrance.

"And now they're going to fuck each other's eyes out," she murmured. "The silly little rich kids."

The thought both elated and depressed her.

Everywhere she looked were variations on the same scene. *Here we go again,* she thought, *tottering round in high heels and pinstriped suits, pretending we know what we're doing. You'd think we'd have learned by now.*

Her gumshoe role was suddenly less glamorous. Drained of invention, she ordered another drink even though the day was getting colder and she didn't much like the wine.

Next door, Stevie plunged his hands into his pockets and laughed, with manly restraint, at one of his companion's meandering anecdotes. So what if she was acting? (He fingered his keys.) The end was what mattered, and the end was pretty clear. Some salad, some wine.

And there, in the distance, his bedroom door left open. He imagined them walking back in silence, each knowing what was coming and neither wanting to waste their breath on small talk.

"Shall we go outside?" she whispered, bouncing him back to the present. "It's such a wonderful day."

Barbara, caught in her more general glooms, had almost forgotten them. She only realized her danger when the adjacent doors swung open with a giggle and a drawl. Cursing her cowardice, she shrank behind the tubs of evergreens that divided the two restaurants. (Yet again, she'd lost the initiative!) But straight away, she relaxed. For it was hard to say which was more contemptible, Stevie doing his solid-as-an-uncle routine or his date laying on the sex-kitten vibes. If anyone should feel embarrassed it ought to be *them*.

"Let *me*," he was saying as he poured the girl a refill, having barely touched his own. Barbara pictured the steady, brown-eyed gaze with which he insisted that publishing was so much more exciting than consultancy.

"Oh no!" His girlfriend's laugh was tinselly. "I'm only an assistant commissioning editor. I don't have glamorous clients. Not like *you!*"

Barbara knew by the tone of her voice that the wretched girl was looking up at him from lowered brows like a bashful dog asking its master for a walk. (In other words: a Princess Diana special.)

"No way," swore Stevie. "*You're* the one worth talking to. Not *me*." (It was a line Barbara had often heard before.)

"Tell me a secret," he went on. "Something that's been bothering you. Something that no one else knows."

This is how it starts, thought Barbara. *This is how he reels you in.*

On they talked, until Stevie rose so abruptly that Barbara was sure she'd been spotted. But he was only going to the loo. "Stage fright?" she wondered, without much interest. Or maybe he was out of rubbers?

This last thought broke into her calm.

She forced her hands not to tremble, her mouth not to scream. It was as if he was in her once more. She heard noises, saw faces. Then she changed into another woman—and another, and another. Nails were pressed into her palms. Seductive murmurs sounded in her ears.

She was every woman he'd slept with since he lost his job. And Stevie was in charge: the writer-director who controlled the action.

To her relief, a mobile phone exploded into action on the other side of the magnolias.

"What is it?" hissed a half-familiar voice. "It's Sunday, for Christ's sake!"

When Barbara peeked through the foliage she found Little Miss Moffat snarling into a handset while pulling down her neckline. "I don't care about *her* side of the story," she was announcing. "It's not *my* fault her novel's shite."

The exchange continued in the disappointingly fragmented way that overheard conversations do until the girl shouted "I don't care! I have to go! I'm in a meeting!" Having slammed the phone closed she reverted, not a moment too soon, to baby-doll mode.

The returning Stevie rested his hand on her shoulder for a beat longer than he needed to. "Oh!" she gasped. "That was my mother on the line."

"Checking up on you?" he leered, dropping into his chair.

"Why?" she laughed, leaning forward. "Should she be worried about me?"

In the silence that followed, Stevie looked at the space below her throat where she'd laid her finger almost casually. She stroked her cheesecloth dress like the heroine of a 1970s Flake chocolate bar ad while Stevie hummed appreciatively.

A muscle contracted, and relaxed, in Barbara's face.

This wasn't the Stevie that she thought she knew—the honest, self-sufficient friend. No more was he her idol. In fact, he wasn't even worth fighting with.

Leave them to it, she thought. *They deserve each other.*

And off she walked, not caring if they saw her.

Behind her came the unmistakable sound of someone choking on their drink. Turning her head, she saw Stevie gawping after her while his girl looked at him in mute surprise. Put-downs rose to Barbara's lips but she bit them back, seeing their futility. Some people weren't worth the bother.

Outside the bistro, the atmosphere had changed.

Stevie was too shocked to run after Barbara, pleading his case. He'd have to plan his words, not gabble them in public. If he kept his cool, things might be okay. And meanwhile he had a job that needed doing more than ever.

His date was surprised by the brusqueness with which he paid for their lunch. He'd seemed suaver than that. But there was no question of a change of plan. He would do well enough, she decided—for the afternoon.

The walk to his place was purposeful. But as they arrived her eye was caught by a balding man on the opposite pavement. He wasn't bad-looking, if you liked that sort of thing, although it was his surreally handsome friend who really grabbed her attention.

She stared over her shoulder as she entered Stevie's house.

"Come on," he whispered, edgily impatient, but she waited in his doorway until the blond man had disappeared around the corner. She wanted to see as much of him as she could so that she could think of him, later, when Stevie climbed on top of her.

10

"This seems nice." Danny pointed to a cluster of marble tables beside some potted plants.

"You think so?"

"We've been up every street in London. This is the best we're going to get."

"It's not the one I had in mind."

"But we'll never find your place."

Christian sat down without replying.

"*If* it ever existed," added Danny, who was more than usually nervous. A mad resolve had been building for weeks and he was determined to put it into action. He'd had enough of unrequited love. ("Never seek to tell thy love, love that never told can be.") This time he was going to tell his friend how he felt.

Christian, though, was in one of his pickier moods.

"This is hardly bruschetta," he announced as the first course arrived. "Garlic bread perhaps, but not bruschetta." And although he was long practiced in using jokes and complaints to deflect other people's emotions, he topped himself by putting on his mirrored glasses as they started to eat.

Danny lacked the nerve to break in. *It's no good,* he thought, as the shutters closed him out. *I'll never tell him now.*

Despair and self-disgust were the usual consequences of failure. And down they would have come if he hadn't felt a tap upon his shoulder. Looking up, he saw an over-tanned face tipped with a half-hearted goatee.

The mouth was grinning at him madly.

"I don't know you," Danny wanted to say. "You're a maniac." Then he realized who had tracked him down.

"Hey!" he stuttered. "Davey! What brings you here?"

doi:10.1300/5902_21

"Work!" said his school friend. "What else?"

Danny introduced them, not daring to meet Christian's eye, while Davey swung a chair the wrong way round and sat between them, Starsky-style. He'd surpassed himself, for London's sake, with his shaved head, cream suit, and kipper tie. The effect was hard to place until he whipped out what he persisted in calling his "shades," gave a cheeky grin, and explained they were "the bona fide, accept-no-substitutes, real thing."

"What brand?" asked Christian, fascinated.

Davey placed the glasses on his nose with rather too much care. "'Police'—like you-know-who's." And he sat back, almost daring you to ask after Romeo and Brooklyn.

Danny sat back too, but with rather less confidence. Here, for his beloved's scrutiny, was the one person from his hometown that he was ashamed of knowing. However, Christian was eager to chat. "Hugo Boss?" he asked, fingering Davey's lapels. Then quick as anything, he winked at Danny.

Unaware that he was being had, Davey responded to Christian's trails with lengthy accounts of the refresher course he'd been sent on, and how exciting London was, and the very many clothes he'd bought, and what a drag it was being away from Katie and the girls.

"How many days do you have left?" asked Danny.

"Four. And it's so intense. Workshops and things." He waved his newest mobile. "Of course I talk to them every day. No expense spared! But it's not the same." His voice dropped below its usual volume. "Not the same at all."

"Ah well," put in Danny. "Not much longer now."

But Davey said nothing.

Never one to prolong an emotional moment—or to admit it had occurred—Christian broke the silence with a stunning non sequitur. "So," he leched. "Yah ever go to the gym?"

Even Davey was taken aback. "Sure," he managed. "Four times a week."

"I bet!" Christian looked as if he might squeeze the other man's biceps. "I go too, but you've got better definition. What rotations do you do?"

Although they were addressed to Davey, Christian's health and beauty questions were for Danny's benefit. Danny knew that "How often do you moisturize?" was not a neutral question, but instead of being impressed by Christian's cleverness, he warmed to Davey's excitement at being in London. Perhaps Davey didn't get what was happening. Or maybe—like his hero, Mr. David Beckham—he was the sort of straight man who wasn't entirely averse to gay-male admiration. Though he'd never have slept with another bloke, he was perfectly happy being eyed up by one.

It was all about narcissism, of course, and exhibitionism: but what's so wrong with that? In fact, it occurred to Danny that his friend would make a better gay man than he himself did. Davey had the looks, the wardrobe, and the spending habits. If it weren't for his unfortunate habit of sleeping with his wife, he'd have done pretty well in Christian's Soho bars. Indeed there wasn't much to choose between him and Christian. Had everything else been equal, Danny mightn't have known which was the bigger berk. For there they sat, quarreling discreetly about who had the more exclusive labels. And though it was windy and the sun had gone in they were still wearing their expensive shades, oblivious to how silly they looked.

And how silly they sounded, too, with their overblown praise of a city that would never know their names or care if they existed. *This is not my home*, thought Danny. *These are not my values*. A different world came to mind, one that he and Davey used to share. You could hear it in the way they shaped certain words or thought twice, even now, before saying "dinner" and "tea." A sense of place and time came down on him so strongly that he could have wept. He grieved for the gap between who he was now and who he had been when he and Davey were competing to be the best in their class. They'd had so many dreams back then, and never guessed they wouldn't all come true.

He realized, now, that Davey's boastfulness sprang from insecurity: He felt uncool because he lived so far from London. Not hearing the artificiality of Christian's accent, Davey was frowning with anxiety about how his vowels should "really" be pronounced. But even while he performed for Christian, he kept grinning at Danny. "It's amazing," he said. "Running into you like this." And he meant it, too, for he was missing that other town: the one he lived in, the one that wasn't London. The one he was erasing from his speech.

In response, Danny's accent grew stronger.

He could have died when Christian asked if Davey's legs were in as good a shape as his arms. Breaking in, he asked where Davey worked out. "I didn't even know we had a gym," he remarked. "There never used to be one." Davey explained that nowadays there were two. One was in the "multipurpose leisure complex" that had replaced the old park and the other was in a disused Baptist chapel. "That's the one I belong to," he added. "It's got more class, somehow."

Christian rolled his eyes at Danny. "More class," he mouthed. When Danny snorted, Davey looked round to see if he'd missed something. Christian gave nothing away—he was used to looking blank. But Danny blushed with shame.

To make matters worse, Davey's hurt gave way to a cheerfully puzzled grin: he was obviously determined to give Danny the benefit of the doubt. In doing so he caught sight of his many-dialed watch.

"Oh, shit!" he cried. "I'm late for my time management class."

Danny was suddenly attentive. "Can't you miss it? They're always crap, those things."

"Better not. They're like rottweilers, this lot. It's worse than school. Remember Tricky Dicky? Or old Mr Cole?"

Danny's laugh was hectic: he enjoyed excluding Christian. "Point taken." Then he took Davey's hand. "Take care," he said, punching him on the chest.

It looked, for a moment, as if this might be a liberty too far. But in the next second, Davey put his arm round his shoulders and squeezed as hard as he dared—inspired, perhaps, by one of Mr. Beckham's goal celebrations. "You too," he said. "You too."

Danny avoided Christian's gaze: he wasn't in the mood for a bitchy postmortem. *Poor kid,* he thought as Davey turned to wave before disappearing into the pounding city. *He's harmless really.*

As if sensing a change in the weather, Christian took his glasses off and let the silence stretch between them. And when he finally spoke, it was to introduce a subject that would give him back the floor. "So," he said, a little wearily. "I suppose you want to know why I went away?"

Danny turned towards his friend. "Yes," he said, keeping his eyes on Christian's face. "I do."

It was hard to say what Christian was looking at. (A crack in the pavement, a lost penny?) In the longest speech he'd ever made about himself, he described the aftershock of fame. The insincere attentions, the demands for a sequel. The people who wanted his money. And the ones who wanted more. "They were the worst, I think. People hate you if you won't come across for them. But if you do, it's never enough. And they kept on doing it to me. They kept falling in love."

Danny shifted. "People in general?"

"More or less."

His attention stayed on Christian's profile. "And that was a problem? The rest of us would be flattered."

"How can people lower themselves? They can't have any self-respect."

A middle-aged couple went by holding hands. Behind walked a woman in tweed.

Danny wondered if Christian had ever been in love. But his friend spoke across him before the question could be phrased. "You have no idea what it's like!" he cried. "You don't have a clue."

"About what?"

"About—being handsome!"

"Thanks a lot!"

"I don't mean that you're not good-looking." Christian's voice was careful. "Because you *are*. But remember what the papers called me? Doctor Dreamboat! I can't stand that sort of vulgarity. And you know what really hurt? People saying I was blessed! I wasn't blessed. I was cursed."

He must have sensed the look on Danny's face, for he hurried on before he could be interrupted. "It's the same with film stars. We say we like them, and maybe we do, but that's not the whole of it. We don't just like them, we want to *be* them. That's why we love it when they fuck things up. It's our revenge on them for being famous."

The waiter who took away their plates raised a sympathetic eyebrow but Danny was beyond such consolation. He was shaking, either from the weather or some other cause, while Christian stared, unspeaking, at the blankness that he felt inside.

For though he had a secret, it wasn't the one that Danny had suspected. If anything, Christian was amused by his name, and by the embarrassment it caused his liberal friends. The terror that ran through his every interaction had little to do with being—or *not* being—Jewish. He had fears all right, but not those ones. Instead, consider this. Perhaps some partner would suss him out if they got too close? Or maybe a journalist would finally be sharp enough to grasp what he knew, and hated, and would do anything to bury? It didn't even matter whether Christian judged himself correctly. It was enough that he believed the sentence. Believed, that is, that he was a bore and a fraud and a nothing. A blank in the mirror. A page that could never be filled. A puppet that only came alive when the world smiled back at him with its misplaced adoration, an adoration he both needed and despised. That was why he'd left. And also why he'd come back.

Danny saw nothing of this. He only knew that to speak now would be to class himself with the desperate ones who had offered their affection and been rejected. Yet the impasse brought relief. For what was there to worry about? Only that Christian would never be his.

"You know, it's odd," he murmured. "The way we flirted for all those years but never went to bed."

Christian smiled but didn't look up. "Yes, I've often thought of that myself."

Danny wanted to scream, "So why don't we try it? What have we to lose?" But another part of him wished he was safely in his train. ("Hopton, Monksfield, Weeping Cross, and Mellford. Downhill, Pelham, Broken Bridge, and Redmill.")

Meanwhile Christian was studying a fly. "I suppose it's a way of drawing people in," he said. "Then keeping them separate. Flirting, I mean. That's why people do it."

"But *I* didn't keep you at a distance," said Danny not hearing his use of the past tense. "I wanted you so *much*."

His friend wasn't convinced. "Are you sure? I mean, I'd never have guessed. Not from how you behaved." Christian shook himself. "It's cold. We should go in." But he went on speaking. "I hated it, you know. Being with a man. Or with anyone. I hated it."

"You did it often enough."

"That didn't stop me hating it."

"Hating what? Being such a tart?"

"The numbers didn't matter. I'd have felt the same if I was married. I can't relax. It'll never change. That's why I write."

For the latest of too many times, Danny softened. His eye was damp but Christian's hand could dry it. So this time he would speak them: he'd definitely say the words. He would say them right away. Without a further pause he'd—

"It wouldn't have worked," broke in Christian. "Don't kid yourself it would have." He ignored Danny's expression. "We know each other too well. We couldn't have made the switch. And anyway," he laughed, "we'd have driven each other mad. You'd have been looking at me like I was a saint, and I'd have been thinking, 'When is he going to *do* something?' I mean, why d'you think I kept having it off? And with nutters every time? I've never made the first move. Not once. I don't have the nerve. I was at the other person's mercy, and I kept getting off with maniacs. Don't ask me why. I don't want to think about it. But at least those bastards didn't think I was some great *brain*. They just wanted to fuck me. If only you'd made a move, Dan. If only you'd *dared*. But it's too late now. Way too late."

Danny's chair might have been about to hurl him into orbit, so fast was he spinning round the earth. "It's not too late," he tried to say. But his confidence faded as he spoke. "It's not," he repeated. "It's not."

Christian twisted round to catch the waiter's eye. When he turned back, his voice was decided. "It'd never work. You're too scared to do what you really want to. You'd treat me too gingerly. And there's no time to change. We've seen too much of each other."

Danny could have slapped his face. But as if recognizing the truth of what his friend had said, he folded his hands and waited until it was time for them to leave.

Can you know someone for a decade and still see things you haven't glimpsed before? In one hour, Danny had learned more than in the previous ten years of his and Christian's friendship. But in later times, when he thought about that day, it wasn't Christian's words that stood most clearly in his mind. Instead he remembered how his friend had signed his credit card slip.

How come he'd never noticed that Christian didn't hold his pen between his first two fingers and his thumb, the way most people did? Instead he rested it on his third finger then wrapped the other two around it. And since his thumb had nothing much to do, he tucked it underneath all three of them.

Danny recalled a childhood game in which he'd been asked how he'd defend himself in a fight. His friends fell about laughing when he showed them. What was so funny? Simply that when he'd clenched his fists he'd folded his thumb inside his fingers.

"So what?" he asked.

"Try it," someone replied, volunteering a stomach. Danny threw a punch and almost broke a bone. For when his fingers hit their target, they also slammed against his thumb.

Applied to a pen, that same gesture forced Christian to shape each letter with laborious perfection. If he'd run forward, gripping hard while pursuing wild ideas, he'd have hurt the very thing he wanted to protect. By forming itself the way it did, his writing hand encouraged the intricacy and the precise deliberations that marked his famous style.

Danny smiled.

There was something so touching about that introverted thumb. But for once this wasn't a smile of surrender; it was one of farewell. In Christian's gesture he recognized, and pitied, the shyness that survives into this thing called "manhood," a strange condition that even Christian's great success could not make natural or easy. If only his friend could admit his need for comfort. But he wouldn't, for he was addicted to distance. Yet even as he wrote his books, his body was cradling itself. Consoling itself.

The gesture stood—or seemed to stand—for so much that Danny loved. But it also made sense of Christian's arrogance. *You can love him for being shy,* thought Danny. *And I do, I do. But shyness doesn't excuse you everything. Lots of us are scared but we still manage to look out for other people's weaknesses. Christian never has. And that's all there is to say about him.*

11

Before her train was halfway home, Barbara had made some useful notes towards her new book—stirred, perhaps, by the admiring looks that she and her outfit were still receiving. It was a timely reassurance, for she knew, when her mobile started throbbing, whose voice she was about to hear.

"Half an hour?" she laughed. "Was that the best you could do for her?"

"You don't understand." His voice was low. "It wasn't how it seemed. It was a business lunch. I got rid of her as quickly as I could."

"Oh, please!"

"No, really."

She decided to toy with him. "Are you sure?" she murmured. "I mean that everything was innocent?" Without actually lying, she suggested that she wanted to believe him. Stevie took the hint and ran with it. Then, when he started to brighten, she inquired as loudly as she could: "So what about that woman from the consultancy firm? Were you fucking her to get a job as well?"

Having said it for her fellow travelers, she was gratified when a punky girl—who obviously disapproved of her outfit—smiled in solidarity. She pressed the advantage home before Stevie could reply. "And fucking that bitch Cassie, too. She's always had a thing for you."

But that was too much. "No!" he insisted. "Never Cassie." And strangely enough, she believed him. For Stevie had never liked women who threw themselves at him.

"Can't we at least be friends?" he begged. "You've done so much for me. I mean I, I can't bear the thought of us not talking."

Perhaps he'd planned the wobble, or maybe he really *had* lost control. By now she couldn't know what was real and what was fake. One day she might write an article about the voice patterns of the New Man—their whiny hypocrisy, their well-muffled selfishness. But for

164   doi:10.1300/5902_22

now she could only shut her phone. It was bad enough being betrayed without being expected to forgive him for it too.

Her inspiration broken, she tried finding Danny, but only got his machine. However, the need for consolation was too ingrained to be set aside. Without Stevie she needed Danny, and without Danny she needed—who?

"Who indeed?" she wondered, ten minutes after her train got in, when she found that she had wandered, half-knowingly, to a 1940s semi in an unfamiliar part of town. A mistake might be in the making but with no boyfriend, and only a mad parent for company, how else could she cheer herself up? Bill Roberts was an authority figure. Like it or not, such men would always draw her.

But when the door opened, it revealed a sharply dressed woman in late middle age. "Are you looking for Bill?" asked the stranger in a voice that sounded louder than it was—probably because the diction was so precise.

"Bill?" stared Barbara. "Oh—yes."

"You'd better come in. Though I should warn you, he's having his nap."

"His nap?"

"Sunday is his napping day." The voice was both astringent and amused. "Though not mine, unfortunately. I'm Audrey Roberts," she added. "Bill and I are twins."

"Twins?" echoed Barbara. She was astonished that Bill had a sibling, let alone a twin. If she'd been asked to imagine such a person she'd have conjured up a defeated pensioner in a beige crepe dress. Instead she saw a subtly made-up businesswoman with angular jewelry and a well-behaved bob.

Horrified by what she'd gotten herself into, Barbara pulled her fur over her absurdly tarty dress.

Her hostess caught the gesture. "Are you cold?" She sounded incredulous.

"Not at all."

"Then may I take your stole?"

Barbara was caught. As Audrey showed her to the drawing room, her eyes moved, inevitably, to Barbara's vertiginous neckline. "I'm sorry," she murmured, "but I don't know your name."

"I'm Barbara Barnes. One of Bill's colleagues."

"Oh," said the older woman, as if that explained everything. "An *academic*. I'd better not wake Bill," she added. "He's only just gone down. Would you like some tea while you wait?"

But as she spoke, the door opened and in shuffled Bill wearing stripy blue pajamas and a frayed dressing gown. "What's the noise about?" He rubbed his face like it was four a.m. "I could hardly get over." He slid towards the sofa, only to recoil on seeing Barbara. "Dr. Barnes! I wasn't expecting you!"

Really, she thought, it was hopeless. All she wanted was to be flattered by a powerful man. What use was a head of department who spent his weekends morphing into Just William? And his sister was as bad, for here she came with a Dundee cake and a plate of sandwiches, like some impossible housewife from a 1950s novel.

To make matters worse, Barbara dropped her plate.

"And the cake was so delicious," she gabbled. "You didn't tell me there was a master baker in the family."

"Audrey can hardly boil an egg," guffawed Bill.

"Then it was you? *You* made the cake?"

This got an even bigger laugh from Audrey. "I can see he's never had you round for supper!"

"So who made it then?"

"One of my sister's clients."

"Really, Bill. You make me sound like a solicitor."

"I'm sorry," said Barbara. "I don't know what you do."

"My sister—" (Bill paused for a flourish) "—is a vicar."

If it hadn't been for her middle-class training, Barbara's mouth would have dropped to somewhere near the floor. "Do you have a local parish?" she squeaked, trying to cover her bosoms with her hand. "St. Oswald's would be pleasant."

Once more, Bill beat his sister into speech. "Audrey's not like us country mice. She works in London. Rather a *good* parish, I think you'll find. No riffraff students for *her*."

The look that passed between them was barely genial. Barbara saw in it a relentless procession of shared childhood birthdays. Inwardly she shook the other woman's hand. If nothing else Audrey could tell the world she'd shared a womb with Bill Roberts and lived to tell the tale.

"But despite it all," her brother went on, "she somehow manages to dash up here to see me."

"Yes, and I find you wiped out by the efforts of the week. I suppose that's why you go to bed when I arrive."

"Sunday's my day of rest. Why shouldn't I have a sleep? I run a university department during *your* days of rest."

Audrey caught Barbara's eye. "It's so typical of Bill to belittle working women."

"I have the highest regard for working women. But I don't think two sermons and a baptism constitute a heavy workload."

"You're jealous I've been promoted!" Turning to Barbara, Audrey explained: "My bishop's nominated me as Secretary of the London Council on Social Exclusion."

"You call that a promotion?" objected Bill. "I've chaired committees for years."

"Yes, on paper clip provision for the Humanities. This is a cross-diocesan group reporting on significant social issues. The last secretary went on to a deanship."

Barbara watched, astonished. Who'd have thought that Bill spent Sunday afternoons in his pajamas while his sister off-loaded food parcels from posh parishioners? More surprising still, she was jealous of their bickering.

Even if they hated each other, siblings had a shared history and a common cause. Nurtured by a common store of memories, they could conspire against their elders, each of them hoping to lead a new and victorious generation. But Barbara had no such resources. Whatever happened, she would always be an only child.

She distracted herself with a third slice of cake.

"My," said Bill. "You *are* enjoying yourself."

She released the knife in an instant.

"*Do* have more," insisted Audrey. "Otherwise Bill will scoff it when we go."

"Did he have a sweet tooth when you were kids?" giggled Barbara.

"Are you joking? He'd have taken the ice cream out of your mouth."

"Do you mind?" cut in Bill. "I'm still in the room."

Barbara asked Audrey if she liked her job.

"Like you and Bill, I enjoy working with young people." ("Bloody students!" exclaimed her brother.) "But the bishop also uses my PR skills."

Being a priest hadn't been an option when she was growing up, she explained, so she'd gone into advertising. ("It wasn't what I'd dreamt of. But these days I can use my knowledge for the Church.")

"Charles Saatchi in a slinky habit," muttered Bill, glaring at her suit. "Couldn't you slob it for once? I'm not the General Synod."

"You bastard!" flashed Barbara's eyes. But before she could smile supportively at Audrey, a half-familiar voice rustled in her ear. It urged her to *Flatter the man and ignore the woman. Laugh at his jokes. Don't upset the boat.* However, when she turned towards Bill a rival speaker whispered *You've more in common with her than with him. Take her seriously. She's a professional. She wants to make a difference.*

Barbara didn't know where to look. Hadn't she gone there for masculine approval?

That's right, said the first voice. *So ditch the woman!*

No, replied the other. *Elbow the man!*

Back and forth she went, like a demented tennis fan, between inner-city poverty and Bill's "exemplary" handling of staff meetings, until she was stopped dead by Audrey's questions about education. How rarely, even with Stevie, had she discussed the theory, rather than the practice, of her working days. Responding to the older woman's well-informed comments, Barbara forgot to show off. Instead, with pleasure and intelligence, she dissected the inspiring, exasperating process that made her who she was—teaching. Teaching, and learning.

For his part, Bill couldn't believe that his sister and a junior colleague were discussing education without reference to *him*.

"But don't you think—"

"Isn't there another possibility—"

"That's plain mad—"

Wasn't it Barbara who was supposed to insert herself into other people's conversations? But here was Bill doing it, like a snappy terrier trying to prove he wasn't past it. He was the kid in the library with a mobile phone, the child who screams for the sake of screaming. But ignoring him felt powerful.

Their female complicity made him want to throw his plate against the wall. But no. Down it went on the table with a forced calm. Then he pushed back his cuff, almost leaping through the air when he saw the time. (It was a *very* theatrical start.) "Ladies," he began. "Delicious though my sister's leftovers have been, I wonder if we shouldn't think about dinner."

Barbara was astonished: it was barely half past five.

When neither woman moved he added, not as confidently as he should have, "Did you hear me, Audrey?"

"Yes, dear?"

"Perhaps it's time someone started on the evening meal?"

"You know, you're absolutely right." She was as expressionless as milk. "You might as well get cracking. Barbara and I will set the table when you're ready." She turned to Barbara with the straightest of faces. "I hope you can stay for one of Bill's big dinners?"

Her brother glared down at her. She stared right back. Seeing that she wasn't getting up, Bill clumped towards the door, tightening the cord of his dressing gown. "I'm going back to bed!" he declared. "You have *no idea* how tired I am."

At which, shamingly, both women burst out laughing.

Of course Barbara didn't stay for supper. Indeed she didn't even let Bill go back to bed. Attending, once more, to the first of her voices, she simpered and flattered, almost undoing her work with Audrey. She'd intruded too long on their privacy, she insisted; she ought to go.

When Bill asked why she'd dropped by, she lowered her gaze.

"I wanted to discuss the university's research strategy." Her murmuring tones almost made admin sound sexy. "I've some ideas that might interest you."

She'd no idea where the tone had come from him until she realized it was the voice inside her head—an accent that she recognized, at last, as her mother's.

"Monday afternoon," he drooled, his eyes alighting on her cleavage as he said goodbye. "Or would you like a drink after work?"

Too late, Barbara realized that her blood-red outfit might be misconstrued by someone who didn't know about her London mission. Indeed the dress was asking to be misconstrued. Glancing from the bottom of the garden, she saw Bill lingering at the open door. When she opened her lips no sound came out.

He asked if she'd said something.

"No!" she cried. "Not a word."

He approached from behind. "Are you sure?"

"I didn't say a thing," she insisted, almost running down the road.

Having cut Stevie loose, she'd felt the need to test herself against a powerful male. She'd wanted to attract Bill as she had attracted Marcus Cranborne, and she'd been sure she could handle him. But when she saw the mixture of amusement, guile, and vanity that lit his face as he waved her off, it seemed that she had faltered and that it was *he* who had finished the day with a sly smile and a sense of having learned something useful.

12

All winter Danny had longed for sun but, like a true neurotic, now that it had come he wasn't sure he wanted it. Convinced that lanky bodies didn't look good in shorts, he stayed inside to not think about Christian.

He'd decided, hadn't he, that there was nothing more to say about his dear, unworthy friend? But hard though it was to block his conscious thoughts, it was harder still to purge himself of the hopes that had dominated his mind without his even knowing it. Tired by the struggle to forget, he had dreams in which Christian knelt by his narrow childhood bed and kissed him on the forehead—a cool, erotic gesture. It was a scene born of bitterness, for who knew what might have happened if he'd spoken out in time? But then deferral had always been his illness. As cause or symptom it powered his depression.

For years, it had been freezing Danny up. Every six months another risk got shelved, and another friendship receded into Christmas cards and birthday cards. Barbara's appearance, and Christian's reappearance, had halted the process. He had begun to hope. But now he cursed himself for living—or for *not* living—and moved still further into numbness. In the days that followed even jokes, his usual savior, were discontinued. Laughter was fine when you were in good spirits. But if you weren't, the wetness in your eyes might turn, mid-tide, into the waves that tore away Atlantis.

"Atlantis!"

The image was more than usually appropriate. For Danny, that famous evening, was sprawled upon his sofa, dying for a pee. A letter lay beside him. Although he had been there for hours it was hard to say how the time had passed. The letter read, he'd gazed unmoving at the faces that passed across the plasterwork above him. Christian. His father. His students. All the men he'd ever loved.

doi:10.1300/5902_23

Had he summoned them or did they come of their own accord? Who knew, who knew. But one of them certainly took him by surprise. He couldn't think how many years it was since he'd thought about the boy from primary school who used to wet himself rather than ask to be excused. Although his name had gone, his face stood clear in the memory. And Danny could guess, as he clenched his pelvic muscles, how the poor kid must have felt.

(But still he stayed on the sofa.)

They were fascinating, these delaying strategies. He wondered if they were a family trait. God knows, his father hadn't been one to take chances. He, too, had been ruled by the sort of caution that could warp entire lives. He, too, had failed to speak out. He, too, had buried his desires.

(Until now.)

Keeping his eyes on the ceiling, Danny willed his pain away. But every time he thought the urge had gone, it returned with greater strength. A fist was clutching his urethra. Soon he'd have to cram his hand into his mouth to stop himself from shouting.

(Yet still he couldn't move.)

It was odd, this news from Dad. "I tried to tell you at Christmas," he had written. "And again at Easter. I had to make sure you were coming. But once you were there, I couldn't find the words." (*And nor could I,* thought Danny. *Nor could I.*)

He pictured the old boy padding round the house, waiting nervously for his son to call. ("I really hope you won't mind," ran the letter. "It'd be everything to get your blessing.") But who could object, wondered Danny. Weren't weddings "the best kind of news"?

(A drop of urine wept from his cock.)

Of course, it was wrong to say they were marrying. She and his dad didn't want the fuss. Not at their age. Not when they'd both been wed before. And not when they'd known each other so long. So if Danny didn't mind, they'd simply live together. She was a fun sort of woman and he was bound to like her.

Of course I will, thought Danny. *How could he imagine otherwise?* And he'd ring to say so once he'd had a pee.

(He started counting. He'd go upstairs when he got to ten.)

That said, it was weird imagining someone else in their house. Someone whom he'd never met. (Two, three, four.) Someone who knew the place as well as he did. (Five, six, seven.) And who knew his dad rather better. (Eight, nine, ten.) It seemed they'd been to the same primary school. (Eleven, twelve, thirteen.) But they'd only recently gotten together. (Fourteen, fifteen, sixteen.) "In the full sense."

It was odd that his dad hadn't said anything before. (Eighteen, nineteen, twenty.) But that was okay. Why shouldn't parents have their secrets too? (Twenty-two, twenty-three, twenty-four.)

Who made the first move? (Twenty-six.) Had she a pet name for him? (Twenty-eight, twenty-nine, thirty.) What did they talk about? (Thirty-one, thirty-two, thirty-three.) Did they watch football together? (Thirty-four, thirty-five, thirty-six.) And where to God had his father got the nerve?

Oh Christ, he was bursting!

Happily, the dampness on his face was just a tear and not some other fluid. But look what it told him! His time on earth was passing. (Forty-two, forty-three, forty-four.) And he had nothing to show for it. Nothing but some moisture round the eyes. That wouldn't get him far. Not unless he made it his vocation. He could cry for the whole damned earth—like monks whipping themselves to purge the world of sin. And he wouldn't find it hard. Not with these red-hot wires knotting themselves in his brain. An aching bladder was the least of it. What really hurt was having to put his clothes on every day just so he could drag his falsely happy face through an indifferent universe full of uncontrollable events and arbitrary forces.

(Fifty-six, fifty-seven, fifty-eight.)

If he let himself sob the floodgates would open in more ways than one. But maybe that was okay? Perhaps he should stay on the sofa, weeping and pissing as his needs dictated. Waves of liquid could come and go as they pleased—baptismal waters to wreathe him in shame: "This is my son the depressive failure, about whom I couldn't give a shit."

He tried to laugh.

To go upstairs or to piss himself? The rest of his life might depend on the answer. (He was already in the sixties. The seventies. The eighties.) But why give up just because his Dad was still on the go? Surely there were friends to be made, decades to be enjoyed. Possibilities to be clawed back.

Somewhere, somehow, a light went on.

Suddenly he didn't want to be there anymore. He wanted to move on.

Careful not to let the waters break, he nudged towards the stairs. Droplets wet his thigh as he dragged his body up. But he squeezed them back. All might still be well. If only he could keep his concentration.

He groaned with pleasure when he reached the top of the stairs. (Not much more to go!) But the effort left its mark. Every part of him was trembling. Heavy bars beat time inside his head. Bright colors flashed before his eyes. (The sun was setting in his face.) Yet he was sure, as he passed the study door, that there was someone working at his desk. And not just anyone, either.

He stepped towards the threshold, his cock already lifting.

Look at those tidy shoulders, that pale bare neck! He'd know them anywhere. And this time he would do it. He'd grab them from behind. He'd kiss them and bite them until his lips were stinging. He'd burn his fingertips on another man's skin. He'd lick and scratch and bite. And he'd make his friend feel good.

One step would bring him to the threshold. Two more and heaven would be his. He closed his eyes, the better to enjoy himself. He kept them shut for three, four seconds—oh such delicious delay! In those same moments the sun made a final leap then sank behind the opposite house. Some other room, on some other street, was being filled with burning light. But now this one stood bereft. And all that he saw, when he opened his eyes, was a leather jacket hanging on his chair.

Danny gazed across his desk. Judging from the dust, it was weeks since the computer had been used. There was a moment of silence.

Then he dropped onto his knees. Who cared if his defenses broke? Let them, let them! Relief was more important.

With one great heave, blood-warm liquid started gushing down his thigh. The carpet darkened. Hot salt fell against his mouth. But still the warmth flowed on. And it was bliss. Such bliss.

It was only when he was done, and when his trousers were sticking to his skin, that the grief returned. He saw bedsheets blowing on a distant line as the air grew sharp with the smell of childhood trauma. "For ten fucking years I've lived like this!" he cried. "But it's never going to happen. He'll never love me. And I'll never have my say."

Panic rose like vomit as he looked around the room. Shelving lined the study. You couldn't see the walls for books. From skirting board to ceiling they surrounded him with other people's words. Artist's monographs sat beside volumes on architecture and music. But it was mostly literature that enclosed him. Slender books of verse and overgrown biographies. Classical drama. And yard upon yard of fiction.

Their names unwound before him.

Tom Jones.

David Copperfield.

A Portrait of the Artist As a Young Man.

Here, in miniature, were the disciplines of a gentleman's library. Here, condensed, were the constituent parts of a liberal education. They were the stuff his life was made of. And what did they do for him, how did they make him feel? They made him want to rush at them to tear them from their places. He wanted to be buried by the very things that had comforted and seduced and mislaid and betrayed him. He wanted to tip the shelves from the walls until the books and the planks and the plasterwork came toppling down on him. He wanted to be as oblivious to the world as the world was to him. And he wanted to hurt them. He wanted to stab at them and score them. It was as if they were people. He wanted to deface them. To talk back to them. To burn them.

He reached at random for a paperback. (He'd pull it out, he promised. Then he'd tear off its cover.) But when he touched it, his fingers spread protectively. The same thing happened with another, and another, and another. How could he think of harming them? They soothed and relaxed him. And they were cool to the touch.

Without knowing what he was doing, he shuffled along the walls, reaching up and down with his hands. He rested his face against the books, sucking nutrients from their spines. He loved them—even the ones he hadn't read. They held other worlds. Other lives. They had made him who he was and it killed him to think he might never add to them. Was that too much to ask? To write something that might feed another person the way these had fed him?

No wonder his study had called up Christian's ghost. His friend already inhabited these books. He was Darcy, Heathcliff, Rochester—absurdly bad fits. And Christian's own work stood among these classics.

Danny eased out *Silence and Remorse*.

Like any other fetish, it required cautious handling: he cradled it with reverence, hoping it would guide him. Touching the pages was like touching his beloved. And here, in the Acknowledgments, the two men came together—for wasn't Danny listed among those whose "intelligence and friendship have informed my argument in real, though unquantifiable, ways"? Yet it was odd, on closer reading, how many other people had "informed" Christian's work. But the book hadn't been inscribed to any of them. As Christian had put it at the time, "There's no way I'm dedicating it to my parents and who else is there, apart from one of my fucks?"

Once more Danny saw him in the British Library—his hair and skin inflamed, his mind unreachable. Perhaps—it came to Danny—they had never really spoken? Perhaps he'd invented their closeness over ten frustrating years. And maybe that was always the way. With books, with people. Communication is a work of the imagination. We fantasize our friends but cannot know them "for real."

Danny dropped the book.

Although it fell awkwardly he didn't straighten out the pages. Instead he surveyed the cliffs of books that hemmed him in. (This time he would do it.) He reached for a shoulder-high shelf. (One nudge and he could splash the contents down.) He could jab at the brackets with the liberated shelf. (He pictured the books crashing to the floor and he among them, freed by the effort.) That was what he dreamed of. Oblivion. Release.

And this time he would do it.

He would do it right away, not even counting to ten.

13

So, thought Barbara, as Bill toyed uncertainly with his chopsticks. *It has come to this.*

To no avail had she avoided Bill's insinuating smiles. It was as though her visit to his house had given him a license to leer. He'd taken to stopping her in corridors to ask if she was still satisfied by her work on women-only communes. Or perhaps the project left something to be desired? Cornering her in the more obscure sections of the library, he would imply that he was humoring *her* lust rather than indulging his own. Then he'd tempt her with a "business dinner" where "things to her advantage" might emerge. Having snubbed him in Ancient History, Philosophy, and Criminology she ran out of excuses and was forced to suggest a briskly elegant Chinese restaurant that would have them in and out in ninety minutes. She also checked the university's harassment code. And so, while Danny was staring at his ceiling, and not peeing, a modestly dressed Barbara was inquiring after Bill's sister.

She wanted to send Audrey a thank-you card, she explained.

Bill flashed his coffin-handle grin. "Are you sure? You mightn't know what you'd be getting yourself into."

"What do you mean?"

He gestured with the menu. "You'll have to help me," he giggled. "I don't know what half these things are." With an attempt at straightening his face he added, "My sister might misinterpret your friendliness."

"I'm not sure I understand," started Barbara, before blushing when she guessed what he was hinting at. "Are you telling me she's gay?"

But Bill had had enough. ("I like the sound of Sizzling Dumplings. Perhaps I'll have *those.*") Then he switched, seductively, to the consul-

     doi:10.1300/5902_24

tants' report on the university. "Of course it's still top secret," he insisted. "Only a handful of people have seen it."

Suppressing images of Amazonian women and homunculoid men, Barbara resigned herself to being the admiring audience that Bill so touchingly required. "Oh, *do* tell me more," she wheedled, playing with a fish ball.

Bill played cruel hard-to-get before collapsing, almost immediately, into showing off his contacts. "According to my informants, the Forward Motion Group has finally talked the Vice-Chancellor round. He's far too cautious, you know."

"So the youngsters had some good ideas?"

"Yes, they're recommending we change our notepaper. Apparently our letterhead doesn't reach the right people."

"Headed notepaper?" Barbara sounded doubtful. "At least that shouldn't cost too much."

"Not in itself. But there's also the new logo to commission. We need to look like a real university. That's what parents want these days. A proper crest. A knight and a unicorn with some open books. Or maybe a computer terminal. D'you think the College of Heralds would let us have a laptop?"

"I don't see why not. You could put a Microsoft logo on the screen and do an advertising tie-in. Bill Gates'd give you thousands."

"Brilliant! If you don't mind, I'll steal that for the Forward Motion Group."

"Be my guest. So what else does the report say?"

"They're keen that we should attend to the fabric of the university."

"I'm glad to hear it!" exclaimed Barbara. "The seminar rooms are a shambles. Will there be a custom-built block?"

"That's not *quite* what they have in mind. They're suggesting we clad the Arts and Science towers in Portland stone and build a neoclassical portico at each entrance."

"But surely that would—"

"They've also looked at seminar teaching."

"Oh, good!"

"—and they're proposing we abolish it."

"Eh?"

"In favor of lectures for three hundred and fifty students at a time."

"But—"

"So there's no need to worry about grubby seminar rooms. They'll simply be knocked together to create lecture theaters."

For perhaps the third time in her life, Barbara was speechless.

"But that's not all!" exclaimed Bill, who was nodding his head as if to emphasize what he knew. "Not by a long shot!" By now the report's confidentiality was forgotten. All he saw were new "fora" for his machinations.

Barbara asked how the changes would be funded.

The question seemed to please him. "In the longer term there'll be public-private partnership deals: and naturally I have some ideas there. But turning the second-year halls of residence into penthouse flats will finance Phase One of the rejuvenation."

"Which is?"

"A public relations drive for A1s and A2s."

Barbara considered the wisdom of universities making their students sound like sheaves of paper. Seeing no point in commenting, she grabbed the remains of the rice.

"The consultants have recommended an excellent PR firm for the rebranding exercise. I wonder what logo they'll come up with."

"Perhaps a literary motif?" suggested Barbara. "Shakespeare and Newton holding hands. The arts and sciences linked."

Bill was cool. "The punters wouldn't get it."

"Since when did you care so much about the market?"

The question annoyed him. "Shakespeare and Newton don't need our help. They'll always be around. But we can't survive without students. We need something sharp. Something scholarly. Something *sellable*. Maybe your Oxford friends would have ideas we could borrow."

Barbara couldn't stop her voice from becoming haughty. "Oxford hasn't had to do much rebranding. I think you'll find that most people already know the name."

"I wish we could say the same!" laughed Bill. "But these plans will bring us closer. Not to Oxford, of course. But Luton we can catch. Don't you think? First Luton. Then Leicester."

She stared with perverse fascination. How he could live with such paltry ambitions for himself, and for his profession? Where was his scholarship, his intellectual program? Numbers were his true preoccupation: student places to be filled, league tables to be climbed. And most of all, his own position on the scoreboard.

But the sad thing was, even his self-promotion was doomed. Barbara had spent enough time with Stevie to know that these days flattery and plausibility were more deadly than blunt force. Although Bill had the necessary lack of integrity, it wasn't clear (as he dribbled soy down his shirt), that he had the smoothness of a modern manager. He was too bludgeoning and charmless. And in his weird, unprincipled way, too honest.

Any more of this and she might feel sorry for him. Fortunately, he proved his unworthiness by treating the waitress who collected the plates to a full and frank appraisal. Barbara gave the girl a sympathetic roll of the eyes. Then he clicked into a sharper focus: "Of course, there are other benefits of moving to a lecture system."

Barbara caught the change of tone. "Because it's a chance to modernize the syllabus, you mean?"

"There *is* that," he said distrustfully. "But I was thinking about logistics." Again he became businesslike. "You can get fifteen people into a seminar. Right? But if you put three hundred and fifty people into a lecture theater you can move twenty times more students through the same course. And with one lecture instead of twenty seminars, some of our colleagues will find themselves with rather too much time on their hands. Which means we can make some serious inroads into our wages bill. Though as you say," he added, "we *could* have a peek at course content while we're at it. I mean, it's a no-lose situation."

Provided you weren't a student, thought Barbara, or a newly redundant faculty member.

"Of course, there will have to be a proper debate," he continued. "We're setting up a 'Your Say' button on the Web site so that staff can contact management with their concerns. But there's only one decision in the end. It's simply a question of slimming down the parts of the university that don't work."

Barbara wondered if this coolly practical appraisal would extend to the English Metaphysicals—never a strong draw for students. She also wondered why Bill was giving her his election spiel.

"*You,*" he said, "are safe. You're exactly the sort of person the department needs. In fact, you might as well know that I'm nominating you for one of our inaugural Good Colleague awards. They're to encourage excellence in everyone from cleaning staff to the Vice-Chancellor's Steering Party. You'll get two hundred pounds, tax free, plus a ten percent discount on your car parking permit." He beamed at her—a wolf in a Fair Isle tank top. "But hard decisions must be made. There are too many wreckers out there. We can't let them win. In fact, we in English can lead the way. I'm not suggesting redundancies. Or not compulsory ones at any rate. But it might be kinder if some people were put out of their misery. We need to encourage them to do the right thing. For their own sake. Don't you think?"

At last Barbara saw why he'd been courting her. It wasn't his advances she should fear, it was his politicking.

"Yes," he added conspiratorially. "I can think of at least *one* person who might thank us if we nudged him in the right direction."

"That direction being?"

"Early retirement."

"On what terms?"

Bill opened his palms but there was nothing in them except a hot towel.

"We have to think about the greater good," he argued. "If we please them, the Forward Motion Group will channel funds in our direction. Indeed they'll have to be nice to us, because they'll never get their plans through unless departments like English side with *them,* and not with the unions." And he grinned at her, thinking he'd finally found someone as unscrupulous as himself.

Just as Barbara prepared to rip whatever strips she could find off his scrawny body, her mobile rang. "Shit!" she cried, apparently meaning the phone. "I thought I'd turned it off." However, the peals stopped before she reached her bag. Looking up, she found Bill applying a matt black number to his ear. Cautious at first—as if the beast might bite—he soon snapped into a worried attention. Rapid exchanges alternated with someone else's monologue before he folded up the phone.

Rather than meeting Barbara's eye he fidgeted with the dessert menu. "Gelato," he said. "I thought this was a Chinese restaurant. That's ice cream, isn't it?" Then he rushed on. "That was bad news, I'm afraid. One of our colleagues has had an accident."

"An accident?"

"Well, no. Not an accident."

"I don't understand."

"He's not so well."

"Something's happened to someone?"

"To be blunt, he's had a breakdown."

"A breakdown! Who?"

Barbara's mind had flown, instinctively, to Danny, so she was astonished when Bill waved towards the waiter and said, not looking at her, "Ronan MacIntyre. That was a . . . friend of his. He's in Broomfield General. It seems he's taken an overdose."

PART THREE

1

Even though she was brimful of the excitement that only bad news can bring, Barbara found it oddly hard to catch Danny's attention when she rang him moments after leaving the restaurant. He usually couldn't hear enough about Ronan. But she was irked, this time, by his monosyllabic answers.

For his part, Danny was thankful he didn't have a video phone. Barbara mightn't have been satisfied by his "Oh?"s and "Really?"s but they were as much as he could manage. It would have been yet more of a stretch, having his wetness revealed. Not even he could have covered *that* one up.

The conversation over, he tried to absorb Barbara's tale. So the lad had flipped? Well, that was no surprise. Rampant ambition always came a cropper in the end.

He picked himself up. (Best to forget the smell, perhaps?) And he could tidy the books when his leg felt better. Too bad, though, that he'd only gotten the first two shelves down. One minute he'd been aiming for *Pride and Prejudice* and the next he was writhing on the floor like an overacting footballer. (Who'd have thought you could do in your hamstring just by vandalizing your house?) And there he'd stayed, glad to have a pain that justified his grief, until he at last he fell asleep, worn out by crying. It was oddly reassuring being cradled on the floor, unable to fall any further. Yet up he'd stretched, obedient to the calling of the phone. There were times, he thought, when he might as well have been a ventriloquist's doll looking for an arm on which to plonk itself.

"A cup of tea?" he wondered, his lips curling in self-mockery. Yes, that was *sure* to cheer him up.

As he moved, as lightly as he could, towards the door, a piece of paper caught his eye. (Why that scrap and not another? From what book, or what file, had it fallen and how had it attracted his atten-

doi:10.1300/5902_25

tion?) Stooping awkwardly he read: "Some Notes on Minor Art."
Very few notes, as it happened—his handwriting went barely halfway
down the page.

He made as if to rip it up but something stopped him.

"Minor Art," he muttered, with infinite scorn, as he put it in his
pocket and limped towards the kitchen.

Daydreaming's odd: you only see how much space it takes up when
you can't do it anymore. Since their last meeting, Danny had been
blocking thoughts of Christian. The hero of a self-help manual couldn't
have struggled harder. ("Who needs NHS waiting lists?" asked the
author of a book he'd picked up secondhand. "Beat the blues with my
ten-step plan to changing Bad Brain Habits.") But the only result, so
far, was emptiness.

He wondered if other people spent so much time re-imagining
their friends. His life was like a makeover show in which he gave his
Objects new characteristics—and all inside his head! Yet who could
say these ghosts weren't as real, in their way, as the flesh and blood
they were supposed to represent? From certain angles, Danny's
"Christian" might be more genuine than the figure that Christian's
parents knew, or that his lays had fucked, or that the man himself saw
when he shaved. But even if it wasn't, and if Danny had misled himself from start to finish, he still couldn't stop making up stories about
his acquaintances. For even as he split himself from Christian, he
began turning to Ronan.

Or rather: to thoughts of Ronan's illness.

Of course, no one knew why the younger man had "done it."

Theories circulated behind raised hands. His boyfriend had
dumped him—or he had dumped the boyfriend. He had been writing
too much—or he had writer's block. It was a cry for help—or he had
really meant to die. The euphemisms varied according to the speaker.
Some spoke of "physical exhaustion." Others preferred "nervous collapse." Bill's contribution was to shout "He's cracked right up" before
laughing nervously. The one clear thing was that Ronan would be off
until autumn.

Although Danny offered no explanations he listened carefully to everybody else's. (You learned so much from other people's attitudes.) Pity, and a dash of guilt, had turned Barbara into Ronan's greatest fan: you'd think she'd never said a word against him. Bill was defensive, while Marcus Cranborne showed a wistful concern. (Maybe he knew how the poor boy felt.)

And perhaps Danny also knew.

God knows he'd spent long enough putting himself in Ronan's head. Had his colleague thrown the pills at his face in hysterical despair or did he count them out methodically? What were they, Mogadon or multivitamins? If he left a note, what did it say? Did he know he'd be discovered? Or did he curse the paramedics who'd revived him?

It was exhilarating, finding out that other people could be wretched. (And not just people in the abstract, but people Danny *knew*!) But the news soon saddened him. For what hope did everybody else have when even brilliant youngsters couldn't cope?

Poor Ronan.

If it hadn't been for his boyfriend's return, he might have been just another tragic story. "A young life cut short ... Enormous promise ... Could have had a brilliant career." Or in the language of their local paper, "Professor Poof Says Enough Is Enough—PICTURES." Thinking of these things stirred a mixture of pity, kinship, and anger. Ronan had beaten Danny to a last resort that should have been his own. (The lucky bastard.) But he'd also shown himself up. (The fool.) And he hadn't even done it properly. (The sad incompetent.)

With so many Ronans knocking round his mind, it was no wonder he felt confused when he finally saw the real one, and at a time and place he wouldn't have predicted.

Danny had a theory that it was easier to get through paperwork when there was no one round to see you. With this in view, he'd started going to work as soon as he woke up: and as he was an insomniac, this made for early starts. Oddly, though, his pile of admin seemed to get bigger the earlier he went in. And he grew increasingly sensitive about being seen. Maybe this was why he jumped one day, at six a.m., when he saw a shadow ahead of him in the English Department corridor. He was about to slip into his office to dial 999, when the rising sun illuminated the back of the stranger's head. Danny might have been dreaming, so often had he seen those curls, except surely his unconscious wouldn't have given Ronan an oversized rucksack and a pair of bandy legs? (How come he'd never noticed them before!)

He could have waited until Ronan disappeared into his office—and God knows he was tempted. But he remembered their attempts to be friendly, and was sad. And his workmate looked so lonely—going into work in the middle of the night! "Ronan!" he called. "How are you?"

Too late, he remembered the last time they'd seen each other.

Judging by the pause before he turned, Ronan was recalling the same scene.

"I didn't mean to make you jump," added Danny. "I just wanted to say I was sorry."

"About my 'accident'? How kind of you to ask."

He tried not to be hurt by Ronan's tone. "No, I mean that time in Sainsbury's. I—I don't know what I was thinking of."

If anything, Ronan looked even more wary than at first. "Yeah, well. I'm not sure what I was up to myself."

"So what are you doing here? At this time of day."

Ronan tugged at his rucksack. "I wanted to get some books from my office. I didn't think there'd be anyone around."

"There never is," said Danny. ("Apart from me" he added, as if that didn't really count.)

They looked at each other: a cautious, dry embrace.

It's terrible, thought Danny, when people behave out of character. It's so exhausting, forming a new set of assumptions about them. Do you try to squeeze some insight through or just collapse into another heap of prejudices?

"Should I ask about the rest of it?" he ventured as they settled, resignedly, into asking and answering the inevitable questions. "I mean, I don't know if you want to talk about it."

The English Department corridor was normally full of academics, support staff, and students. Later in the day a line of lecturers would be praying for the prompt arrival of the photocopier repair man. Clusters of students would be tangled round the notice boards and the coffee machine, arguing, gossiping, and laughing in a variety of accents, languages, and tempers. And Lisa Lewis would be sorting out five different problems while Marcus Cranborne offered wisdom from the classics. But at 6:40 a.m. Danny and Ronan stood in ghostly silence, their arms planted to their sides. They found themselves whispering even though no one was there to hear.

"It was impossible," said Ronan. "I couldn't go on."

"Was it work?" pressed Danny, thinking of his own situation. "Or something else?"

Ronan forced his baritone into a throaty murmur. "Work? I don't know. Maybe."

His gaze was staringly intense. Trying to evade it, Danny looked towards the monumental windows that ran along one side of the corridor. It was disconcerting, seeing half a dozen pigeons banging their beaks on the glass to be let in, and once you noticed them they were hard to ignore. So while Ronan discussed the impossibility of ever being good enough, Danny watched mucky-bottomed birds shitting on the window ledge.

Ronan said he *had* been expecting his boyfriend to come back. "But I know I took a risk. You hear stories about people not turning up when they're supposed to."

Danny nodded sagely. "That's what did it for Sylvia Plath," he remarked while studying a pigeon foot.

Ronan unfolded his story—first warily, then with insistence. The problem, it seemed, was his hard-nosed father. How could an only son match up? It would have been impossible even if that son had been straight.

"I wish I had a different kind of dad," Ronan kept saying. "Someone who'd help me be who I want to be."

Something in his tone put Danny on his guard. "I'm sure you'll come through," he said in a falsely jocular voice. "Now listen, it's been great seeing you, but I've got tons to do this morning. Maybe we could have a drink sometime?"

"I wouldn't want to inconvenience you." Ronan's voice was sour. "I mean, perhaps you've got some shopping to do?"

Danny blushed to the roots. "No, really," he insisted. "What about a beer on Friday?"

This time Ronan hesitated. "I'm not sure. I mean, I'd like to. But, well—maybe we could leave it for a while?"

"Sure," grinned Danny. "You're the boss."

"Oh," said Ronan. "Great."

But he didn't sound very thrilled to hear it.

Because Ronan kept canceling his own suggestions it was another month before they had what Danny, with heavy irony, called their "date." The delay gave Danny lots of time to brood on his colleague's illness. In his imaginings Ronan became a boy in the newspapers with slashed skin, a teenager driven to self-harm. No longer was he a pushy junior lecturer. Instead Danny saw the ghostly figure that he'd met at six a.m. in the English Department corridor. Danny liked this new guy. He was as malleable as a case study.

A major skirmish, in the phoney war before they met, was where on earth they'd go. Ronan favored the Spread Eagle but Danny held out for the Gardener's Arms. ("They've finished their refit. Let's see what it's like.") He couldn't have said what disturbed him about going to a gay bar with Ronan, yet when he'd carried his point he prepared for their evening with almost as much care as if he'd been going for a *real* date.

Sadly, the venue wasn't one of his better ideas.

Time off work plus six pills a day had given Ronan the puffy, blown-up-with-a-bicycle-pump look of a late-period Judy Garland. His acne had returned, and to cap it all he had split from his boyfriend. ("I think it's what they call collateral damage.")

"It's almost a relief," he added. "But then I'm always doing that. Falling in love with Mr. Oh-So-Wrong."

Embarrassed, Danny looked towards the bar. ("The relaunch party's next week," said one barman to the other. "Nothing special. Just cocktails and nibbles.") The Gardener's Arms, which used to be pleasantly old-fashioned, now had bright yellow walls with aquamarine furniture and an almost total lack of custom. It wasn't a setting that encouraged intimacy. Despair was the more likely effect.

It's madness, thought Danny, *trying to ape London on a shoestring. In fact, that's what makes us look provincial.*

If he'd learned anything from his Covent Garden dalliance it was that staying true to your values, however quaint they might seem, was better than playing catch-up in a game you'd never win. That needn't mean being small-scale or unstylish, for who says life outside a capital has to be like *that*? It was simply a willingness to be the person he most often felt himself to be: a middle-aged gay man, currently single, who was born in one regional center and who lived and worked in another. Such things were only shameful when examined through Christian's cold and skeptical eye—an eye that was secretly self-hating.

He brought his attention back to Ronan.

"People will respond to me differently," the younger man was saying. "When Deirdre came back from her bypass, it was like she was already dead. Every other word was 'poor Deirdre.' I don't want to be 'poor Ronan.' It's far too fucking early. I mean, with all this free time, I wouldn't be surprised if I finished my book ahead of schedule."

If there was desperation in the boast, Danny didn't hear it. Rather than responding, he waited until Ronan dried up and they had nothing left to do but smile at each other with vague goodwill.

"A rocky evening," muttered the youngster, too softly to be heard. Then he snapped into life. "God, this place is grim. Come on! I'm taking you to the Eagle."

"Do we have to?"

"Yes! Use it or lose it—that's my motto."

It would be, thought Danny, eyeing his colleague's body. As he followed him half-heartedly, he tried mouthing the words "Poor Ronan": and they felt good upon his tongue.

"So what about you and your ex?" he asked, as they headed for the Eagle. "Any chance you'll get back together?"

Ronan's look was sharp. "I shouldn't think so."

"Oh, that *is* a shame!" Danny's insincerity was almost chic. "So why d'you think that is, then?"

Ronan should have been flummoxed by Danny's tone, but like a good sport he spilled the beans. Perhaps it helped that the problem, for once, wasn't incompatible sexual tastes but the opposite. ("It shouldn't have been allowed. The way we turned each other on.")

Danny's smile became harder to maintain. "So what went wrong?"

"Too much of a good thing."

"Meaning?"

"He had to be on top all the time."

"Oh."

"Not that I minded being underneath. I mean, I like it that way. But I want a fight as well. That's what's *really* sexy. A bit of friction. Not just slotting into someone else's view of you."

"There was all this talk about open relationships," he went on, "but I'd never hear the end of it if I so much as eyed another bloke up. I couldn't be doing with that. I mean, I liked him being powerful, but there are limits. And anyway, you can't be very secure if you have to control your boyfriend's every move. I want something different next time. Something sexy. But something I can deal with too."

I wouldn't get too eager, thought Danny, studying his figure. *I mean, who's going to have you when you look like that?* Yet Ronan himself seemed unconcerned. He'd already been direct about his medication. ("I'm on these," he'd said, waving a strip of foil-backed tablets. "And no booze, dope, or E.") And now he swung into the Eagle as easily as if he were walking into his living room.

"Aren't you nervous?" asked Danny.

"Not anymore. What 'bout you?"

But they were surrounded before Danny could answer.

"Hi, Rone!"

"Good to see you!"

"How's it going at the Uni?"

"D'you want your usual?"

"So who's your mate, then?"

Danny stood aside while half a dozen guys kissed Ronan on the lips. "I didn't know you were such a regular," he said.

"Oh, yeah. Regular as clockwork, I am."

It seemed inconceivable that Ronan's natural habitat should turn out to be their local gay bar rather than a high-powered academic conference. Yet maybe it was so.

His friends continued to drift by to tease him about his work. ("Do they pay him by the sentence?" "Yeah, but he gets a special bonus for words of more than fifteen syllables.") Laughing along, he told Danny that he'd been reluctant about going out after the hospital released him. "But that was silly. This lot warned me about Richie. Never trust a man whose name can be abbreviated to Dick, they said, and they were right."

He smiled from behind his mineral water. "They visited me in hospital. Or some of them did. They're my friends. They saved me, in a way."

Danny focused on Ronan's belly while listening, restlessly, to the gospel according to MacIntyre. ("This place isn't just about sex. Not that there would be anything wrong with *that*. But it's about hanging out as well, and having a laugh.") "You should try it," he added, sensing Danny's resistance. "I mean, you worry me, Dan."

But Danny wouldn't hear. "Where's the loo?" he laughed. "It's so long since I've been here that I've forgotten where to go. I could give you directions in Soho but I'm clueless at home!"

Ronan pointed unsmilingly to a door beside the jukebox.

Danny put down the lid and locked himself in the cubicle. Head in hands, he tried to untangle his feelings. All evening he'd been split between a wish to identify with Ronan and a need to patronize him. Ronan had been the braver of them: he had made his pain explicit. But even though he'd scarred himself, he refused to be a passive symbol of someone else's grief. He was like a bullied child who'd spoken out, a victim who shamed the world by displaying his bruises. "Why should I hide," he seemed to say, "when it's *your* fault I've been hurt?"

Then there was the shame of their supermarket scene.

Had Danny, any more than Ronan, been "sane" that evening? And which of them, now, was closer to health? Through the thin partitions Danny heard the beat-beat-beat of the jukebox and the raised voices of the pool players. One of these hailed Ronan with a mock salute. There was a lesson here if he could take it. If only he could take it.

When he returned, his voice was brightly artificial.

"So how's the film coming on? I suppose Barbra Streisand has optioned it by now."

"The film?"

"*Hello, Dolly!* meets *Shaft*. Send in the Crack Dealers. The Ladies Who Lap Dance. I've Seen the Future and the Future's Queer. *That* film."

"I tore it up. It was crap."

"You *do* surprise me."

"At least I was trying to move things on."

"Yes, and look where you are now. A crappy gay pub in the middle of nowhere."

"It isn't crappy! These are my friends. I told you."

That shut Danny up. So he tried another tack. "But you've got to admit it's phoney. All that stuff you spout at work. It isn't real. It's just people with pierced tongues telling the rest of us we're past it."

Ronan looked as if he'd been hit in the face with a live mackerel.

"See!" He opened his mouth. "No ring! But if someone else wants one, good luck to them. Live and let live, that's what I say."

Danny was incredulous. "But you're *always* telling people what to do. I can't count how many times you've put me down over things like that."

"No, I haven't."

"Yes you have. What about that time you said you'd never pass judgment on someone else's mental health? You made me sound like Jerry Springer! It was as if I had no values whatsoever. At least not compared to *you*."

"Can't you see?" hissed Ronan. "It was a sensitive subject. I mean, use your imagination."

Danny wanted to shout "It was sensitive for me as well!" But he didn't dare.

"I come on too strong," admitted Ronan. "I know I do. I'm like Dad. I always have to prove myself. But I don't know why you feel so threatened. All I'm interested in is finding new ways of doing things. I mean, look at the guys in here. I love them, I do, but it's ridiculous the way they keep going after the same things. They're either shagging in Ibiza or buying fitted kitchens. And they want their boyfriends to be the same as them. Same age. Same height. Same everything. But why can't we shake things up a bit? That's what queer theory's about. I mean, don't you get tired with the old ideas?"

Danny wouldn't concede that he'd often thought the same. "I'm not into novelty for the sake of novelty," he said. "We get enough of that at work."

"But what about novelty as a way of changing things? You can't change the world unless you start asking what it should look like."

"But what about people who want to stay the same? What about me? *I* don't want to change."

"Fine. I can't force you. But why can't I nudge things on? You use your word and I'll use mine. After all, we both fancy men."

"Yes," laughed Danny. "It's just that every time I hear the word 'queer' I reach for my—"

"Cum?" broke in Ronan—not a particularly sophisticated joke, but it changed their evening. Newcomers entering the bar a moment later saw the two men firing responses without a pause. What brought the change? Simply that Danny turned Ronan's joke back on him.

"And if you hear the word 'cum' you reach for your—?"

"Tissues," said Ronan. "Which make you think of—"

"Sneezing."

"Hay fever."

"Allergies."

"Shellfish."

"Mussels."

"Pecs."

"On the cheek."

"Or the cheeks."

"That's naughty."

"But nice." (Ronan licked his lips in a parody of lust.)

"Christ!"

"What?"

"I can't tell you what I'm thinking."

"Try me."

"No way."

"Go on."

"No!"

"Just for fun?"

"Well. Maybe—"

Word-long sentences are compulsive. They're gone before you realize what you're risking. As well as "acne," Ronan offered "paranoia," "competitiveness," and "podge" (at which he squeezed, half-fondly, at his stomach). Danny produced variations on Ronan's themes (such as "being looked at" and "feeling a failure") plus peaches of his own like "baldness" and "repression." Inevitably there was also a "Barbara Pym."

Each hoped to learn about the other: the trick was to remember the words that *he* said while trying to control your own. Even so, if you're used to holding things in it's exhilarating to balance on a cliff edge, tossing up words that you'll never be able to claw back. Although Danny reddened to the armpits when he mentioned "Christian," Ronan merely heard a reference to religion. Other patterns were more compromising. For example, their references to sex might have been harmless if Ronan hadn't given "SM" in response to "waking up at six a.m." (What was he saying?, wondered Danny. That spanking was a cure for insomnia?) Once that particular cat-o'-nine-tails had leapt from its bag, they found themselves riffing back and forth with "masks," "whips," "chains," and "handcuffs." And the thread recurred in the most unpromising of contexts. So when "car crash" gave rise to "whiplash," they returned, inevitably, to the same territory.

Neither knew what the exchange "meant"; they just enjoyed having it.

At the last orders bell, Ronan's friends came forward once again. "When I was on steroids," consoled one, "I put *stones* on. But it didn't stop me getting off." And he scribbled the name of a dining club where larger chaps got the recognition they deserved.

Danny and Ronan shifted around outside, not sure how much affection was required. A handshake? A hug? A brisk "take care"? In the end, Danny's avuncular pat on the back seemed right. But he still managed to muzz things up by looking back when he got to the corner of the street. Ronan was standing outside the pub, staring after him. Danny had held the look for half a second—it was like their standoff in the supermarket—before turning on his heels and walking briskly on. That was bad enough, but then curiosity got the better of him. Craning round a moment later, he found that Ronan was still there, only now there was a man by his side. They were laughing, and pointing after him. The other man looked familiar, but maybe it was just that he and Ronan seemed so well-matched—same height, same hair. Same everything.

Danny veered home, annoyed he'd looked back.

But perhaps, despite their touchiness, a link had finally been made between him and Ronan? When he stretched his legs under the duvet he felt the pleasurable unease that comes when you've started revealing yourself to a new acquaintance. It wasn't an emotion he'd felt very often. But as he fell asleep, his eyes jerked open. (Why, he wondered, are our bodies so resistant to sleep?) With the clarity of a biblical vision he realized that the man outside the pub was Freddie. *His* Freddie. Freddie from the junkshop.

Freddie and Ronan—

Ronan and Freddie—

For a single stabbing moment he was angry. Then resignation descended in its usual dispiriting way. Why be surprised? He should know by now that some men got endless action while others—didn't.

Yet for all of his bitterness, someone *did* lie close to him that night.

Falling through time and air he found himself in Sainsbury's with Ronan's breath upon his neck. The scene changed with a toss of his head. Squinting through blackness at the dots of people leaving The Spread Eagle he caught, and kept, Ronan's eye. They put their hands on each other's shoulders and stared, and stared, and stared. Then he saw the two of them bent over a table speaking quickly and nervously about—what?

2

It was as much as Barbara could do not to say, "More tea, vicar?"
But even though its time had finally arrived, she thought she'd save
the line a little longer. Meanwhile, she giggled inwardly at her situation.

"Resplendent" (for that was surely the word) in one of her mother's
1940s "costumes," she set the teakettle on its silver stand then picked
up the serving tongs. "Anyone for petits fours?"

"My!" said Audrey, moving her eyes from Barbara to Barbara's
mother. "You *are* spoiling us."

You'd think, from her gracious nod, that Mrs. Barnes had iced the
violet fancies herself, or at the very least ordered them in person from
the cook. "I'm so glad you could come," she murmured. "I always enjoy meeting Barbara's friends."

Oh yeah? thought Barbara. *First I've heard of it.* But her handiwork
cheered her. The new (or rather, the antique) tea set was just the sort
of present her mother liked. What with that, the new paint job, and
her homemade seed cake, Barbara deserved an Oscar for Best Production Design. But for all her retro-chic effects, the real miracle was her
mother's mood.

"What a charming brooch," said Mrs. Barnes, examining Audrey's
chest. (She was evidently looking forward to the afternoon's festivi-
ties.) "You clearly have an eye for accessories."

"I can't claim any credit for this one," said Audrey, fumbling with
her neckline. (Like the others, she wore a dress cut for an older summer than this. Its long-hidden colors ran with joy as she unpinned the
cameo.) "It used to be my godmother's," she explained while Mrs.
Barnes held the jewel to her eye. "Victorian, I imagine, and not the
highest quality. But it has sentimental value. As they say."

doi:10.1300/5902_26

"No, no, my dear," protested Mrs. Barnes, as she drew her finger over the crack that spoiled the setting. "It's a *truly* fine piece."

Trying not to laugh, Barbara looked into her lap while Audrey smiled at Mrs. Barnes, and Mrs. Barnes smiled at Audrey. Each woman ate a petit four. Although no one appeared likely to risk a cream horn, Barbara couldn't regret the fifty-five quarter turns she'd lavished on the pastry. Not only did they look deliciously vulgar, they'd also be waiting on their doilies when she got bored with the day's main business. For God knows she hadn't much time for all *that*.

Still, she had to admit that the more she saw of Audrey, the more impressed she was. For example, it had been clever to wear an inferior brooch. Her new friend had known, by instinct, not to threaten Mrs. Barnes. Mind you, it was easy for *her*. It would be no big deal if she and Mrs B. fell out. (Which meant, of course, that they were bound to get on.) What's more, she and Mrs. Barnes had their unexpected tastes in common.

"Perhaps," ventured Audrey, "it's time to go upstairs?"

To a woman, they rose.

"What do you say?" asked Mrs. Barnes. "The main bedroom?"

"Yes," said Barbara with an air of getting things over with. "The dressing room's way too small."

So up they climbed—the heroine, the heroine's mother, and the heroine's lesbian friend.

Despite the drama of the moment, Barbara's main emotion, as the bedroom door swung open, was relief that she'd overcome her mother's snobbishness about DIY: the room looked almost decent. If Mrs. Barnes had known that Audrey's visit was mostly an excuse for Barbara to clean the house up, it would have taken more than a new teapot to win her round, but as it was she closed the curtains with girlish pleasure before turning expectantly towards the others.

"Mother prefers not to use natural light," explained Barbara.

"Things look truer without it," agreed her mother. "After all, no one goes dancing in the daylight."

"My word!" Audrey's gasp was involuntary. She was dazzled by the fabrics that the older woman was drawing from her closet. "Isn't that a Balenciaga?"

Mrs. Barnes put a finger to her lips. "Have a look. What do you think?"

Barbara, no more than any child, could see the whole of her parents' lives. Among many other obscurities, the years before her birth would always be uncertain. But sometimes there were hints—like the way her mother's fingers played upon the "costumes" she was showing Audrey. Or the stories that had come back to her when she'd been scrubbing her mother's woodwork in preparation for the visit. Kneeling before the skirting boards, she'd heard echoes from Mrs. B's adolescence—the creaking of the wood as her mother sneaked downstairs in borrowed dresses and homemade accessories to dance, and dance, and dance. (Was that *really* how her parents met—at a party that she'd dared to gate-crash?)

Barbara never guessed, when she was being raised on these tales, that she'd see—for real—the house that her mother had wanted to escape. And nor did she picture her mother returning to that house.

Yet there they were.

She wondered what her life would have been like if her mother hadn't run away with her father. She (or rather, some other child) would have grown up here, in this other world. She would have known her grandparents. They wouldn't have had to shift around, avoiding her father's creditors. And she needn't have been a party to her mother's precarious ambitions. For unlike the truly privileged, who don't give a damn how people see them, Mrs. Barnes had always been terrified of exposure. Barbara, on the other hand, had been able to take her upbringing for granted, even to the point of fighting it. (Which, now that she thought of it, might be another reason for her mother's hatred.)

These things came to her as she watched Audrey and her mother bending lasciviously over a cashmere wrap, their fingers linked in admiration. After a moment's struggle, she let her jealousy pass. It was enough that Audrey should give her mother a pleasant afternoon and herself a guiltless one.

"I'll leave you to it," she murmured. "You don't really need me."

If her mother heard, she didn't disagree.

It was strange, thought Barbara—this friendship she had formed with Audrey. Despite knowing lots of gay men, she'd never had lesbian pals. But then even Danny was a man, and men had to be attended to. But women—? Barbara wasn't so sure about women.

Recently, though, her eyes had opened wider. Stevie's treachery had made her pause. And she'd been aware, from the start, that Audrey had a different way of doing things. The first time they met for lunch, Barbara wanted to treat her. ("Let's go somewhere really nice. I owe you for that delicious tea!") But the more Barbara insisted, the more Audrey objected. She hadn't even baked the cake, she laughed, so why should Barbara pay for her?

When Barbara finally grasped the absurdity of buying a three-course meal for someone who'd made you a cup of tea, she apologized for her pretensions, flicked back her hair, and decided to flirt like hell. She'd never done it with a woman. (Flirt, that is.) And Audrey was a promising target. Barbara fancied living dangerously. It could be a new way to test her power.

However, Audrey was ready for her. "Let's not get carried away," she smiled, as if their lunch venue was the only thing at stake. "I know a place off Fitzroy Square. It's cheap and cheerful but we can talk. And that's the main thing. Isn't it?"

As they ate, Barbara was possessed by unfamiliar pleasures. Audrey didn't have to drop any hints about how they weren't each other's types, though, for Barbara's elation wasn't about physical attraction. It was about feeling relaxed.

Audrey was attentive and intuitive. And she knew when to make a joke. Excited by talking to a stranger (not to mention a professional listener), Barbara gave an unexpurgated account of her and Stevie's affair. An account, that is, in which she didn't portray herself as either heroine or victim. By the end of the meal, on which they went dutch, she and Audrey were sufficiently pleased with each other to arrange another meeting. And it was Audrey's idea—born after several more lunches—that they visit Mrs. Barnes. Together.

At first, Barbara was appalled. ("But she'll say we're an item. Or accuse you of molesting her. You don't know what she's like.")

"Tell you what," suggested Audrey. "You do the food and I'll wear something femme. Then she can show me her frocks. She'd like that, wouldn't she? And it would be a treat for me."

"But you're so—" (Barbara blushed.)

"Businesswoman-dykey?"

"No nonsense, I was going to say."

"It comes to the same thing," laughed Audrey. "But I like girly clothes. Not on myself, of course. But on women who can carry them off."

And so it was, after much persuasion, that Barbara brought Audrey to her mother's for tea and fabrics.

By now Barbara had moved to her mother's yard—a dank rectangle with an outside toilet. (Disused.) If she herself had grown up there, she'd have wanted to get out. For she, as much as her mother, had been ambitious: they just dreamed of different things.

The green-streaked walls depressed her.

Looking up, she pictured the scene in her mother's room. Audrey stroking silks and wools. Her mother showing off her most intimate belongings. Voices lowered in reverence. Two women sharing. Bonding. Complimenting each other's taste. Contemplating each article of dress—

Barbara returned abruptly to the house.

But it, too, discouraged her. Why had she bothered painting it? Her "touches" merely emphasized the surrounding tawdriness. And the dampness turned her stomach. She wanted to repudiate the house and everybody in it. It seemed to taunt her with something of herself—her Sunday slobberies, her wish to let go.

Sighing theatrically, she went upstairs to resume her daughterly duties. She was hoping, rather meanly, that her mother had turned—for Audrey's delectation—into Frankenstein's granny. But when she clumped into the room she found them poised upon the bed. Between them lay a 1940s fashion catalog full of impossibly elegant silhouettes—charcoal shadows stretched to a dubious perfection.

Her mother's voice was testy. Where had she disappeared to? And why did she have to barge back in again? If she wasn't interested in what they were up to, why couldn't she leave them alone?

Barbara screwed her mouth into an exasperated pout. But before she could say anything, Audrey winked at her.

Jealous, resentful, and admiring, Barbara returned the signal.

As she did so, a question flicked into her brain:

"Was *this* what it was like to have a sister?"

While Barbara and Audrey spent lunches laughing uncontrollably at tales of stalking errant lovers, Danny tried, in his quieter way, to stop the past from blocking up the future. If she'd known what they had in common, Barbara could have helped him. (And vice versa.) But he'd never told her how he felt about his friend. And though he'd have liked to see her, he didn't yet feel able to wish himself on someone else. It was easier to stay at home, adding to the strange piece he was writing on minor art. It was hibernation. A time of repair.

And he needed it. Watching his students sunbathing on the Arts Tower car park, he wondered how many years it would be before they realized that sunny Mays often led to washed-out Julys. Mind you, he was cheered, one day, by an e-mail advertising a government funding scheme "for research projects where the outcome is unknown. That is, for projects where failure might be an acceptable outcome." Like friendship, he thought, or life—a clouded endeavor where success is rarely total.

Although he still hurt, it was with the pain of letting go, not the ache of unspoken desire. He'd somehow had his say, and the scars had begun to knit together. In the meantime there were exams to be marked and students to be dispatched on more lucrative careers than his own. Bill Roberts held his annual competition for the most deliciously illiterate exam howler, a competition that Bill's students usually won. Despite much promising material, Danny refused to enter. Instead he was moved to tears by the naive, half-formed handwriting of students raised on word processors. There was something poignant about their awkward grapplings after facts, arguments, and interpretations. What would become of them?, he wondered.

It was in this ambiguous mood that he lifted the phone one day and dialed Ronan MacIntyre. The impulse struck him as a friendly gesture, a sign that he wasn't shy about seeing a convalescent colleague, even when that colleague was having it off with one of his own crushes. (The lucky bastard.) Without planning to, he used the cheerfully brisk tone that people turn on pensioners and children. To his surprise, Ronan asked him round for dinner the next evening. ("I've got things to do at home," he explained. "And I'd like to show you my place.")

Yes, thought Danny, *and that way you'll have more scope for dangling Freddie under my nose.* However, he was touched by the mixture of nervousness and bravery in Ronan's voice. His funny coughs brought to mind a young man with spotty skin, or a nephew needing help. The image excited Danny with such tender aggression that he heard himself accept the invitation, even as he wondered, rather uncharitably, what Ronan's cooking would be like.

The conversation over, Danny felt strangely restless. After three and a half pages of *Jane Eyre* and his sixth cup of tea of the day, he made a token perusal of his thesis. That done, he took out his observations on minor art. Even though these tentative explorations absorbed him more than his academic writing had ever done, there was still something distracting him. It wasn't a sound or an object. It was more like a thought trying to be born.

He replayed Ronan's voice in his head. Hearing it jump up and down, the octaves loaded him with a wish to protect his younger colleague. The lad had seemed different since his illness. (Since *both* their illnesses, he meant.) But when he tried to sort through his complicated impressions, another set of lips came into view.

He tried to stare them out.

"I do not need you," he told them. "I'm past all that."

"But you'll come running back," they replied. "You always do."

"No, I won't."

"Yes, you will. You will."

(Those lips, those eyes—how they froze him!)

"Not this time," he managed. "This time I'll be strong."

The lips parted. Their smiling was an ivory blade. "But he doesn't fancy you," they mocked.

These lips belonged to no man—not even to Christian. They were the voice of Danny's deepest fears. But somehow, somewhere, they'd become attached to the man that he had loved. "You're old and bald," they laughed. "And you've wasted your life. He's found someone his own age. His own height. You're too tall, too thin. You've never lived and it's too late to begin. No one wants you. No one. And me least of all."

Danny's gaze nearly faltered. But with sudden inspiration he thrust his hand into his desk and pulled out a folder. Running downstairs he laid his draft obituaries, with loving care, on the living room grate. A moment later he added the rest of the folder, plus a firelighter.

The cardboard took a long time to catch but he had no wish to pull it out. Instead he felt an odd sense of power. It was almost as if he was ready to take control.

3

Barbara was relieved, as she stood stock-still in the middle of the car park, that she wasn't the only one trying to work out what was different about the campus. Colleagues stood like sentinels beside their cars. Then one by one they laughed and pointed at the bright green window boxes dotted on the Arts and Science Towers. What's more, a couple of giant-sized terra-cotta tubs had been plonked at the building's foot, where workmen were filling them with pampas grass and Swiss cheese plants—odd choices, one might think, for an outdoor site in the Midlands.

Unable to move, Barbara looked the building up and down as if appraising the sex appeal of an unfeasibly tall man. Despite their brutalism (or perhaps because of it), the towers possessed a weird integrity that had no use for window boxes and ornamental plants. What next? A bright yellow cartwheel and some milk churns? Or perhaps a water-feature to go with their leaky roof?

As she stared, she felt an unexpected sadness. It was like finding a gnome with a fishing rod at the entrance to Tate Modern. The towers were noble, in their way. But now they looked embarrassed—shamed by their owner's lack of faith.

Just as she told herself off for being sentimental, someone poked her in the back with more intimacy than could ever be welcome at eight a.m. in the staff car park. "Oh," she muttered. "It's you." It was hard to imagine a less enthusiastic voice.

Fortunately Bill had enough enthusiasm for two.

"Isn't the new look great?" he bounced. "Of course, it's just a holding measure until we've released the funds for the portico. But we thought window boxes would go down well on Open Days. That's the sort of thing parents notice, you know."

        doi:10.1300/5902_27

"So how are *you?*" he managed before continuing his self-glorifying account of the university's expansion plans. These included everything from an "East-meets-West common room" (to attract ethnic minorities) to a "series of groundbreaking joint degrees." Notable among these was the new program in English and Hotel Management, where students could specialize in Wordsworth and the Lake District, or the Brontës and Yorkshire, with Seamus Heaney and the Bogside as an option for the more adventurous.

It was 8:20 a.m. and already Barbara felt ill. However, there was no need to attack Bill with a stun gun. For when they reached the pigeonhole room, he found a letter that made him turn away without a word. ("Men!" she spluttered. "Will I *ever* understand them?")

Mail-wise, it was a good day for Barbara: not too much brown paper and only sixty-five new e-mails to join the 1,537 undeleted ones on her machine. These were mostly conference announcements. The Northwest American Society for Eighteenth-Century Studies was soliciting papers for its annual "Due South of the Rockies" bash. Possible topics included "Out to Lunch—Cutlery and Silverware in the Poetry of the Mid-1730s," "Puritan Sex Games—Filmic Rewrites of Richardson and Defoe," and that old favorite, "The Rhythm Method Reassessed: The Art of the Rhyming Couplet." After all *that,* the participants would be more than ready for "Professors on Prozac," the University of Alabama's panel discussion on "timetabling trauma and seminar stress." Other possibilities included one-day conferences on "The Erotics of Space" (in Lyme Regis) and "The Politics of Porn" (in Aberystwyth). Meanwhile a lecture series on "The Radical Academy" was being jointly hosted by King's College, Cambridge, and a well-known computer corporation.

This was followed by exciting news from the university's Staff Progression Office:

Are you a MANAGER? Have you been MANAGED? These inhouse workshops have been rigorously assembled from a series of cutting-edge studies. Project management is an ever-proliferating field of inquiry. Academic debates need not concern us this time, however. Our concern on this occasion is in the area of practical policy implementation. These interlocking workshops have been projected as constructive interventions in your (evermore!) busy lives. Your first task is to select which workshop(s) you intend to attend:

(I)   Are you a MANAGER? First we must ask, What IS a manager? Managers are people who manage. There is more than one way to manage. Deans and Heads of Department manage—but so do administrative assistants and tea-shop liaison staff. This is a workshop that will improve your management skills. Our objectives will include: how to evolve clearer project definitions; ways of improving project delivery; end-of-project assessment exercises; disseminating best (and worst!) practice; and coping with shortcomings in project realization. Unsuccessful projects cause fatigue, rework, and a loss of commitment among project workers and adjacent stakeholders. Consequently, one emphasis of the workshop will be the foregrounding of adequate aims communication.

(II)   Have you been/are you now being MANAGED? First we must ask, What does it MEAN to be managed? There is more than one way to be managed. We all have line managers. (Apart from the Vice-Chancellor!!!!!) Cleaners and clerical staff are managed—but so are senior academics and policymakers. This is a workshop to help you cope with being managed. Being managed is stressful. In this strand, our objectives will include: how to understand and implement the aims of your manager(s); how to process feedback on your work progress; how to deal with negative evaluations of your output; how to action self-critical learning measures; and—of course!—how to learn from your failure(s).

ADDITIONAL OBSERVATIONS:

(i) Attendance at these learning opportunities is entirely optional.

(ii) Attendance/non-attendance at these learning opportunities will be noted on your Staff Register and may be considered during your Annual Performance Review.

(iii) It is recommended that you attend at least ONE of these workshops. Many of us, however, are both MANAGERS and MANAGED. In which case, it is recommended that you attend BOTH workshops. (NB: If in doubt about which category/categories you fit into please approach the Staff Progression Office for advice.)

Having deleted this valuable message, Barbara turned to her non-electronic post. Audrey had sent a card from an antipoverty conference. (Rome had never looked so lovely.) Next came the usual catalogs from Manchester, Edinburgh, and Cambridge University Presses; she binned them without a glance. Then, as the pile of envelopes went down, and as she began to think about the stack of unmarked essays in her in-tray, she found her heart beating faster and her palms covered in a cold thin fluid.

Could it be true—?

She turned the letter over, not sure what to think. Then her future seemed to open, and she gave a quick, comprehending laugh as longed-for opportunities swam into view.

Several rooms away, Lisa Lewis listened, in amazement, to Bill's humming. What could it possibly mean? One part of her pondered the ups and downs of her boss's mood while another bit of her worked through a spreadsheet with enviable efficiency. Yet this wasn't all, for she also smiled to herself, and bit her lips to stop herself from laughing. And though it was safe to assume that her amusement had nothing to do with the charts on her Mac, it was harder to guess its cause.

Every so often—when the coast was clear—she took a hardback notebook from her bag, wrote a phrase in it, then slipped it out of sight. The book was heavy with questions, underlinings, and exclamation marks. In it, overheard remarks were rearranged and improved until they became entirely different to how they were before.

Scenes were sketched, revised, and cut. Others had been removed from their original context and Sellotaped elsewhere. The overall effect was so anarchic that no one—least of all Lisa—would have guessed how well the book would sell when it finally appeared, two years later. (*After* she had moved to a new job.) But with material like hers, how could it have failed?

Next door to her Bill, still humming, had torn through mounds of cheap manila.

He'd been clearing a space for the thick cream envelope he'd spotted in the mail room. These days only the Vice-Chancellor's Office was allowed expensive stationery, and earlier that week a space had opened in the Vice-Chancellor's Steering Party. (Poor Edward's heart attack had been so sadly unexpected.)

Bill was sure, as he slit the heavy paper, that pleasing words lay ahead. However, the letter fell from his hand before he'd finished the first paragraph.

"Jesus Christ." The words were a whisper.

Then he banged his fist so hard that Lisa dropped her notebook, while across the corridor Danny leapt from his chair as if he'd been electrocuted.

Bill's eyes grew tight.

How on earth could a class on Andrew Marvell provide grounds for a complaint "from a student whose anonymity we must protect"? So what if some Katie or Rebecca hadn't liked his course? The university didn't have to take their whinging seriously. As far as he was concerned, he had nothing to be ashamed of. For all he'd done, if he remembered the incident correctly, was dismiss feminist approaches to the poet.

The girl (whatever she was called) had claimed that the line in "To His Coy Mistress" about worms burying into a woman's "long-preserved virginity" made her fear that "something horrible" was going to happen to her. Bill had said that *that* didn't seem particularly likely, but the joke was wasted on her. Instead she accused Marvell of writing "a fantasized harassment narrative" that "implicitly valorized assaults on women." Bill had remarked that that sort of thing might go down well with Barbara Barnes, but this was a class on seventeenth-century poetry. Literature expressed the human soul: it had no place for political correctness.

But Ms. Whatsername wouldn't back down. And although Bill didn't encourage students to disagree with him, he couldn't help admiring the fierce resistance with which she spewed out books he didn't recognize and authors he'd never heard of. Perhaps that explained what happened next. But he was adamant, even now, that his actions had nothing to do with desire. He'd simply touched her hand and told her not to be so tense. He'd seen it as an attempt at human kinship—a way of reaching out. And nor had she objected. She'd just fallen into one of those sulks that students do so well. He'd taken her refusal to meet his eye as a begrudging acceptance of his point. Only now, a fortnight later, does it turn out that she saw it as an attempt to silence her. (Or, even worse, as an inappropriate overture.)

He'd been unlucky, in retrospect, that the other kids had missed the class. (Never known for high recruitment, his courses also had hefty dropout rates.) And instead of mocking colleagues such as Ronan, he wished he'd imitated them by keeping his door open when seeing people.

What Bill didn't realize—or wouldn't concede—was that the mess was a result of not taking students seriously. A non-incriminating apology might have gone a long way, but he wouldn't countenance anything that looked like giving in. Nor could he admit that the woman might have a point. Which was why he had to fight back, before his enemies briefed against him.

Damn!

He could have strangled this neurotic Ms. for upsetting his plans. But there was no more time for fist-banging. Instead he'd get Lisa to dig out her file; it was bound to contain something he could use against her.

But first, first, *first*—he had to remember her name!

"Why am I even thinking twice about it?" murmured Barbara.

All round the university, cleaning contractors performed their secret ministry on lavatory U-bends and polystyrene cup-strewn common rooms—but, with her day's work done, she was still reading and rereading her former tutor's letter.

His offer was tempting, to say the least.

"Come back to Oxford," he'd written. "You know it's what you want. Provincial universities are all very well but it's not like being in the center." The job, if she got it, would bring her closer to North Oxford mansions and midsummer garden parties. With it came book grants and May balls. Small classes. Privileged students. Cultured colleagues. And when the public sector was run by managers, not academics, surely it was easier to thrive where there was some money in the system?

And yet—

What was Oxford if it *wasn't* a "provincial university"? At least her present colleagues didn't mistake themselves for the center of the intellectual universe: apart from Bill, they knew their own obscurity. But compared to Ronan—or even to Danny—most of the Oxford dons she knew were academic versions of the Queen Mother (may the Gracious Lady rest in peace). That is: old, rich, and spoiled. And the remainder were exploited youngsters.

For the second time that day, Barbara wanted to protect her workplace from someone else's gaze. It was kind of her tutor to ask her to apply for this job. But although she'd told herself a hundred times that her current post was just a stepping-stone, she resented her university being described as "the sort of social experiment where you never see the sun." And not even her respected supervisor had the right to tell her what to think. Yet that's exactly what he'd do once she was there. He'd tell her who to approve of and who to despise. But most of all he'd tell her what to write about and what to teach. That might have been okay once, but not now. For, bizarre though it might seem, new universities believed in having new courses, and their employees liked designing them! But in Oxford she'd be stuck with an ancient syllabus and colleagues who'd fight her every move.

"I don't know if coming here was the right thing to do," one of her leftier friends had famously said after taking up a fellowship in Cambridge. "But I figure I'll be helping to educate a radical elite." At the time Barbara had applauded but now she wasn't sure. For since when had chatting to rich kids about books ever changed the world?

Tired of her dilemma, she went to the window. Even at that great distance Bill was creepily familiar as he sliced his way across the deserted car park. She giggled to see Danny loping after him a safe distance. With *his* timetable, it was no surprise he'd been working late. The wonder was that he could skip along so cheerfully!

She smiled to see his happiness.

He meant a lot to her, she realized. And yet their friendship had been interrupted. She was sure it wouldn't take much effort to get their closeness back. (*Would* it?) But it shocked her, as she watched him spring along, that she hadn't the barest notion of what his life was like. And if she left, she never would.

She stood at the window long after Bill and Danny had passed out of view. The town lay around her—comfortable, unpretentious, "real."

Should she stay or go?

She had no idea.

4

Was it the weather, or the way that whole afternoons had started passing without thoughts of his beloved? Perhaps it was the return of his appetite. Or maybe it was the letter he'd scooped off his mat on the way into work. His dad was having a moving-in-together party with his girlfriend. "We hope you'll bring a guest," the note read. "Anyone at all you'd like us to meet."

The "at all" was underlined three times.

Whatever caused it, Danny's lightness lasted well after Barbara saw him leaving the campus. It was true that dinner with Ronan and Freddie was more a duty than a pleasure, but his curiosity was piqued. And his confidence had grown: he didn't feel nervous till he rang the bell.

Bloody rich kid, he thought, peeking up at the house. You couldn't get places like that on a professor's salary, let alone a junior lecturer's.

He was conscious, as he waited, of the large brown envelope lodged in his bag, beside his wine. He felt ungainly and the delay didn't help. Maybe Freddie and Ronan were doing it behind an upstairs window. And perhaps there'd be a tour of the house in which he was invited to examine their rumpled bedding, like a state official picking over the debris of a royal honeymoon. He smirked at this until the image got out of hand and their pairings started twisting through his mind, garish and inviting. However, when the door finally banged opened, Ronan was unerotically brisk. "Shut the door. I'll be as quick as I can but I can't make any promises."

Charming, thought Danny as his host disappeared through a door under the stairs.

You'd think an evening at Ronan's would be efficiently organized, if nothing else, but by the look of him the lad hadn't so much as washed his hair. And as for the house! Why hadn't Ronan had it deep-cleaned and decorated after "Daddy" paid off the mortgage?

 doi:10.1300/5902_28

Danny smiled: he was remembering his own father telling him on the phone that it was never too late to fall in love. His smile came back to him, unexpectedly, from the other side of the lime-green hallway. And since there's nothing more powerful than a mirror in an empty room, he let himself be drawn to it.

Even though his face hadn't changed over the past ten months, the image seemed new. He considered his eyes, his lips. His close-cropped temples. The line of his mouth. He rapped his knuckles on the glass—lightly, and with amusement. Over his shoulder he could see the door through which Ronan had disappeared. He watched it for a moment then turned and walked towards it.

Later on, when he thought back to that evening, he couldn't work out when the noises started. Had he reached the door or was he still moving? He just knew that as one cry ended, another began—sharp, half-human yowls.

Pictures burst through his head in the briefest of flashes.

A telephone that rang and went dead on Christmas Day. Pigeons pecking on a windowsill while two men talked about their lives. Ronan's unwashed hair. His dirty clothes and peeling walls. A voice that went up and down the scales. And a boy who slashed his skin.

By the time his fingers closed around the doorknob, Danny could feel the moaning echo through his body.

"What is it?" He yanked the door open. "What's going on?"

Ronan was crouching on the floor: his face was bloody.

"Are you okay? Show me where you've cut yourself!"

The younger man laughed euphorically—madly, even.

"It isn't funny! I'm trying to help."

Ronan's palms were cupped together.

Oh God, thought Danny. *Please not the wrists.* Then he realized his colleague was holding something out to him.

"Look!" cried Ronan. "Aren't they wonderful?" In his hands were the tiniest kittens Danny had ever seen. "I didn't realize she was so close," explained Ronan. "That's why I'm running late."

At his feet a smoke-gray cat was stretching itself in langorous ecstasy, like a feline Saint Teresa. Kittens clung to her in open-mouthed adoration.

"These two took me by surprise," he went on, as he laid them by their mother. "But that's the last of them.

"I don't suppose *you'd* like one?" he added in the innocent voice that pet owners use on these occasions. "If they're anything like Evie, they'll have a warm and caring disposition. A bit snappy on occasion, but only when provoked."

"Well, ahm—"

"Think it over while I change." He led Danny into a disconcertingly messy kitchen. "Have a gin." His voice was brisk. "There's tonic in the fridge."

"What about Freddie? D'you want to me to let him in?"

"Freddie?"

"Freddie from the junkshop."

For a moment, Ronan's face was blank. "Oh, *Fred!*" he laughed, as he ran towards the door. "Your beau. I shouldn't think *he'll* be coming. Sorry to disappoint you, but it's just the two of us tonight."

Danny stared into the space vacated by Ronan's bandy legs. They were strangely moving, he decided.

And oddly sexy.

Humming under his breath, he examined a meager heap of cookery books, each of which had the air of having been used precisely once. Unable to find much inspiration in *Low-Fat Meals with Pulses, Grains, and Seeds*, he dropped his gaze to the kitchen table where a lidless tube of acne cream had oozed over an unpaid electric bill. An old pizza box lay underneath. Looking for a patch of freshness on which to rest his eyes, he spotted two sparklingly clean litter trays resting on the single tidy corner of the floor. Beside them was a plate containing a half-eaten lump of meat—lamb's heart, by the look of it.

Fantasies are most powerful when they're open-ended: we don't always give them conclusions. And so it was with Danny's. The anticipation with which he'd left work was connected, somehow, to the suspicion that he and Ronan were . . .

That one of them might . . .

That they could . . .

But instead of writing in the dull conclusions that life might have supplied, he'd left the sentences unfinished. After all, it was merely a question of whether or not they slept together. And however fascinating that might be in the abstract, the question seemed less compelling in Ronan's kitchen. How long could dreams flourish on take-away pizzas and/or plates of bulgur wheat and beans? Faced with such fare, Danny felt disinclined for dinner let alone for sex.

Raising his eyes from the cats' bowls, he forced himself to study the photographs on Ronan's notice board. He liked animals as much as the next person but there was something unsettling about finding so many legs and tails jumbled together. Ginger cats frolicked on a haystack, gray ones stalked a robin, and a tortoiseshell went flashing in a sun trap. Many of the pictures had been ripped from magazines but a few were digital printouts featuring the cat under Ronan's stairs. While Danny wondered why the photos looked familiar, a long black tom plopped through the cat-flap and stalked around the floor, ignoring his hand. After sniffing its half-eaten heart, the creature sprawled on the floor with an air of arrogant challenge. Then Danny realized that it, like the others, was posing for a previously unrecognized genre—cat pornography.

A pounding on the stairs announced Ronan's return.

The startled cat ran off as his master entered, squeaky-haired from the shower. It was even harder, now that Ronan was cleaned up, to reconcile his fair-haired youthfulness with the tackiness of his house. He seemed to feel the disjunction himself for he tried to pull his acne cream off the table when Danny wasn't looking. "I get like this sometimes," he apologized, as he filled a bin-liner with rubbish. "Life's too short for housework."

"I'll drink to that!" said Danny, who was cheered to see that besides the tonic, Ronan's fridge held a bottle of Cava, a green salad, a bag of coffee beans, and half a side of cold salmon. Danny sipped his drink while his colleague bustled round with a pinched nose and cautious fingers. And to be fair Ronan's acne *had* been clearing up. There weren't such mounds of it—only some flakes on the back of the neck.

Danny laughed out loud, remembering Marcus Cranborne's sinister voice at the start of the academic year. Ronan looked at him questioningly but he refused to explain. Instead they fell into a silence that was either nervous or companionable depending on your point of view.

"I got this ready-poached," said Ronan as they sat before the salmon. "From Waitrose."

Danny's mood, which had been improving, took another jump when his host asked if he'd heard the news about Bill.

"What news?"

"Nothing much. Only that the university has started an inquiry into his teaching methods."

Enjoying Danny's shock, Ronan explained how the student in question had come to see him earlier in the term. ("She's taking my queer theory course. We discussed the pros and cons of making a complaint and she e-mailed me last week to say she was going through with it.")

Danny held his breath. "Does she have a case?"

Ronan paused to remove some bones. "Oh, yes. Though it's not a major offense—as these things go. They won't sack him. But with a bit of luck we'll get a new Head of Department."

Danny couldn't help but grin. "Of course it must be terrible for the girl," he added, perfunctorily, as he tried not to stare at Ronan's still-wet hair and pale blue jeans. Plumpness suited him—he was like a Giotto that'd had too much spaghetti. Even the hated CCCP T-shirt looked good on him.

"Hey!" said Danny, reaching for something at his feet. "I want you to have this." He handed over the package that he'd brought from home. "It's some notes I've been getting into order. Nothing special, of course. But you'll be the first to read them."

"They're about minor writing," he added, by way of enticement.

"Oh."

"But if you'd rather not—"

"No, no—it isn't that." He'd be pleased to read them, explained Ronan. It was just that writing wasn't an easy subject, right then. In fact he was so disillusioned with his book that he was sure he wouldn't finish it.

Danny was astonished to hear himself urge his colleague on. "But you must! You've so much to say."

Ronan grunted. "But who in their right minds would listen?"

"Ideas trickle down," said Danny. "We raise them in our courses. Then our students talk to their friends. The word gets spread. And there's your film," he added. "Why don't you work on that as well? You could set it here: it doesn't have to be LA. Everything helps when you want to leave a trace."

"Ambition's a curse."

"But that's what moves things on. For better or for worse."

It wasn't relaxing, working out how to change the world through words, but what else could they talk about? Neither wanted to part, but nor were they comfortable moving closer.

"So what's this about you and Fred?" said Ronan archly. "Is there something I should know?"

Danny couldn't think where to look.

"You know he likes you?" asked Ronan.

"But he's *your* friend. I saw you together."

"We went to the same school. I'm not sure that counts."

"So you're not—together?"

"Oh please!" Ronan made a face. "He's much too wet. Anyway, he keeps asking me about you. For some strange reason."

He rose, abruptly. "I'd better check on Evie. D'you want to come?"

Danny traipsed behind with fear, excitement, and reluctance.

Like bridesmaids dressed in black, the kittens in the box room revolved around their mother, sucking and mewing, and showing off their bloody pelts. Ronan peered at them lovingly. "Don't you want a closer look?"

Danny's muscles ached as he stooped beside the glowing stepfather. He felt hot. Everything was closer than it should have been. The cats. Ronan's thighs. The indescribable junk of the room. Ronan was telling the cats that they were the main things that kept him sane, that they were so beautiful that they almost made him believe in God. It was too much to bear—the pathos and the bathos. Tears came to Danny's eyes, just as they did when he saw notices tacked to lampposts about missing pets. How often were they found, he wondered?

As if sensing his pity, Ronan's tone got sharper. "Mind you I can't cope with four of you. I'll have to make do with a couple. Jacques and

Michel. Or maybe one of you's a Judy?" He got up. "But it's good homes for the rest of you—or else you're off to the knacker's."

There's nothing sexy about embarrassment, thought Danny, recalling his behavior in Sainsbury's. Although he and Ronan had changed from who they were back then, the bristling of his sweat was making him conscious of his body in a similar way. He wondered how the evening would end: with him going home, or with a quick grope above the litter trays? Neither seemed inviting.

He sighed, too weary to disguise his discomfort.

Hearing him, Ronan's voice grew moist. "What's the matter, Dan?"

The name sounded odd in his colleague's baritone.

"Oh—nothing." He was conscious of his fear, and of the smell of Ronan's hair.

"It can't come as a surprise," added Ronan, "but I like you. And I don't enjoy seeing you this way."

Danny remembered Christian and his own mad love. *Poor kid,* he thought. *I know how you feel.*

Perhaps it was this that made him lean across and kiss his colleague, for the first time, on the lips. A quick peck. Then: nothing.

He stood up straight.

Ronan followed suit.

"Look at us! Two experienced guys and this is the best we can do!"

So they tried a little harder. Danny put his arm round Ronan's shoulder in a gesture that was both fraternal and erotic. Or so it seemed when he looked down into the younger man's face.

"The thing is," said Ronan, "I like being near you. When I see you, I want to get closer. I saw you on a train, once. It was the first time I noticed you—like that, I mean. You had some nice stuff on and you looked so—tall. Then I realized I was always looking out for you. At seminars and things. Hoping to impress you." (It was the shyness of his smile that Danny went for.) "I think I overdid it," he laughed. "I mean, I'm such a pushy bugger. But you know what? These days, I prefer you like this." He brushed his hand on Danny's sweatshirt. "It's more you, somehow." And up he looked, with either innocence or guile, his eyes as wide as they could go.

Danny smiled down at him with new satisfaction. Now that the kid was better, maybe they could do something with each other . . .

Or for each other . . .

Or *to* each other . . .

The sentences were still unfinished, but maybe he was getting closer? Except Ronan had started preaching again. ("I tried to get through to you in the pub. But you weren't prepared to listen.")

"All right, all right," snapped Danny. "I get the picture."

Fortunately, Ronan got a stronger call on his attention. "Leo! Where have you been? Tormenting your sister, I suppose."

The tomcat from the kitchen swaggered onto the rug between the two men and gazed reprovingly at the empty fireplace. Gravely, Ronan told him he should know better than to expect a fire in July. Not satisfied, the cat turned its back on its master and viewed Danny with marginally more interest than before. With its swagger and its wiggle, it looked like John Wayne at the end of the final reel.

"Come on, Leo!" cried Ronan. "Don't be mean."

Relenting, the cat jumped on his lap.

Ronan laughed triumphantly and started petting him with another-worldly abstraction. "Look," he said, sweeping his hand down the animal's spine. "He knows what he likes, doesn't he?" The cat wriggled under his touch, twisting this way and that but always pushing his head into Ronan's palm and nudging at him until he got another stroke. "This one's taught me everything I know." He giggled while the cat whined its pleasure. "He goes after what he wants and he isn't guilty when he gets it. That's the secret, isn't it? I mean, what's wrong with wanting to be happy?"

"Easier said than done," muttered Danny. He wasn't sure if he was jealous of the cat, or of Ronan, but he certainly felt left out.

"I know," said Ronan, rubbing Leo's throat. "I've always asked too much of myself. But I'm trying to relax."

The cat started moaning—a deep-throated sigh that Ronan imitated as if he was returning a love-cry from his mate. Their duet awoke a strange memory. Was it really true, as Danny had read somewhere, that there were barbs on a tomcat's penis? Apparently no one knew for sure if the female cat screeched in agony or joy when the tomcat drew it out.

Ready for another game, Leo turned on his back and glanced invitingly at his master. "Who's my best boy?" said Ronan, not caring how he sounded. "Who's the best boy in the world?"

But as soon as he touched Leo's stomach, the cat threw up its paws, clutched him tight, and bit his hand.

"You little bastard!"

He tried in vain to free himself.

"It isn't funny!" he objected, hearing Danny's laugh.

At last he flung off the cat, who walked away looking pleased with himself. "Little fucker," he repeated, as he examined his hand. (Luckily, the skin was unbroken.) But oddly enough, Danny was cheered. He knew what to do now—what the limits were, and the thrills. (And the dangers, too.) "Give me that," he ordered, grabbing his friend's hand.

He couldn't remember the last time he'd felt so aroused.

"Here," he said, inspecting it for welts. "I'll make you feel better."

But as they went upstairs, the only thing he could think of was Ronan's cry of pain when the cat's long white teeth had come down on his plump white hand. It was enough to make a man mad, he thought, as he all but pushed Ronan through the door and onto the bed.

ABOUT THE AUTHOR

Vincent Quinn teaches English and Gay Studies at the University of Sussex in England, and is co-founder of the Centre for the Study of Sexual Dissidence. *Worth Fighting With* is his first novel.